A CABOT CAIN THRILLER

ASSAULT ON
KOLCHAK

CALIBER
B O O K S

Also from ALAN CAILLOU

CABOT CAIN Series
    Assault on Kolchak
    Assault on Ming
    Assault on Loveless
    Assault on Fellawi
    Assault on Agathon
    Assault on Aimata

TOBIN'S WAR Series
    Dead Sea Submarine
    Terror in Rio
    Congo War Cry
    Afghan Assault
    Swamp War
    Death Charge
    The Garonsky Missile

MIKE BENASQUE Series
    The Plotters
    Marseilles
    Who'll Buy My Evil
    Diamonds Wild

IAN QUAYLE Series
    A League of Hawks
    The Sword of God

DEKKER'S DEMONS Series
    Suicide Run
    Blood Run

The Charge of the Light Brigade
A Journey to Orassia

Rogue's Gambit
Cairo Cabal
Bichu the Jaguar
The Walls of Jolo
The Hot Sun of Africa
The Cheetahs
Joshua's People
Mindanao Pearl
Khartoum
South from Khartoum
Rampage
The World is 6 Feet Square
The Prophetess
House on Curzon Street

ASSAULT ON KOLCHAK
Book One

CHAPTER 1

A terrifying, chaotic fury had descended over the city.

The chaos, at this late stage of the war, was understandable; but the fury was something quite different. Everybody was fighting everybody else, and nobody really was quite sure where loyalties lay. The devotion to ideals had been smashed, and all that was left was a desperate need for disentanglement, for a recovery, if that were at all possible, from the holocaust. They cried stop, enough, but the holocaust kept rolling, growing in force, in momentum, in vengeance and the city was in its path.

The city was Budapest, and it was a long, painful time ago; the wounds are not yet healed.

The Hungarian Army collapsed, and out of the East came the violent, rapacious masses of enemy troops, pouring down out of the lush mountains and across the dusty plains like an unstopped avalanche. The land was black with their tanks and armored carriers, and the air was heavy with the smoke of their guns.

The advancing, victorious troops had been told: *the city is yours, do what you want with it...*

They stared at the beauty they found there, then they despoiled it. They looked for the first time in many long, violent months at the beautiful women, and they despoiled them too, because this was part of the pattern which had been set by invaders in the beginnings of history. Budapest was a city renowned for the beauty of its women.

In the first three months of the occupation, eighty thousand cases of rape were reported. Divide the city's one million population into male and female; don't count the women under fifteen and over sixty, and a figure of eighty thousand means that one female in every nubile three was raped in those first twelve shocking weeks. Murders—called executions—were uncounted; but convoys of thirty, fifty, sometimes a hundred trucks were seen at night carting away the bodies of the patriots for mass burial or burning. A million people fled Hungary in fear. The figures, the records, are all there; it's only necessary to read them.

The rest of the world was too busy with its own troubles to care.

In the great Hall of the Zrinyi castle, the restless, impatient man was striding up and down in his long leather overcoat, stopping once in a while to warm his hands at the fire that burned in the center of the room. It was two o'clock in the morning, and after the heat of the day the night was cold.

There were logs of wood in the storehouses, and even some coal; but the fire burning on the flagstone floor was made of the silk drapes from the tall windows. Blue smoke was crowding up to the high-vaulted ceiling that had been carved for the delight of King Matthias five hundred years earlier. The smell of them was ripe, pungent, and a little strange too, as though all the history that was going up in flames for the pleasure of one man had its own sweet scent.

He was short, and stubby, and powerfully built, and the leather coat that reached almost to his ankles, open at the front to show his field-gray uniform, seemed a little incongruous. He had thick black hair, straight and slick under the Colonel-General's cap that was set on the back of his head. He had a heavy, stolid-looking face with a thick, drooping, old-fashioned mustache and lively eyes, eyes that were the slightest bit curved up at the sides, as though there were Mongolian blood somewhere but not very much of it. He looked, at first sight, like a peasant; but there was a sharpness too, an autocratic arrogance that somehow seemed out of place and unexpected, and the air of competent authority was immense. Peasant or not, the moment he spoke there was evidence of a shrewd and ruthless mind, an ease of manner that denied his origins. In the old days he would have been killed off as an upstart, destroyed because of a competence that was out of keeping with what would have been called, then, his station. But now, men like these were needed, men whose minds were alert but whose hands were calloused, with bitten, grimy nails. He had grown to maturity in a new world; and now he was back in an old world that he knew of only by history. The expansive elegance all around him was proof of it, and it amused him.

The other man stood watching him. He was tall and slim and cultured, and it seemed that he was trying, successfully, to hide a very real fear; there was a brooding anger in his eyes, but his voice was quiet and controlled, and even polite.

He said, looking at the burning silk, watching the Colonel-General warm his hands at the flames: "There is wood, there is coal. If you had told me, I would have had the servants bring some."

The Colonel-General laughed quickly: "The servants? Where are they, Zrinyi? *Count* Zrinyi? I'll tell you where they are, they're fleeing for their miserable lives, heading for the forests."

Zrinyi said calmly: "Yes. To fight you."

The Colonel-General shrugged. "Let them fight. They'll be cut down as soon as they show their miserable faces." He laughed shortly. "And why aren't you running too, Excellency?"

Zrinyi answered calmly. "Because my place is here, I'm the head of the family, the holder of the title, and my place is with my people."

Outside, in the great yard where the stables were, there was the rattle of machine-gun fire; a woman screamed. Zrinyi ran to the door, and a guard stepped forward with his bayonet lowered. The Colonel-General said, not turning his head:

"Don't worry about it, Zrinyi, there's nothing you can do. There's going to be a lot of shooting, probably, so you may as well resign yourself to it. It's time for sleep. I'll take the rooms on the top floor, my officers will have the rest of the house. You can have the head gardener's cottage. The servants, those that are left, will stay where they are, and they'll serve us, not you. Nothing will be removed from the house, nor from the grounds, You'll keep to your quarters, and you won't use the phone or the mails. My aide is called Captain Telek, and like me, he's a Tartar, which means he won't stand for any nonsense. If you've any problems, see him. If I have any, he'll see you. Where's your wife?"

The question came suddenly, out of context, but Zrinyi was waiting for it; he'd been waiting for it all day. He said evenly:

"The Countess is in the country, visiting her family."

The Colonel-General said: "I'm given to understand that she's a remarkably beautiful woman."

There was a little silence, and then Zrinyi said: "Hungary is full of beautiful women." There was a touch of resignation in his voice, but the Colonel-General laughed and said: "You may go to your new quarters now."

There was the ripe smell of food coming from the kitchens, and the sound of a woman's laughter through the open doors. Zrinyi walked slowly across the room, and at the door he turned and asked:

"May I know your name, Colonel-General?"

Again, the little silence. Then the Colonel-General said clearly: "My name is Kolchak. Colonel-General Vladimir Kolchak."

The cottage was dark when he got there; the head gardener had long since gone and was somewhere in the city, holed up in a dark cellar with the Partisans, waiting for news of other Partisans. But as he fumbled around in the darkness and lit the gas jet, a shadow rose from a chair in the corner. It was Perczel, the Major-Domo, an old, old man who went about his duties with an arthritic limp. There was an angry light in his eyes, and Zrinyi said, surprised: "Perczel? I thought you were with our new masters?"

The old man nodded. "I was. They sent me out to round up all the servants who are left. I'm giving them time to get away if they still can."

"Good. What was that shooting?"

"They machine-gunned the horses."

Zrinyi was sick to his stomach.

The light was low, and the old man fiddled for a while with the jet until the mantle glowed, and when he turned back to look over his shoulder, the narrow cheekbones were framed in the yellow light, outlined against the dark recesses of the room.

Perczel asked, hesitantly: "What will happen to all of us now, sir?"

Zrinyi sighed. "I'm afraid you'll be working for them. I don't know how long they'll stay. It can't be forever, but in the interim...It won't be easy now, I'm afraid, for any of us." He asked abruptly: "Did you see your mistress?"

"Yes, sir, I saw her. Frederica and Isolde are with her."

"They're the only two girls we need worry about, I think, though Carla...If only we'd had more time!"

"They came so fast," Perczel said sadly. "It's surprising so many of the men were able to get away."

Zrinyi said: "If you're asked where your mistress is, I said she'd gone to the country to visit her family. The question is, how to get her and the girls out of the house. And where to send them," He said again, impatiently: "Time, there just wasn't enough time."

Perczel just listened, saying nothing and nodding in agreement.

Zrinyi said: "I fear the Colonel-General. I'd be happier if we had a peasant lording it over us, but Kolchak...I can't quite make him out. He has the hands and face of a *moujik*, but he talks like an educated man, and that's a combination I don't like." He was suddenly aware of how very old Perczel was; the skin on his cheekbones was losing its ancient tautness and beginning to sag. There was a bruise on the left side of his head where one of the soldiers had hit him. He was a good man, a kindly, gentle man at the end of his years.

Perczel said now, almost fearfully: "Whatever kind of man he is, we must get Madame out of the house very soon. There are more than four hundred of them here now, and sooner or later they will find her."

"Not if she stays where she is. But the question is...will she? It was hard enough to persuade her to hide. And of course, she will be deeply concerned about the child."

The young boy, their son, was with his mother; he was five years old. They were all together under the castle in what Zrinyi thought of as the tasting room.

It was a small cellar, comfortably furnished and pleasant, that was tucked away to the side of, and a little below, the main wine cellar of the castle. Centuries ago, the small room had been converted into a well-hidden hiding-place for some of the family's jewels. A stone wall had been built, with just the merest slit for an entrance, and that in turn had been hidden by one of the huge wine casks, too heavy to move—if you wanted to enter the hiding-place it was necessary to crawl on your hands and knees under the cask and worm your way through the lower part of the tiny cleft; you could walk for hours in the cellars without coming to the end of them, and even then, from quite close by, you could not guess that beyond the great cask there was yet another room—small, but big enough for a dozen people to hide in if necessary, provided they kept still and quiet. The Countess was there now, with the child and the two nubile girls, hiding from the dangers above and around them.

There had been time enough to take some food down there, and there was always water in the demijohns; and above all, there was safety there from the prowling soldiers in the house above.

She had agreed to go there reluctantly, only when the troops had forced their way into the castle, battering down the door which would have been opened had they knocked, and she had carried the child into the tasting room with the two young girls; and they were still there, waiting for him, somehow, to come and get them out. And to take them away, somewhere...

Until then, he was sure, they were safe. He laughed suddenly, without humor. "When the Romanians were here, my great-aunt and her children were in that room for more than eight months, and nobody found them."

"I was there," Perczel said. "I remember well. I took the Contessa news of the war every day, while I was selecting wines for the Romanian officers." He sighed. "Eight months, and there was no word of complaint from any of them, in all that time."

He had lit the small fire, the old man, and Zrinyi stared into it moodily.

He said at last, speaking very carefully: "Perhaps I don't have to tell you this, Perczel, but...we've survived, you and I, and everyone on this estate, for nearly fifteen hundred years. We've survived by giving way at the right time, and then coming back when the time is right too. Tell the men who have stayed behind...remember it yourself. We must treat these people correctly. They are now our masters, and we must accept that, for as long as may be. We will help them as little as possible, but we must not try to fight them, because for the time being, at least, it would be a useless fight. I've no doubt that later on..." He was silent for a long time.

But somebody found the tasting room before the night was over.

He heard the screams, Zrinyi, and recognized his wife's voice among them, calling him in terror. He raced along the gravel path in the gray of the first light, and a bullet hit him in the side of the neck, just grazing the flesh and not stopping him. A bayonet sliced open his hip as he ran for the stone stairway. And in the cellar itself, a swath of machine-gun bullets cut across his thighs and his knees and brought oblivion as the floor came pounding up at him to strike him in the face and break his nose with the impetus of his fall.

He saw the child using its tiny fists. He saw the two girls cowering and heard them screaming. And he saw his wife with her dress ripped off her lovely body. He saw that Kolchak was there, looking at her, saw him turn to glance briefly at him as though barely aware of the interruption; he saw him jerk a thumb at the stairway and saw the two soldiers thrust his wife toward them. And as she stumbled and fell, everything went away and there was only blackness and silence.

And when, at last, he came to his senses, it was ten days later and the invaders were gone. She was there, his remarkably beautiful wife, looking perhaps a little older but still as lovely as ever, and the word *survival* flitted briefly through his semiconscious mind. He remembered holding her hand, very tight, and saying nothing. He remembered the look in her eyes, both hesitant and determined at the same time. He remembered wondering if ever again he would know what she was thinking.

The end of the summer came, and the hungry winter, and then the spring. And in May, the child was born. It was a girl.

CHAPTER 2

Zrinyi sighed, and said:

"And that, my friend, was nearly a quarter of a century ago. For Fenrek here, Kolchak is a name in a file, no more, But for me..."

It was a kind of place, the castle, where time seemed to stand still. It was here that the events had taken place, and as I looked at the high architraves and the carving on the stone walls, it seemed that Kolchak might still be there somewhere; I could almost hear the screams of the women. Outside, the roses had grown again, and died, and grown...but here, in the cool shadows where our voices seemed to echo with a memory of the past, the seasons were all one, merging into a present that never passed on. I could imagine him, Zrinyi, as a younger man, elegant, detached, cool to the point of arrogance. But now, he was almost trembling; smiling, and telling his story drily, almost as though there were a sort of deprecatory humor in it; but still trembling, He walked with a limp now, on two artificial legs.

He moved to the buffet, taking my empty glass and pouring me another Cognac. "For all those years, I've dreamed of putting these hands around Kolchak's throat and strangling the life out of him, and it's never been anything more than the kind of dream we use to comfort ourselves when things are bad. But now"—he gestured vaguely—"now, at last, we have one thread that might lead us right to him. A green and golden thread that's fragile as a spider's web but tangible enough to...I don't know. Perhaps I'm hoping for too much. I'm too old, and too tired, and too...broken."

"Now," Fenrek said. "Now we have the necklace."

Fenrek, Colonel Matthias Fenrek, Department B-7 of Interpol, Headquarters, Paris, an old, old friend and one of the brightest men in the business. He was fifty-five years old, and looked thirty; a slight, muscular man with a tanned and eager look about him. He had a cheerful, easy-going manner that didn't quite succeed in masking an astonishing competence. He used his hands eloquently when he talked, waving them around all the time like an Italian taxi driver.

He turned to Zrinyi now and said suddenly: "He left the army just after...after the incident at the castle, did you know that?"

Zrinyi shook his head. His eyes were very alert, waiting.

Fenrek said: "Well, 'left' is a bit of a euphemism. His excesses were too much, even for Moscow. He killed a young girl who turned out to be the daughter of one of Moscow's favorite people, so they recalled him, and like any sensible man whose sins have found him out, he packed up and went. And it wasn't only everything of value in the castle that went with him. According to the files of the War Crimes Commission, he took with him at least twelve truckloads of loot, over the border into Yugoslavia where he had a shootout with some Partisans, then somehow or other into Switzerland. We found twelve Russian truck drivers up in the mountains there, each one with a bullet in his skull. Exit Kolchak into history."

There was a long, long silence. Zrinyi was propped up on a hard high-backed chair that was upholstered in ancient Belgian tapestry, his hands hooked over the armrests; it made him look predatory. It seemed that it was his turn to speak, but he was dreaming, and Fenrek said at last, prompting him, and speaking very gently with a slight smile on his handsome face:

"We came here as friends, Istvan."

He came out of his daydream, picking up the thread of Fenrek's thought. "Yes, yes, I know that." He took a deep breath, ready for the plunge, and looked at me with a surprisingly cold, challenging expression on his face. Old and tired, he had said, and broken; he didn't look it now.

"All right," he said. "Let me forge for the moment my normal Hungarian subtlety, and borrow some of your laudable American frankness." He made it sound as though laudable and crude were the same word. "There's a great deal of money involved, by anyone's standards, and I'd like to get my fortune back, of course, But yes, I want Kolchak's head on a platter too. Legally, illegally, I don't care which. Does that make me a potential murderer? I suppose it does."

Fenrek's arms were waving like windmills again, "He's wanted by almost every police force in Europe, and that means two things. First of all, it means a certain moral justification, if that's what you're groping for..."

"And secondly," I put it, "it means he'll be hard to find."

"Precisely."

Zrinyi did not answer. He stood up and went to the window, looking out into the rose garden. There was a bright, white moon outside, and the pale cream of the Sweet Aftons was reflecting it weirdly. The dark reds of the splendid Charles Mallerin Hybrids were black in the moonlight, and only the Sweet Aftons were glowing. An owl was hooting somewhere, and I heard the distant croak of a bullfrog down by the river. He said, not turning round:

"The necklace, is it a lead, or isn't it? I don't know very much about these things."

Fenrek answered cheerfully. "Of course it's a lead, if only a slender one. Let me tell you how these people operate." He got up and began to pace around restlessly, and then thrust his hands deep into his pockets. He stood like an orator urging on the masses.

"They stole, during the war, enormous amounts of jewelry, paintings, tapestries, antiques, anything that was of value and transportable. The Nazis, mostly, and some of their looting efforts were spectacularly successful. We know where most of *them* are now—in South America. But that's a very wide continent, and it's not easy to define their whereabouts with much more precision, except on one or two memorable occasions. And you can't go hunting through nearly seven million square miles, among a hundred and twenty million people, with nothing more to go on than the knowledge that they're there somewhere. And those, in any case, are the Nazis. It's not likely that Kolchak, a Communist, would be among them, so that merely leaves us the rest of the world to comb through."

I said politely: "You were going to tell us how they operate."

The arm waving stopped momentarily, then went on again, just as though I hadn't spoken. "In most of South America, there's a certain political freedom for Nazis, and this is where most of them went—with their loot. Take a man like Ludenheim. Ex-S.S, wanted by Poland, Czechoslovakia, Russia, for mass slaughters all over the occupied territories. He escaped to Paraguay. And he took with him nearly two million dollars worth of paintings and quite a lot of gold bullion. For about fifteen years he managed on the bullion, but at last he ran out of ready cash and sold a Madonna by Correggio to a dealer in La Paz. From La Paz it went to Buenos Aires, from there to New York, from New York to Paris, from Paris to Amsterdam—which is where someone finally caught up with it. The Dutch police traced it all the way back to La Paz, which took them nearly two years, and then the trail came to a dead stop. All we know is that Ludenheim was the man who sold it, and that he got thirty thousand American dollars for it, about a third of its true value—which is not too bad, really. He sold a Rembrandt two years later, and a Van Eyck six months after that, and this time...this time, they got him. But he's one in a thousand. All over the world the looted treasures are slowly turning up, more and more of them as more and more time passes and the money begins to run out. Sometimes they lead us somewhere; more often, they don't. The closer you get to the original source, the stronger the wall of secrecy. Often, it's impregnable."

I asked a question that seemed to me very important. "In relative figures, how much loot was taken by the Communists as opposed to the Nazis?"

Fenrek smiled thinly. "A relatively infinitesimal amount. They're so much nicer people, the Communists, aren't they?"

Zrinyi said sourly: "Yes, aren't they?" He was suddenly very angry. He looked at me very hard. "I've told you, I want Kolchak's head. In your view, does that make me sound like...like a gangster?"

Fenrek laughed. "It makes Cain sound like one."

"And that doesn't seem to worry you in the slightest," I told him.

Fenrek was suddenly very serious. "We're all Hungarians here, Cain, you're the only American among us. And there's a lot about us that you don't know, isn't there? Has it ever occurred to you that the Hungarian isn't quite like anyone else in the world? We find it very

15

easy to justify the reproachable by stripping it down to essentials. Personally, I'm a policeman, and I've a high respect for law and order. But if someone raped my wife I'd hunt him down to the end of the world and far beyond, and I'd slice him in little pieces, and I'd tell St. Peter on Judgement Day: 'If you don't like it, then go to Hell.' So let's have no more damned nonsense. If you're going to take the job, take it, for God's sake. If not..." He broke off.

I repeated: "If not?"

Zrinyi said tightly: "If not, then my son Nicholas will try. My wife thinks...I think, that this is a family matter, that it's morally reprehensible to call in a stranger, a hired gunman, to do something that is clearly a matter for me or for my son." He gestured at his legs. "I'm not much use to anyone nowadays, and Nicholas...Nicholas is a good boy, a fine young man, but I'm aware of his imitations. He fought tooth and nail against bringing you into this, but Fenrek's a man I admire and whom I've known for more years than I care to count. And if half the things he says about you are true, then it's obvious that you have the necessary talents and abilities that we don't have. Nicholas is desperately hoping you'll turn me down, Mr. Cain. But he's not capable of it, and if he tries to find Kolchak...Yes, he just might do it. But he'll get himself killed in the process, of that there's no doubt in my mind at all. He's rash, he's impetuous, and...he's not really very bright."

He was already expecting me to say no. But Fenrek was a close friend and a good man, and he'd said, urging me with all the persuasiveness at his command—which was considerable: "At least listen to what they have to say."

I said, draining my glass of its last golden drop: "Let me look at this green and golden thread of yours that might just hang a man."

As we went into the pleasant little drawing room, the dark, brooding young man got to his feet and looked up at me. "Well, you couldn't be anyone else but Cabot Cain, could you? I'm Nicholas Zrinyi." He turned to introduce the woman sitting on the couch, but Fenrek spoke first. He said gravely:

"Cabot Cain, the Countess Ilona Zrinyi."

She held a hand out to me and I touched it briefly; it was ice cold. Her voice was low and soft and very pleasing; her English was smooth and easy, but touched with an accent that was French, perhaps, more than Hungarian—the accent of the cultured European cosmopolite. Her steady gray eyes were on mine, reading the thoughts there with a practiced ease. She said: "You are very welcome here, Mr. Cain." I murmured something appropriate, and she looked quickly at her husband and back to me, and asked: "I hope you don't find what we are asking you to do too...distasteful? Or have you already made up your mind that you are not a hired killer?"

They thought alike, these people. She was tall and rather willowy, with astonishing pale-gray eyes and very fair hair, an attractive woman in her early fifties, poised and sure of herself, very calm and composed and just a trifle...is hostile the right word? If it really was hostility, then it could only mean that she too was more interested in Kolchak's blood than in getting back the personal fortune they had lost. I wondered about that, and saw Fenrek smiling gently as though he were reading my thoughts and enjoying a sort of grim humor all by himself.

I said: "Why don't we call it fortune hunter? It sounds better, no?"

She accepted the rebuke gracefully. "Forgive me, Mr. Cain. But it's hard to expose our desperate need for...for revenge to a man we really don't know very well except at second hand."

To expose the savagery under the cultured facade? Somehow, the frankness endeared her to me. She was a woman easy to admire on sight. There was something sad about her too, as though the very personal things that Zrinyi had been forced to tell me had pained her deeply. This was a world in which the private tragedies were always kept concealed, out of the eyes and minds of others; and yet the need for opening up the old scar and excising the poison had been so strong that even this secret had to be shared.

She smiled and said: "Is it absurd to say: 'if only we'd known you a little longer?' I suppose it is."

I shrugged. "All you really need to know is that I'm a friend of Fenrek's. That should be recommendation enough."

"Yes, of course."

It was strangely intimate here in the small room after the huge impersonality of the Great Hall. A neat, feminine room of chintz-covered chairs and painted lampshades; there was even a small handloom in one corner with a cut-silk tapestry on it, half-finished in a Flemish design of extraordinary intricacy. I turned and took the young man's outstretched hand; I saw the sullen look in his eyes, and he held onto my hand with a very strong grip as though asserting his own strength too. He asked: "And did they tell you too that I want this job for myself?" There was no attempt to disguise his hostility.

I said: "Yes, they did. And they also said you weren't capable of it."

"And you are? It's not really a job for an athlete, you know."

I thought: oh-oh, here we go. It's hard for a man of my size to look like anything but a prizefighter. But I didn't want to push him; I could sympathize with him easily enough.

I said: "If I take it, I'll need help," and left it at that.

Zrinyi had opened a drawer in a fine old Italian console and had pulled out a small oblong box of hard, brightly-polished leather; it had a burl to it like walnut. The inside, when he opened it, was dark red velvet, a deep, burgundy color that somehow made me feel I wanted a glass of Chéteauneuf-du-Pape. And on the bed of velvet, a long thin chain of brightly shining emeralds was resting. He looked at it for a moment before he took it out and handed it to me. "Tell me what you think of it, Mr. Cain."

I took the fragile necklace and stared at it, mesmerized. It was one of the most beautiful things I had ever seen. Rose-cut oblong, very unusual, twenty-four, twenty-eight, thirty-two narrow-cut emeralds, sparkling with a hypnotic brilliance, each finely mounted in a filigree of open gold-work, so delicate it seemed it would break if you sneezed, all carefully matched...No, there was one that wasn't quite right.

They were all watching me and waiting. Fenrek seemed to be enjoying some secret joke. Nicholas came up and stood just beside me as though he were guarding it with his life. I knew what they were waiting for.

I said: "As beautiful a piece as I've ever seen. Sixteenth century?"

Zrinyi nodded. "Yes, of course. At no other time in history did they cut emeralds quite like that, a lost art. It was made for King Ulaszlo the Second, in fifteen hundred and fifteen, a present for his favorite mistress, whose name..."

I said: "Magda Zrinyi"

There was a painting on the wall that had attracted my attention when we first entered this charming room. I walked over and looked at it, and Nicholas was there again beside me, keeping an eye on the family jewels...A dark, gypsy-looking girl in a bright blue velvet dress, with the conventional pink cheeks and laughing eyes of the period, a plump, pretty girl with black eyes, red lips, and cream-colored skin. A fine painting of the Venetian School with a touch of the Florentine in the scholarly modeling of the hands. I thought it might be by Andrea del Sarto, or one of his pupils, perhaps. A fine painting of a fine young woman. Against her splendid breast the necklace did not shine as brightly as the one I held in my hand. I heard Fenrek say, with a sigh: "Beautiful, isn't she? He was a lucky man, Ulaszlo."

I turned to Zrinyi and said: "Ulaszlo was one of the Jagiello Kings, I recall, and there was a famous Jagiello collection of gems that was bandied back and forth between the Hapsburgs and—who was it?—Cardinal Bakose? And then broken up about two hundred years ago. Am I right in thinking that this piece is one of that collection?"

I could feel Nicholas' eyes hard on me. "That's a recondite piece of Hungarian history for an American to know about."

I shrugged. "It's all on record. It's there for anyone who bothers to read." I could feel the delicate texture of the stones in my fingers; it's an extraordinary thing about emeralds; they seem to burn. I said: "I suppose you know that one of the stones is not an emerald?"

Fenrek laughed, and Nicholas said grudgingly: "You've got sharp eyes, Mr. Cain. Yes, one of them is a replacement."

"And that was done—when? While it was in your possession?"

Zrinyi shook his head. "No," he said. "When it was stolen, the necklace was intact."

"Interesting."

"It's a damn good copy," Fenrek said, "but it would never pass expert examination. So why?"

I said: "The interest isn't in the *why*."

The Countess was sitting there silent, her eyes cast down; I wanted to know more about her. I went over and put the necklace back in its wine-colored nest, and turned to her and said: "Tell me about the rest of the collection."

She wore a long green dress, and now she moved a trifle and placed it around herself just so, as though the image were important; it seemed she would hold the pose forever, a pale composure, waiting for the rest of the world to pass her by. Her delicately-boned face and high forehead gave her an old-fashioned look, with a firm, strong mouth for good measure. She was still very beautiful. Twenty-five years ago she must have been ravishing, I thought; and then I decided that this was not a happy choice of words.

She said: "Eight pieces of the collection have been in our family since the sixteen hundreds. They were willed by Ulaszlo to the illegitimate daughter he had by Maria. They were stolen from us by the French, recovered from them by the Turks, looted by the Romanians—and finally they found their way back to their rightful home, this castle." They were all grouped around us, listening, as though there were pleasure even in the retelling of the family history.

She continued. "Eight pieces, each one of them priceless, both intrinsically and for its historical value. There's the emerald necklace, which at last has come to light. There's a splendid tiara of diamonds, rubies, emeralds and pearls. There's a diamond bracelet, three ruby and diamond rings, a small gold snuffbox encrusted with pearls by Cellini. And finally, there's an immense and rather vulgar ruby bracelet with three pendants hanging from it, the pendants being really of more importance than the rest of the bracelet because they came from the first of the Jagiello crowns. Unhappily, for the last three hundred years, two of the pendants have been missing; the bracelet as we know it contains only one of them."

I said: "Cardinal Bakosc? I seem to recall a story..."

She smiled. "Bakosc was a man of expensive habits, and his taste in jewelry is legendary. He gave the three pendants away, one to each of his most favored mistresses. But then he had a change of heart and tried to recover them. He only succeeded in getting back one of them before he died. And so, now the bracelet has only one pendant; and the rest, the most valuable part, is still missing. Missing for three hundred years. And that's all of them, Mr. Cain. Eight pieces of history. We still have drawings of them, quite old, but accurate. Nicholas?"

The young man nodded and went out. When he came back, in a little while, he handed me a portfolio of sketches.

The Countess was saying: "The Germans, of course, were our allies, but when they took over the castle as their H.Q. we were careful to hide our collection away. They were too much of a temptation. And then the Russians came, and..."

"From the Russians," Zrinyi interrupted, "it was hard to keep *anything* hidden."

It didn't make sense. If I'd hidden a collection of jewels like those, nobody would have found them, ever.

"Even so," I said, "a small box could easily enough be hidden securely on an estate as large as this. Buried somewhere..."

"It was," Zrinyi said, "It was buried in the copse at the back of the stables, but..."

"But?"

He was very moody all of a sudden. The Countess would not meet my eye. "It was very hard," she said, "to hide anything from a man like Kolchak."

Zrinyi came back to life. He said suddenly: "Perczel, a man named Perczel, a servant. A very old man whom I'd known, and loved, since I was a child. He told them about the jewels, and he showed them where to dig. And he told them about the tasting room under the cellar."

"And you've so easily forgiven him?" Fenrek asked.

There was a very long pause. "Yes. Yes, I have forgiven him. I can only guess what they must have done to him. He was a fragile old man, fragile enough to break easily."

"And he was a Communist," Fenrek said. "He'd do just what they wanted him to do."

Zrinyi grunted. "So you've always told me. But I'll never believe it." The legend of the faithful old servant was hard to kill, especially for a man like Zrinyi, one of the old school who took it for granted that their family retainers would lay down their lives for their masters without question; perhaps they would, who could tell? It didn't seem to matter very much now.

I turned the leaves of the portfolio Nicholas had given me. There were sketches in black and white, colored tempera drawings, some of the details in oil. The paintings embraced a period from the sixteenth to the eighteenth century. I said: "May I keep these for a while?" The Countess smiled. "Of course."

Zrinyi picked up the necklace and stood looking at it for a moment. He said slowly: "Even a piece of glass, Kolchak said, outlives us. And this...this is more than a reflection of what went on twenty-five years ago. It's seen more suffering than all of us in this room will ever know, it's part of our heritage." He turned to me abruptly. "Can you know what I'm thinking, Mr. Cain? Once, not too long ago, I was an immensely wealthy man, by any standard. Today, all I have is..." He gestured vaguely around the room. "My paintings, my furniture, my castle, it looks a lot, doesn't it? But in spite of it all...We live in a political society that frowns on personal wealth, at least officially. But I pay dues to all the right parties, I'm careful to say all the right things, and so, like a dying anachronism, I am permitted to survive with rather more than *they* think is good for me. I used to lay great store on the art of survival. It's a peculiarly Hungarian characteristic."

Nicholas was laughing suddenly, showing his strong white teeth, his sullenness and his anger gone. He said: "Some of the finest treasures in the world, but don't ask for more sugar in your coffee, because there isn't enough to go round."

Zrinyi was suddenly laughing with his son; it seemed to bring them very close together. He sobered, then, and said:

"All this time I had resigned myself to the loss of a personal fortune, persuading myself that under the benevolent government which presently guards our welfare I would have no use for it anyway. And then, suddenly, out of the blue, Magda Zrinyi's necklace is on display in the window of a French antiquarian. It even has a price tag on it. One million francs, or two hundred thousand English pounds, or five hundred and sixty thousand American dollars, whichever the buyer should prefer."

I said: "That's a lot of money to pay for a man's life," and Fenrek said cheerfully: "A typically Hungarian remark, Cain. So soon?"

"I assume," I said, "that you did pay something like that to get it back again?"

"Indeed we did," Zrinyi said. "We collected all the money we could lay our hands on, we borrowed from friends, we sold a few trifles over the border when that benevolent government was looking the other way. Yes, we paid for it."

"And now it's a rope to hang a man." I looked at Fenrek. "I suppose your men tried to trace it back?"

Fenrek shrugged. "It was sold to the antiquarian in Paris, in the Rue St. Honore, by a highly respected dealer in antiques and jewelry. He, in turn, bought it from a woman at the Georges Cinq who seemed to have title to it. Or at least the next best thing—a good story. And the woman has never been traced."

"But you know her name."

Fenrek was enjoying himself. He said: "She called herself the Countess Ilona Zrinyi, and showed a passport to prove it."

I said: "To prove it to whom?"

Fenrek looked at me sharply, with a suddenly thoughtful look in his eye. "To prove it to the dealer, of course. He was satisfied as to her integrity, and he bought the necklace and resold it to an antiquarian. The antiquarian notified the police as a matter of routine, but the necklace isn't on anyone's list of stolen or looted property, though the War Crimes Commission keeps a pretty comprehensive one."

"Why not?"

Zrinyi answered my question smoothly: "We've never tried to hide the fact that the collection is ours, how could we? But at the same time, we haven't been too noisily boastful about it either, since the war. The Big Brother who keeps an eye on us also has a delight in baubles; for the benefit of the people, they call it."

"I see. Let's get back to Kolchak. I assume the Commission is looking for him already?"

Fenrek nodded. "They've been looking for twenty years. He's just one of a thousand."

They had all taken seats now, like conspirators, round the heavy oak table, carved, I noticed, in a Venetian motif; early Brustolone; some iconoclast had sliced his initials deeply into its beautiful old surface, probably, I thought, with the point of his bayonet. It seemed to bring the old days of the Occupation back again, Only the Countess remained on the sofa, her composure held, but a strange, sad look in her eye.

Fenrek said, guessing what I was thinking more than answering my question: "He's wanted, Kolchak, for capital crimes all over Europe. The Poles want him for murdering those eleven hundred Polish officers in Rossosz. The Germans want him for supervising the slaughter of thirteen thousand prisoners of war. The Czechs want him for personally wiping out the whole of the Zvolen High Command, eighty-two officers and men burned alive in a silo. The State of Israel wants him for handing over two thousand Jews to the exterminators in Riga. And the Russians want him for two comparative trifles—the murder of twelve of their drivers and the killing in a kind of sex orgy of Commissar Hecht's attractive young daughter. So if you're thinking—and you were, weren't you?—of the moral implications, I suggest they really shouldn't worry you too much."

Fenrek always knew what I was thinking. But to set the record straight, I looked at Zrinyi and asked: "Are you asking me to get Kolchak for you, or to bring back the jewels, or both?"

Zrinyi's face was very hard, "Both. Or either."

I took time out to think about it all. Zrinyi went out and came back with the Courvoisier bottle and poured me a glass, then poured for Fenrek, and Nicholas, and himself. He held the bottle up to the Countess and smiled, but she shook her head. I said to Fenrek: "Tell me about Commissar Hecht's daughter." I knew Hecht was a man trained carefully by the Russians for eventual placement in Poland, a clever, dangerous man whose loyalties were never too clearly on one side or the other; I'd never known before why he'd abruptly defected, for what he called "personal reasons" to the West.

Fenrek said: "An exciting woman, rather than pretty. Over-sexed, a little bad-tempered, and full of mischief. Five feet two, a hundred and four pounds, twenty-seven years old at the time of her death."

I said: "It's her death I want to know about."

"She was one of Kolchak's girls for a while, and one of Kolchak's little weaknesses was a taste for whipping. He flogged her to death. Unintentionally. I believe he was genuinely sorry that he'd killed her; if a man like that can ever be sorry about anything."

"A man who never has any regrets at all? That's a rare kind of man."

Fenrek smiled. "Yes, and it narrows down the field considerably. If you can get close enough."

I said: "Don't laugh. I want to know what this man eats for breakfast. If I'm to hunt him, I want to know how long he boils a four-minute egg."

"There's a file," Fenrek said. "In Paris, I'll show you the file. All you need to know at this moment is that Kolchak is tough, resilient, cunning, a man with no scruples and no morals, a man who is quietly, stolidly, and constantly in control of everything around him. A man who trusts nobody, a man who likes to do his own dirty work either for that reason or because he gets a personal satisfaction out of it. I'll tell you this, friend; if you ever get near Kolchak and he knows it, he won't send anyone to kill you, he'll come himself, to slice you up for goulash."

I said: "And that too is a little weakness, isn't it?"

He nodded happily. "We're getting closer to him all the time, aren't we?"

I stood up and went over to the Countess. She looked at me without surprise as I sat down beside her. I said: "You are not happy about this, are you?"

She took a long deep breath. "I could tell you, Mr. Cain, that the idea of revenge pains me. I could tell you that it brings back incidents I'd much rather forget. Or I could tell you I'm ashamed that we're all of us plotting the destruction of a human being. But I won't. I'll tell you the truth. I think, and Istvan thinks, and Nicholas thinks, that what we have to do is a compulsion too strong to fight, even if, intellectually, we decided we ought to fight it. And so, were all agreed. Only..."

She broke off and looked at her hands for a while, then looked at me before continuing.

"It's sad that there's no one in the family who is capable of satisfying our needs in what is, after all, a matter of family honor. Does that sound old-fashioned to you, Mr. Cain? In your world, I suppose it would be."

"Perhaps. My world learned a lot from yours. Perhaps we didn't learn enough." I felt it was urgent to change the subject. I smiled at her. "And there's one member of the family I haven't met, isn't there? Where is she?"

The Countess put a hand on mine in a gesture of astonishing intimacy; it was as though we bad known each other for quite a long time. She said, her voice very quiet:

"Leda? Leda is in Paris, Mr. Cain. She knows only a little of what you have been told. All this time, we've kept it from her. My husband knows, I know, my son knows, and our dear friend Colonel Fenrek knows. Now, you do too. There's no one else in the world. And she must never know, will you promise me that? Whatever you decide to do about this thing...promise me that, at least?"

I was already nodding my head when Nicholas came over and stood beside me. He was always right there, keeping an eye on something or other. He said roughly:

"And if she ever finds out from you, Cain, that she's a bastard, I'll personally kill you. God help me, I'll kill you."

I rather liked him for it.

CHAPTER 3

The newly-cleaned columns of the Church of St. Mary-Magdalen, or the Madeleine as the vulgar call it, were shining as brightly in the April sunlight as they had when they had first been carved three hundred years ago. They'd never been satisfied with those columns, I remembered, and were always knocking them down and putting up fresh ones to please the architect, or Napoleon, or Louis the Eighteenth, I remembered too that the fine old building, one of the most delicately proportioned in the world, once almost became a railway station.

It was a good time, I thought, to be in Paris. The water was still swirling in the gutters from the night time street cleaning, and rubber-booted men in blue smocks were swishing their long burlap brooms, smelling the scent of roasting coffee in the bistros which meant they would soon be off duty. There was the friendly clatter of chairs being set out on the pavement, and a heavy dray, drawn by two huge Percheron horses, was turning out of a narrow cobbled side-street onto Rue Royale.

It was too early in the morning for the tourists. Even those who were determined to make every second of their holiday count were still sitting in the lounges of their hotels, waiting for the American Express to open, preparing for the days exhaustions. Even the sweatered young American girls with their copies of the Stateside papers were not yet on the streets. A cool wind was blowing across the Place de la Concorde, up from the river, I asked the waiter for a *filtre* and a Calvados; there's nothing like a tot of applejack first thing in the morning. Watching the *quartier* coming to life, I thought: Paris should always be like this. I'm more at home in rougher places, where there are forests and jungles and marshes and deserts; but once in a while a breath of civilization is refreshing. A handbarrow, loaded down with oysters, was pulling up at the kitchen entrance on the corner, and a waiter came out, rubbing his hands and unloading them onto the stand; Belons and Claires for the tourists, and the bright green Marennes for the more demanding of the gourmets...

Then Vallence came up.

A plump, fussily-dressed man in a dark business suit and thick-lensed glasses. I couldn't help a sigh; he was less than five feet tall, and that always, with me, makes for embarrassment. I'm six feet seven, and even Fenrek, whose slender grace makes him look considerably taller than he really is, looks like a midget if he stands too close to me. And, as I stood up; Vallence stared, but recovered quickly and made a quick little bow, then thrust out a pudgy hand and said: "Colonel Fenrek?"

I said: "Yes, I'm Fenrek. It's good of you to see me."

I sat down quickly and slouched a bit. Vallence took off his glasses and polished them, and sat down and said: "So much more pleasant on the early-morning streets than in a dingy office. You were absolutely right. And this is a good little place, a good place." He put his glasses back on and peered at me, and said: "Your call mystified me a little, Colonel. The police have already informed me, of course, that the Zrinyi necklace I bought was, in fact, stolen. They have also absolved me absolutely from any blame in the matter."

The attentive waiter was hovering, and when I raised my eyebrows Vallence said: "Just coffee, please." When the waiter had gone, he made a broad gesture that reminded me of Fenrek and said: "In my business, these things do happen, you know, though not very often. That's why, as a matter of routine procedure, the police are informed every time we acquire any gems of exceptional value or interest. In the case of the emerald necklace, as you must be aware, there was no record anywhere that would indicate that my acquisition of it had even the slightest tinge of illegality. Before I bought it, I searched the records most carefully. And the history of the emeralds that the lady gave me was, as you must agree, a very plausible story."

I already knew what I wanted to know from M. Vallence. He was just talking too much and too fast. There was a very real fear under the studied ease, and he hadn't waited for me to say a word about his dealings. *Qui s'excuse, s'accuse*...

The coffee came, and he wiggled the china top of the filter as though he were in a hurry to let it seep through and get out of there.

He said: "And, of course, I informed the police promptly of my purchase. Even then, there was no...no suspicion of any trouble. It was only when someone told the Zrinyi family that it was on sale at the Rue St. Honore that...that the trouble started." He took a sip of his coffee and burned his lip, and smiled quickly and said: "So you see, Colonel Fenrek, Interpol's interest in me personally is a little disturbing."

It was only common courtesy that made me push him any further. I said:

"The woman in the Georges Cing, the woman who gave her name as Ilona Zrinyi, What did she look like?"

He said promptly, reciting: "Tall, fair-haired, very well-dressed and elegant."

"And she spoke French?"

"Er...yes."

"Accent?"

He shrugged. "The slightest trace, perhaps, of a Hungarian accent."

That did it. I said: "And she showed you a Hungarian passport?"

"Yes, she did. In the name of Countess Ilona Zrinyi."

"A good one, the passport?"

"I beg your pardon?"

"It was a phony. Was it at least a good one?"

He hesitated. "As far as I could tell. I am not an expert in these matters."

"And so you accepted her story and her necklace."

Vallence said very carefully, as though he were finally going to put me in my place:

"Colonel Fenrek, I went to great lengths to assure myself of the likelihood that she was indeed the rightful owner of what she was selling. In this business, it is always likelihood, and only likelihood, that matters. We can never be absolutely sure that at sometime or other in its history, any piece of antique jewelry has not been stolen, But if there are no records to show this, then we are perfectly justified, after we have taken reasonable precautions, in proceeding with the purchase and the resale." He came to a full stop, and when I didn't answer, he spread his hands and said: "We all know that the Hungarian Aristocracy are selling off their jewels to pay for a form of life they don't really enjoy anymore." Full stop again.

I got up and said to him pleasantly: "Interpol agrees entirely with the police opinion, M. Vallence. My only object in asking you to meet me was to see if perhaps we could trace the necklace back just a shade further than the police were able to do."

"And you think...you think you'll be able to do that?" There was no nervousness there; it had all gone.

I said: "Yes, perhaps we will. We've been very lucky in this case." I smiled a sort of disarming smile. "We have a good idea where it really came from, and I'll be making a little trip very soon. Good to get away from the office, you know what I mean?"

"Oh, really? Well, that's, er, splendid. Er..." He hesitated. "Where would that be, Colonel Fenrek? If it isn't too indiscreet to ask?"

I gave him the right kind of look, friendly but reproachful. "Well, one of our secrets, I'm afraid. Meanwhile...thank you once again for seeing me, you've been most helpful."

He stood up and took my hand. I couldn't help noticing that he glanced around to see what sort of a spectacle we were making, with him coming up to my navel in his elevator shoes; he couldn't have liked it very much, and he sat down again quickly. As I put some money on the table, working out the fifteen percent and the twenty percent and making the tip and the service just right, Vallence seemed suddenly very happy. He said: "If you'll forgive another indiscretion, Colonel...Surely, in your profession, most men like to appear somewhat more inconspicuous? Isn't it a disadvantage to be so...so splendidly built?"

I thought that was a rather nice way of putting it. I podded with just a touch of ruefulness. I said gravely: "It is indeed a disadvantage sometimes. Did you pay the lady by check or cash?"

Unperturbed, he said: "By cash, as you must know, Colonel. She suggested that the present Hungarian government might cause her some difficulty if she tried to bank so large a sum. And we none of us agree, do we, with their ideas regarding the wickedness of personal wealth? So I acceded to her request. A perfectly normal one under the circumstances."

"Yes. Yes, of course it is. Good day, M. Vallence."

The oyster man had finished unloading his barrow and was getting a free Calvados just around the corner. As I passed him, I said: "All right, Henri, he's all yours."

He tossed back his drink and grinned at me, and said in execrable English: "Okay, Mr. Cain, you leave him to me."

A tiny little Peugeot 204 convertible, fuel-injection and all, raced out of Rue St. Honore, which is a one-way street, against the traffic, and turned into Rue Royale in a hurry. He nearly bumped off me and smashed a bumper as I crossed the street.

Fenrek wasn't in his apartment when I got there, so I said hello to the waddling old concierge, went on up in the creaking elevator and let myself in with my own key. It was one of those pleasant old houses of graying stone on the edge of the Bois de Boulogne, on the Boulevard Souchet that runs from Auteuil to Passy; there were cypress trees in the tiny front garden and not much else except some hopeful daffodils that weren't doing so well.

The maid began to prepare some more coffee, and I opened the desk drawer and found the Vallence file where Fenrek had left it for me. I was halfway through it when the Colonel came in. He looked exhausted after his night's labors. He hung up his coat in the hall and called out: "Well, how was it?"

He came in and we went out onto the verandah through the tall French windows and looked over at the bright greens of the Bois in their fresh spring growth, with the buds on some of the trees still bursting, and the birds fluttering about them noisily in their search for the insects that were feeding on the rich new sap. From this rooftop height we could see the couples strolling on the grass verges, arm in arm, with all the time in the world and not much to do with it. Looking at them, Fenrek said: "As though the present can be prolonged by languor." He grinned at me and said again: "Well, how was Vallence?"

"A bloody liar."

"That's precisely what I was afraid you'd think. But you're wrong."

"And your file is a lot of poppycock. I hope you've got more than that on Kolchak."

"We have, you'll see. But Vallence is clean."

"He's a very nervous man, and he's hiding something he's terrified we'll find out."

He said, waving his arms again: "I thought so too at first, but we went over Vallence from head to foot and he came out smelling as fresh as a glass of *pastis*."

I said: "Do something about your daffodils down there. Some blood meal would work wonders with them."

"All right, what makes you think he was lying?"

"The accent."

He hesitated, "Say again?"

"He told me that the woman who sold him the necklace had a Hungarian accent, and showed a Hungarian passport."

"If the accent was strong enough to be noticed, then the desk clerk at the hotel would have asked her to hand her passport in, right?"

"Yes, that's normal police procedure. For a foreigner."

"And the Sûreté, maybe even the clerk, would have seen at once that it was a forgery."

"Yes, probably..."

"So, her French must have been good enough to fool the clerk that she was a native Frenchwoman. So how come it didn't fool Vallence?"

"Dammit," Fenrek said. "She had to have a Hungarian passport if she was claiming to be Ilona Zrinyil."

"Then why—and perhaps more to the point—did she fool the clerk? The Georges Cinq is not exactly a dump you know. The staff there can tell at a glance, at a word, precisely where their guests come from. They've been doing it for a hundred years."

I hate playing detective, especially with the experts, and I couldn't help feeling a trifle belligerent. I said: "You're sure this mystery woman really existed?"

Fenrek nodded. "She existed all right, the police spent a long time looking for her. She was registered at the hotel as Marie DuBois, from Bordeaux. She met with Vallence twice, on the fifteenth in the hotel lobby, and the next day in her room."

"Description?"

He shrugged. "Vague, a very vague description from your expert clerk. Sufficiently like Ilona Zrinyi, I suppose. Tall and slim and about the right age, with gray eyes and fair hair. Gray eyes are common enough, and blond wigs are easy to find. There was never any need to fool anyone except Vallence, who couldn't possibly know the real Ilona Zrinyi."

"Why do you say that? Suppose he had known her?"

The shrug again: "A hell of a long shot."

"Uh-huh."

He said: "The woman stayed two days and left. Exit into history again."

"Fingerprints?"

"They keep those damned hotels too damned clean, Nothing."

"Vallence is a professional dealer in gems and antiques. That presupposes a lot of travel. I suppose you checked?"

"The police did. In the last twelve months: London, Prague, Mexico City, Rio de Janeiro, London again, Brussels, and Geneva. Each time he imported something of value, declared it, paid the duty, and sold it. I tell you, Cain, he's a highly respected man in his field."

"Just the kind of man I'd choose if I were floating out looted treasures one at a time. He's wealthy?"

"Very."

There was the tinkle of a little bell, and we went back into the stately room its high walls pale gray and its drapes a deep amber-colored velvet. The coffee was on the table, a silver service on an enameled tray, with little eggshell cups of English bone-china; Spode, about 1850 or so. The maid poured for us, a plump, pleasantly middle-aged woman from Auvergnes. When she had gone, Fenrck said:

"Isn't it bone meal you're supposed to use on daffodils?"

"Blood meal is better. Higher in nitrogen. Bone meal is

phosphates, good for turnips."

"When are you seeing Leda Zrinyi?"

"Taking her to lunch. I spoke to her on the phone last night. Her mother had already called her about me. How well do you know her?"

Fenrek sat down and balanced a fragile cup on the end of his up-thrust bony knee. He put his hands behind his head and stared up at the ceiling, and said:

"She's a nice girl, if that's not too old-fashioned a phrase. Bright as a new franc, better looking even than her mother, impetuous, and...trouble-prone. She's the kind of person who always gets the wrong end of the stick. But she's a...a nice girl. I'm very fond of her. You'll see what I mean."

He had asked me before why I wanted to see her; but I didn't even know myself, I just thought that I ought to; I wanted to know the girl whose father I was expected to hunt down and who just might get one of us hurt in the process.

We finished our coffee in silence. Fenrek wasn't the kind of man you have to talk to all the time to keep things going, and this was one of the things I liked about him. There was no strain in the silence, just a feeling of calm and comfort. At last, he put the little cup back on the table and said, with a sense of frustration:

"I'm just beginning to realize that I brought you into what is an absolutely hopeless search, you know that?"

"Difficult, but not hopeless."

"Hopeless. There've been a hundred cases with stronger leads than this, cases where the man we're all after has been seen and identified a dozen times, and still...nothing but a brick wall waiting at the end of a long hard hunt. You're hunting for one war criminal out of thousands, and Kolchak's not even a Nazi. If he were, it would be a lot easier, they're better documented. We could get help from the Israelis, and all the other amateur agents. Some of them are pretty damned good. But this man's a Russian, a Communist. That puts him in a category all his own, and far away from the usual places. It's tough enough with the Germans. The Eichmanns and the Stengels are rare cases; they were both well-documented and had been watched for two or three years before anyone moved in on them. In Kolchak's case, we've got nothing. We don't even know if he's still alive. Or if he is, in what part of the world."

I said: "South America, for sure."

He cocked an eye at me, a very shrewd look on his face, "You know something that I don't?"

I told him: "There was one stone in that emerald necklace that wasn't an emerald, put there since it was stolen."

"So? A piece of fine garnet, from Russia, probably. So?"

I said: "It wasn't garnet. I took a long hard look at it; it's a thing known as $CUCO_2CU(OH)_2$. Garnet is usually $_3CaO.A1_2O_{3.3}SiO_2$. That's the grossular, of course. The Pyrope type..."

"Oh, shut up, for Christ's sake!"

Fenrek was weak on chemistry, and he knew that I knew it. "All right, all right, what's its common name?"

I told him. "Malachite. Density four, hardness three point five to four. But there's no trace at all of the usual radial structure, and that identifies it as a rare kind of malachite that is sometimes found in beds of chessylite. It's caused by the action of meteoric waters on copper sulphides. You want the composition of chessylite? Or shall we make it easy for you and call it azurite?"

Fenrek waited; he looked pained.

I said: "That kind of malachite is only found in Brazil. Nowhere else in the world."

He knew better than to argue. I took a Master's in Petrology, a long time ago; just a hobby, really. But he protested, none the less, with the true policeman's obsession for fact, I never think much of facts, myself, they're too misleading. He said, with a touch of sarcasm that didn't become him:

"All right, a Brazilian stone. It could have been put into the necklace in London, in Vienna, in Paris..."

"No." I remembered the fussy little Vallence, and said: "Vallence made a good point. He said that in his business he has to deal in likelihoods. Well, so do I. The malachite was a perfect copy of the emeralds, so whoever cut it must have had at least one of the original stones to copy. The danger would have been too great had the job been given to one of the big European houses, because someone in any of the more important houses would surely have begun to ask questions about those rare, oblong, rose-cut stones; or at least wondered about them; or even remembered them at the wrong time. The job could not possibly have been done by any important European house. Ergo, that points to a place where the skills are high—very high, it was a beautiful job—and contact with the rest of the world of gems is relatively constrained. Again, I'd say that points a very definite finger at Brazil. They've got the best craftsmen in the world, but owing to the receding market there, thousands of their skilled men are out of work, and it wouldn't be hard to find a man who could do so skillful a job and keep quiet about it."

He was beginning to agree with me; all you have to do is *tell* them...He said somberly: "Either keep his mouth shut—or be silenced easily."

"If any one of the great stonecutters in the places we all know disappeared—and this was done by a master, I assure you—then probing fingers would start poking around where Kolchak wouldn't want them. But if some unemployed Brazilian were brought out of his *favella* to do the job and then disappeared, there wouldn't be quite so much fuss. A sad point, but an indisputable one."

Fenrek sighed. "Well, it's good thinking, I suppose..."

"You know damn well it is."

"...but it's a little tenuous, wouldn't you say?"

"Maybe."

"And Brazil's a damn big country."

"Population, fifty million odd. All we have to do is smoke out one man."

Now he said it: "*Pouff.*"

And then the doorbell rang, It was the oyster man, Henri, whose real name was Jean-Marie Castelet, a Detective-Sergeant from the Sûreté. He brought a basket of bright green Marennes, packed in wet seaweed, and handed them silently to the maid, and then accepted a glass of wine from the Colonel which he contrived to drink while standing rigidly to attention. He was a cheery, red-faced fellow who carried a little too much weight; but once he had his eye on a man, he would never lose him. He knew more about the tricks of tailing than any man I've ever known.

When he had finished his wine, he set down his glass as

though he was afraid his chubby fingers would snap the stem, and he fished into his pocket and brought cut a piece of paper. He said:

"Without a doubt, Colonel, it's in code. The subject went straight to the Post Office and sent this telegram."

Fenrek took it from him, looked at it, laughed quietly with a sort of saving grace and read aloud: "*The Giosil Company is very interested in the Ouro Verde property and will possibly visit you soon, Signed, Vallence.*" He said to me, not hiding the grin: "Ouro Verde, that's an estate just south of Setubal, in Portugal, a multi-million dollar tourist complex, hotels, restaurants, night-clubs, little villas on the ocean, that sort of thing."

I said: "Keep talking. Then tell me where the telegram was sent."

He laughed loudly, and said: "Elena da Costa, Poste Restante, Ipanema, Rio de Janeiro, Brazil. Does that prove everything for you?"

"I told you, I deal in likelihoods. You know what Ouro Verde means in Portuguese?"

"Green gold."

"In other words, emeralds. How do you spell the name of that company, Giosil?"

He told me, and frowned, and said: "If the first *i* were an *e*, it would indicate an interest in stones, wouldn't it?"

Mocking him, I said: "Try using one letter before each consonant, one vowel before each vowel."

He worked it out a trifle laboriously, I thought, for such a good brain. "F for G, E for I, N for O...My God, that's Fenrek!"

"Does that prove everything for *you*?"

There went the arms again. The Sergeant watched with quite a show of admiration. Fenrek was very excited. He said eagerly:

"Yes, it clinches it for me, and I apologize. But do you realize, my friend, that we're being watched? Or else how the hell would Vallence know that you and I were even friends?" He said explosively: "'Fenrek interested in the emeralds and will possibly visit you soon.' How did he know of *my* interest in the case?"

I shrugged. "He doesn't, really."

"But...my name, for God's sake!"

I said: "Yes, I forgot to tell you. I used your name when I

spoke to Vallence, you don't mind, do you?"

"You son of a bitch. Why?"

The idiom didn't even sound strange coming from him, but I couldn't help laughing at his indignation. He said: "And you don't forget things like that quite so easily. You son of a bitch. No, I don't mind, since it apparently gave the desired result."

I said: "It's a clumsy code, isn't it? One letter transposition, amateur stuff, I wonder what that means?"

Thoughtfully: "Y-e-s..."

"And yet, the mere mention of your name is to tell them that it's Interpol they have to worry about. To a bunch of amateurs, your name wouldn't mean a thing."

"Precisely what I was thinking."

"I know that."

He turned abruptly to the Sergeant: "All right, Jean. Thank you. Where's Vallence now?"

"At his office. Boulevard Haussman."

Fenrek looked at me and I shook my head. "He's told us what we want to know." He nodded and told the Sergeant: "All right, leave him alone now."

When he had gone, I poured myself a final cup of coffee before the maid came in to sweep the things away, looked at my watch, and remembered my luncheon date. I said: "Who do I see in Brazil?"

"You need more leads than you've got before you go traipsing off to South America."

"What's his name?"

"Da Cunha. Roberto da Cunha Silva Filho." He sighed. "I'd better tell him you're on your way. What about Vallence?"

"Your baby now. I've finished with him."

"The woman?"

"Probably of no importance. He knew his story would be checked, and met a girlfriend in the hotel for the sake of appearances. What they did, what they talked about, that's their business. I don't suppose for one minute she ever had the necklace. Vallence probably brought it back with him the last time he was in Brazil. When was that?"

"Two months ago."

"That makes sense."

Fenrek said: "I'm just wondering what the punishment is for impersonating an Interpol officer."

I banged my head on the door as I went out. It's a couple of inches lower than it ought to be, and I always forget. Always.

Someone had scraped the side of my car when I got down to the street. It's a Jensen FF, English chassis and American engine, the best of both worlds. A six and a quarter liter mill with a Carter four-barrel carb and four-wheel drive with the new Maxaret disc brakes. It's an immensely strong and powerful brute of a car, the model with the roof of brushed stainless steel, only I'd taken it round to Radford's and had them cut the top off; there's no car made, not in the last thirty years, that will seat a man my size in comfort. I take it with me almost everywhere, but I thought South America would be just too far; pity. The trouble with having a degree in Automotive Engineering is that it sours you against the run-of-the-mill cars that, frankly, aren't always as well designed as they might be. That in turn means that you have to pay fifteen thousand dollars for an automobile instead of three.

I drove down to the Pont de Passy, and then took the Right Bank as far as the Louvre, because it's a better drive, crossed over to the Island, and then by the Petit Pont, my favorite of all Paris' thirty-two bridges, to the Left Bank. I parked in Place St. Michel and walked along the beautiful Quai des Augustins to the Laperouse, which has always been one of the truly great restaurants of Paris. Its brown facade and wrought iron balcony brought back a lot of happy memories; and also a reminder to duck as I went in—the doors are very low here. When I had spoken on the phone to Leda Zrinyi, she had suggested a bistro nearby; but I wasn't staying long in Paris, and I wanted at least a couple of first class meals. No good visiting the gastronomic capital of the world if you're not going to pander to your palate a little.

She was ten minutes early when she came, and I wondered if that were a sign of eagerness. Just like her brother, she said when I stood up: "Well, you can't be anyone but Cabot Cain, can you?" She laughed and said: "They already told me what to expect."

I knew her age, of course; she was born in the last year of the war in Europe, and as Fenrek had said, she was better-looking even than her mother. It wasn't the legendary type of Hungarian beauty, though her eyes were properly pale and her hair very fair indeed; she had her mother's calm, controlled assurance—but only on the surface, the kind of young woman you feel you don't really know for quite a while. Tallish, a trifle thin, and very easy-moving with a happy sort of articulation to her limbs. She wore white, and though the summer hadn't come yet her arms and legs were well tanned; she looked like a schoolgirl just back from holiday. When we had spoken on the phone, there seemed to be a suggestion that she wouldn't have much time for lunch, so the first thing I asked her was: "Well, how long do we have?"

She gestured at the decor; there were ancient scratchings on the plate-glass mirrors where long ago attractive young women like Leda Zrinyi had cut their names with diamonds. She said:

"My first time in Laperouse. I decided I'd better take the rest of the day off. I'm not rushing a meal in a place like this, not for anybody." I thought that showed a nice sense of values. She said: "The rest of the day, I'm all yours."

She worked in a small and fashionable dress shop on Rue Dauphine. Not much money, but good clothes. She said: "We have a certain Madame Henriette who's a bit of a virago, but when I told her it was a friend of the family from Budapest...She's very good, really."

"Then after lunch, a drive out to Fontainebleau, how does that sound?"

"It sounds marvelous."

We ordered their famous Crayfish Georgette, and through all the small talk I was delighted that she never once wanted to know what it was that had prompted me to ask to meet her. When they brought the *plateau des fromages* she selected a green-marbled Septmoncel, which comes from the Franche-Comté and is manufactured by the herdsmen in the Jura mountains in minute quantities. The sommelier beamed when I ordered a vin *jeune* with it, a Chateau Chalon, and asked me if I came from the Franche-Comté myself. He blinked when I said: "No, from San Francisco." I think I hurt his feelings. Chateau Chalon is one of the seven greatest wines of France, and we lingered rather long over it, but by half-past two in the afternoon we were speeding down Route Seven through Corbeil and on to the lovely forest of Fontainebleau.

We drove over to the gray-green Gorges d'Apremont and parked, and then wandered around the rocks for a while, looking at the oak trees and the heather, and feeling very remote in both time and space from the bustle that we had so recently left.

She sat down on the bank of a small stream in the shade of a huge chestnut tree, and folded her arms round her knees, and I stood beside her and thought, suddenly, what an extraordinarily attractive girl she was. But she looked unaccountably lost, with a touch of hidden sadness in her. I was reminded strongly of her mother, and the reminder was something to do with family, with the old chains binding parents and their children that don't seem to be as important today as they once were. It was quite natural for a girl of her temperament to go out and make her own way, but somehow it seemed to me she'd be more at home with the others back in the castle. I asked her about it. "Do you miss Hungary? Do you like it here?"

She smiled, a slow, soft smile. "Any civilized woman likes Paris. Yes, I like it; yes, I miss my home too." Like a child, she plucked a long blade of grass, held it between her thumbs, and blew a trumpet sound out of it. Then she looked up and said: "Is that all you want to know about me?"

"Before we're through I'd like to know a great deal more about you."

I sat down beside her, and she said: "So you're going to find the family jewels for us. Do you think you can?"

"Perhaps. I'm going to try."

"Why."

I said gently, teasing her: "I'm a fortune hunter. It's the closest thing I have to a job."

"From what I know of him, he's a terrible man, Kolchak. It might be both difficult, and dangerous."

I wondered how much she really knew about him. One thing, at least, she'd never learn from me.

It was very pleasant out there under the trees and among the rocks, with the gentle trill of the water as a supplement to the sound of the April wind in the trees; the scent of pine needles was coming to us across the little gorge where the stream ran.

I said: "If necessary, could you travel out to Brazil?"

41

Startled, she looked at me: "Brazil?"

"I believe that's where Kolchak is. If he's still alive." For the life of me, I couldn't explain, even to myself, the reasoning that lay behind the question. It just seemed that somehow, it would be a useful thing to have a woman along. Perhaps, almost unconsciously, I was thinking of Ilona Zrinyi and her regard for the family honor; I don't know.

She said: "Now? Right away?" It was an acceptance.

"No, not now. It will probably not be necessary, ever. But if it should seem to be desirable, I'd like to be able to call on...on someone at least connected with the family."

There was a little pause. At last:

"In your world, do people just dash off like that, at a moment's notice, halfway across the world?"

"If it's necessary, they do. And it's far more satisfying than planning for weeks on end. Fenrek says you're an impetuous young woman; are you?"

She laughed. "All right, just send for me. But I don't have any money, does that matter?"

"No. I'll take care of it."

It brought us very close together, somehow. With Zrinyi and the rest of the family, even with Fenrek there, I'd felt more or less an outsider. They'd been friendly, and considerate, and anxious not to show the barrier that lies between the Hungarians and the rest of Europe, or the stronger barrier that we've put up between the Americans and the rest of the world. For them, ours is a very alien culture, and I was always conscious that for them, a native citizen, one of their own kind, would have been more easily acceptable. But Fenrek had said, unequivocally: "Cabot Cain's the only man for you." And so...

But with Leda, I felt none of that strangeness. She'd sloughed off most of her isolationist Hungarianism; she was a European now, and that's a fish of a very different color.

She admired the Jensen when we started back, and on the spur of the moment I said: "Would you like to try it out?"

She looked surprised. "You trust me with it?"

"I trust you."

"A lot more horses than my *quatre cheveaux*."

"Just don't press the pedal too hard. It's the kind of car that goes exactly where you point it, and goes there right away, with a certain amount of alacrity. That's all you have to know."

She drove well, like a racing driver, her thumbs up over the wheel out of the way of the spokes, gripping lightly with her palms and fingers. Her fair hair blew back in the wind, and she said:

"I didn't know they made a convertible."

"They don't. We ran a can opener round the top."

She said, pleading: "Can I try just one short burst of speed?"

I liked the way she held her elbows well into her side, and didn't cross her hands when she turned the wheel, but used them both to push and pull. I said: "As long as you can handle it."

She put her foot down, and the car shot forward like a living thing, growling its impatience. A startled Mercedes pulled over sharply as she swept past him. He chased us for a while, and then gave up and slowed down, even when Leda, with a long-drawn breath, eased off on the pedal.

I went up to her apartment when we got back to Paris. A small, charming place with two rooms, kitchen and bath (of sorts) in an old, seventeenth century building that was so near to the point of collapse that there was a five-degree cant to the floor. Fourth floor, no elevator. The slope to the floor was strong enough to see with the naked eye, but she shrugged it off with: "Don't worry, they tell me it's been like this for the last two hundred years, hasn't moved an inch since then." The furniture and furnishings were the kind of thing you can still find for peanuts in the Flea Market—if you know where to look and don't look like a tourist. Charming and functional, with everything there for a young girl living alone. There were two small windows, cretonne-curtained, that overlooked the pretty little courtyard of the Church of St. Julien-le-Pauvre, and one wall was a bookshelf crowded with books in French, English and Hungarian. But the item that caught my eye the fastest was a small spinet, the two-and-a-half-foot model, that stood in one corner with a tapestried bench beside it.

Leda watched me, a very pleased expression on her face, as I touched the delicate patina of the fine old wood. I said: "May I?" and struck a single note. It was half a tone above normal pitch, the *ton de chapelle.*

She said: "Almost the only thing I brought from Budapest. It was made by Annibale Rosso."

"Oh? That makes it about fifteen seventy."

"Fifteen seventy-two."

"I hope you know what it's worth."

"I do." She sat down and played one of the French Fantasias of Telemann.

I said: "There's a man for you. In twenty years he wrote six hundred overtures, nineteen Passions, twenty Oratorios, and twenty operas. Besides the little trifles you're playing now; thirty-six of them."

The view from the window was fine. We were just high enough to see all the bustle of the Left Bank below us, the narrow streets, and the plane trees, and the patches of brilliant, well-cared-for green.

She finished playing and said abruptly: "I had a letter from Nicholas, he's very fond of you, did you know that?"

It surprised me. "No, I hadn't noticed."

She wandered around the room, putting things in order. She found a stocking under a chair and tossed it carelessly into the bedroom. "Yes, he is. He wrote me a long letter about you, a very long letter. He feels you're doing what he really ought to do, but none the less he thinks you're the better man for it. I don't doubt that you are." She broke off suddenly and frowned. "Reading between the lines, I thought I saw a...a kind of obsession that this should be something for *him* to do. Do you know why?"

I shrugged. "Family jewels, a family matter, that sort of thing."

"But there was almost a personal involvement, as though Kolchak had somehow harmed Nicholas personally, I could read an almost savage hatred that...that he seemed unable to hide. Were very close, Nicholas and I, and he doesn't quite realize how easily I understand what he's thinking."

Parents never really know just how much their children understand; I wondered if Leda knew more than her family gave her credit for, whether their well-kept secret was, at the least, almost a suspicion. I tried to make her change her tack. I said:

44

"I'd feel a bit sore myself under the circumstances. As far as they're concerned, I'm an outsider, with an alien culture. And a culture that I don't suppose they really approve of very much, either."

She laughed then, and the danger was gone.

I wandered about the room with her, picking things up and putting them where they belonged as though half the apartment were mine, as though we shared it together. I did some mental arithmetic for her on the costing she was doing for the dress store, and we sat on cushions on the floor and had some *vin ordinaire*, and she grimaced and said: "It's not Chateau Chalon, is it?" We listened to some of her albums, and she looked at me once and said gravely: "Does everyone think you're a prizefighter? They must, does it bother you?" I said: "No, it doesn't bother me. In my world, most people have more respect for the body than for the mind. I can't hide my size and shape...so I hide my brains instead, is that bad?"

She laughed and said: "Yes, it's terrible! Fenrek was telling me about you. I simply don't believe more than half of it."

"Never believe anything Fenrek tells you."

"He's the nicest man in the world."

"Next to me."

Unexpectedly, she leaned over and gave me a quick, friendly kiss on the cheek. She said: "You don't count, you're one of the family."

"I'm a hired hand is all. And that's a terrible recording."

She got up and changed it, and I got up and wandered round the tiny apartment with her. We made some small talk, and she showed me some of her books.

Looking out through the narrow windows, I could see a Mercedes parked, illegally, in the corner of Rue de la Boucherie. It was the same one we'd seen on the way back from Fontainebleau.

I'd seen it on the way there too.

CHAPTER 4

Every time I go to Rio, I get there just after a storm. Not the kind of storm that hits the West Coast of the U.S.A., where I live, but a storm that can drop twenty inches of water on the town in a single day, sweeping away vast mountain-sides where the slums are and taking with them a hundred or more of the sad little tin-sheet hovels of the *favellas*. That day the newspapers said that three hundred and more had been killed, swept out into the glorious sea and drowned in channels of flowing red mud.

But now, the sun was hot and bright, and the great phallic emblem of the Sugar-Loaf mountain rose up out of the bright blue water against a bright blue sky, gray and green and topped by the little white restaurant in its garden of hibiscus and pines. One of the orange cable-cars was creaking its way up there, a thousand feet above the red tile roof-tops, as we drove along the wide tree-lined sweep of the Flamenco.

Fenrek's man Cunha was there to meet me, a plump, dark-skinned, happy Portuguese-Brazilian in a dark-brown business suit. He drove like a madman in his locally-assembled Volkswagen, scaring the wits out of me, taking short cuts against the traffic in one way streets and once overtaking a long line of cars by driving along the sidewalk. A policeman yelled at him, but he took no notice except to yell back a vigorous insult and run the red light. He saw the look on my face and shrugged. "Everybody does it, why should we have to wait, it's a free

46

country."

The beach at Copacabana was crowded, and kids were flying brightly-colored paper kites and playing *futbol* on the hot sand. I saw a mailman there, stripped down to his shorts and lying asleep with his head on his mail sack. If he slept for too long, or got carried away by the warmth of the sun and the sound of the surf, he'd dump his mail when no one was looking and report back with his empty sack; another day, another *cruzeiro*...

We turned up Paula Freitas and cut in behind a Willis that was trying to park, and went to the Chez Mazot for lunch. A good place, I'd been here before in the old days. We had the shrimps on a skewer and a couple of bottles of ice-cold *cerveje*, and when the coffee came, strong enough to melt the spoons, Cunha pushed back his chair and finally took off his jacket; the temperature was in the early hundreds and the humidity chasing it for the honors. He said:

"And now, Senhor Cain, tell me in what way I can help you."

The little verandah on the sidewalk, lined with privet in boxes, was empty, though it was crowded on the air-conditioned inside. From time to time a waiter poked his head out and raised an eyebrow and brought more beer when Cunha nodded, but we were left comfortably alone; nobody chases a diner out of his seat in Rio, there's all the time in the world; as there should be.

I handed him a piece of paper on which I'd written down the message Vallence had sent to the Poste Restante in Ipanema. "There's a woman named Elena da Costa somewhere, to whom a man named Vallence sent this message. I'd like to find her, first of all."

"Ha! Every other family in town is named da Costa, every other woman is named Elena. But I'll try."

"I don't even know if that's her real name."

He said, pursing his lips: "To get delivery at a Poste Restante, she'd have to show identity papers of some sort. Of course, they're easy enough to forge if it's necessary. But with a name as common as Elena da Costa it wouldn't be worth her while. We'll see what we can do."

I said: "And secondly...This might be a little more difficult." I broke off and said politely, gesturing at his again-empty beer bottle: "Wouldn't you rather have some *conhaque*?"

"Just tell me, I'm quite sure that I can help."

"All right, I will. I suspect that somewhere on the police files there'll be an unsolved murder."

"You really think they keep files?"

I ignored him. "A stonecutter, a first-class craftsman, probably unemployed, or at least not employed by a particularly big outfit. Someone who could be called upon to do a very difficult and unusual job. You know about emeralds?"

"Of course. Half our economy here is founded on gems."

"You know the oblong rose-cut?"

"Er...yes."

He didn't, of course, but it didn't matter. I said: "Someone cut a piece of malachite to resemble an oblong, rose-cut emerald. The circumstances were such that he couldn't have been allowed to live to tell anyone about it."

"I don't know how many stonecutters there are in Rio—maybe a couple of hundred thousand. Yes, Mr. Cain, I will have a glass of *conhaque*. Thank you."

I told the waiter, and then said: "Out of all those possibles, you can eliminate a few improbables. This man was an expert. He must have been given an immensely valuable emerald, cut in a sixteenth-century fashion, to copy. And it must have been someone who could be silenced, one way or another, as soon as he'd finished the job."

He said slowly: "That points to one of the unemployed cutters from the *favellas*, wouldn't you say? A man who wouldn't be missed. It's a very distressing thought, isn't it, that if a man is successful, someone's going to wonder what happened to him if he's killed. But if he's poor, no one really worries very much." He said piously: "When I reflect on things like this; I wonder if there is any hope for the human race."

I said: "My thinking precisely. But somewhere among those unhappy people, there was once a man who cut a piece of malachite for the man I'm after."

"You have, of course, an approximate date?"

I said cheerfully: "Any time in the last twenty years. Or twenty-five, at a pinch." He looked shocked. I said: "Well, start a few months ago and go back. With any luck at all, it might have been fairly recent. A necklace was sold, and it's at least a likelihood that the repair to it would not have been made while it was just lying around in someone's safe. More probably, it was done when the decision was made to sell it."

He frowned, "Even so, why should anyone put a false stone in an emerald necklace? Even the best malachite wouldn't stand up to expert appraisal."

"No, and that was a mistake, wasn't it? My guess is that not all of the stones would have been tested, so one out of thirty-two might have squeezed by. Sold illegally, the seller would only get a third of its true value anyway, so it was worth a try not to have any more taken off because one stone was missing. But as I say, a mistake. Ever hear of a man named Kolchak?"

He shook his head. "Only in Colonel Fenrek's cable."

"Uh-huh."

"You have good reason for thinking he may be here?"

"Tenuous reasons, Fenrek called them. And I suppose he's right."

We had some more coffee, and I saw that all the customers were leaving. Watching them go, Cunha smiled and said hopefully: "Off to the siesta, it's a custom here."

I said: "Yes, I know, let's go for a run down the beach."

He protested, but he didn't really know just how high I rated with Fenrek and so, very reluctantly, he agreed. He patted his paunch and said:

"Well, a slow stroll perhaps. I'm not really as energetic as all that. We have to conserve our strength, you know, or when we come to need it, it's all gone, wouldn't you say?"

He walked me round to the hotel. Two blocks, and he wanted to drive in that damned sardine-box of a Volkswagen. We bought swimsuits on the way and changed into them, and then set off along the hot sand at a slow trot. He gave up after two hundred yards, and I left him there and ran the three miles to Ipanema, then another three along the Praia de Leblon, did a hundred push-ups or so to get the sleep out of my lungs, and then ran back.

I found my new friend lying lazily under an umbrella with a slim and pretty *Mameluca* girl, part Portuguese, part Indian, part

Negro. A lithe young animal of a girl with very high, pointed breasts and a waist so small it was going to snap in two at any minute. He grinned at me and said:

"Her name is Maria da Costa. She has a sister named Elena, and two cousins named Elena, and an aunt named Elena. I wonder if you'd like to take your pick." The girl was smiling at me, looking up with her eyes wide and mischievous, and I said:

"I'll choose her any day."

She laughed, showing strong white teeth, her eyes bright and full of fun. She said: "So let us go, big man, now."

I stood with them on the hot sand, and da Cunha squinted up at me and asked: "You must have gone as far as the Arpeador?"

"Four miles beyond it."

He stared at me as though I were quite mad. Strange; the plumper a man gets, the less important he thinks it is to keep the body working properly.

I sat in the sun and chatted with Maria for a while. It was good to hear the Portuguese of the true *Carioca* again; it's a cheerful, happy-go-lucky dialect; just like the people. A Negro vendor in a floppy straw hat came by, selling pineapples, and we shared one together, letting him slice it up expertly with the razor-sharp machete they call a *facao*; he squatted on his heels with a happy grin and fed us all. The sweet juice dribbled down Maria's chin, and she stood there with her body bent forward, her elbows away from her body, her long fingers spread, very slim and feline and extraordinarily attractive; not pretty; good looking. She saw me looking at her, and stretched up one hand to see if she could reach the top of my head; some girls passing by laughed at us, and everything was very pleasant.

Cunha said: "This is the life, isn't it?" I agreed, but told him there was work to do. Reluctantly, he patted Maria's little behind and we went back to the hotel. He said, hopefully: "To sleep?" He looked very pained when I sent him down to the police station to start the ball rolling.

He met me again the next day at noon, when I was down in the gym on Barata Ribeiro, working out with the punching bag. I said:

"You're just in time, I was going up to Corcavado to look at the view."

He said: "Ah, splendid, my car is outside."

"On foot."

He paled a little. He said uncertainly: "Surely you jest?"

"No, do us both good."

It's not much more than ten or fifteen miles, but it's a climb of two thousand feet or so, and I needed the exercise. He said:

"Perhaps I should have the car follow us, just in case?"

"I'll buy you a beer at the top."

He said earnestly: "I'll never make it, Mr. Cain. Never."

"And you can tell me all the good news on the way."

Well, to keep him happy, we drove the Volkswagen as far as Laranjeiras where the ratchet-railway begins its long haul to the top. He looked enviously at the train that was just starting up, and I said:

"This way, through the forest, we'll take the old road. And for God's sake get rid of that jacket."

He nodded miserably and took off his coat and tie, and I laughed and said: "I promise you, you'll feel a lot better for it."

He was a Brazilian, and his misery wasn't going to last for long. He brightened up when we stopped to look over the treetops at the great lagoon spread out there below us, with the islands green and lovely, and a few white clouds in the sky. There were palms and ferns, and rubber trees, and bougainvillea and honeysuckle, and a thousand unnamed plants in a thousand different colors; the air was soft and clean and fresh, and there were great patches of deep, cool shade as we moved in and out of the trees. We crossed the railroad track, and moved over one of its rickety bridges, and climbed up and up and up till the whole of Copacabana and Ipanema and Leblon were laid out far below us. Cunha stared and said:

"My God, have we really come from down there? Wait till my wife hears about this."

We reached the first of the plateau at four o'clock, and I looked at the expression on his face and said:

"All right, I'll give you a beer and half-an-hour's rest."

There is an old hotel there that looks like a railway station, with a big verandah overlooking the sea. A red slash in the side of the mountain showed where the recent rains had wrought their havoc, and there were up-ended banana trees everywhere, all down the steep slope. We drank some cold beer and took in the scenery for a while, and then Cunha looked at his watch and said happily:

"Time's up, let's see if we really can reach the top."

The road was washed away here, leaving a perilously narrow portion that jutted out over the immense drop, and there were signs that said: "NO TRAFFIC PERMITTED"; the cars were rattling noisily past them, at high speed, as always, squeezing by with millimeters to spare. The waving greenery at the broken edge was the tops of trees on the lower slope, more than a hundred feet tall.

We reached the final platform at last, with the gigantic concrete statue of Christ, ninety feet high and weighing more than eleven hundred tons, and we found a grassy spot to sit on where there was nobody much around and the view across the bay to the mountains above Niteroi was unbelievably splendid, and I said:

"All right, you came with news, let's have it."

He leaned back against a tree and spread out his pudgy legs, and said, beaming: "I thought you'd never ask for it." He took a deep breath and said: "Well..." He was wet through with perspiration, but happy. He lit a little black cigarette, threw the match carelessly into the grass, and blew out a long puff of blue smoke.

"First of all, Elena da Costa. There's a woman of that name registered for the collection of mail in Ipanema. She shows her identity card, of course, and we checked the address given on it; there's no such place, so it seems likely that this is the woman you're interested in. The clerk there remembers her, and says she comes in fairly regularly, once a month or so, and that most of her mail comes from abroad."

"Out of the thousands who pick up their mail there he remembers one woman? How come?"

"Two reasons. The fact that the mail is nearly always from overseas and he's a bit of a stamp enthusiast. Secondly, and more important, every Brazilian remembers a good-looking woman. I don't have much of a description—the clerk is not really very bright. All he could do was keep saying, with considerable enthusiasm and a foolish grin: '*Linda, muito linda*, very beautiful...' A small, dark woman of thirty or so."

"Once a month? That presupposes no great urgency ever, and

also regular visits from somewhere up-country."

He nodded, and pulled a piece of paper out of his trouser pocket and said:

"Wilhehm Werther, an unemployed stonecutter, disappeared eight months ago and hasn't been seen since. The circumstances lead me to suspect that this might be the man you are interested in. Two other stonecutters were killed, or at least died, both of them in the last five years. One, run over in downtown Rio, the other washed away from a *favella* in a rainstorm. Both were employed by Sterns, a big and famous house, and therefore not quite what you wanted. Werther, however"—he frowned before continuing—"with Werther, the whole thing's fishy."

"Tell."

"Nine months ago, he told his wife he was going to São Paulo to look for work. He hadn't had any for more than a year, though he's a first-class cutter. As you know, the business is not what it was a few years ago, and a lot of good men are out of work. All right, he went off for what he said was going to be a few days, and his wife never saw him again. They didn't get on very well together; or perhaps I should say they really hated each other. No children. However, he did return to Rio, three weeks later, but not for long. Just long enough to pick up his girlfriend, a young woman named Dorothea da Gloria, and go. Dorothea lived with her sister in Flamenco, and fortunately, they were very close, good friends as well as sisters. Whenever Werther came calling on Dorothea, the sister would sleep out on the verandah. Now, when Werther made his quick and secret visit back to Rio, Dorothea told her sister, very excitedly, that she was going with Werther to Fuerte Quemado. And she also told her that she was under the strictest orders not to breathe a word to anyone of her destination. And since that time, no one has seen or heard of Wilhelm Werther. He may not be dead; but he's certainly disappeared."

"No one has seen him—in Fuerte Quemado either?"

Cunha looked at me strangely, "You don't know this place?"

"Fuerte Quemado? No, I've never even heard of it." That wasn't quite true; there was a little bell ringing somewhere, but it didn't mean very much.

Cunha threw away his lighted cigarette-end and fished out the pack. This time he offered it to me hesitantly: "But you don't smoke, do you, Mr. Cain?"

I shook my head, and he lit up and said: "Fuerte Quemado is up on the Bolivian border, on a mountain above the River Marmore. A tiny, colonial town, built by a group of adventurers from Captain Orellano's men back in fifteen hundred forty, led by a Captain Amado."

Orellano was the man who had given the Amazon its name, the first of the great explorers. During his search for the headwaters of the great river, he'd been attacked by a tribe of what he reported were female warriors (which is how the river got its name), although they were probably just plump, long-haired, highly-painted Indian men; some of the tribes up there are so fierce that you can't get close enough to tell the men from the women without getting your head chopped off. The Amazons had captured Amado and a hundred of his men and dragged them off, and I seemed to recall that they'd escaped later and built a mountaintop fortress above the Marmore. It hadn't done them much good; a couple of years or so later, the local Indians had eaten them all.

Cunha said: "During one of the rubber booms in the early nineteen hundreds, Fuerte Quemado became quite a prosperous city. But there was only one way into it, a very difficult track up the mountain, and an earthquake moved the side of the mountain a couple of miles off in nineteen seventeen, and that was the end of that. The only way in now is by helicopter." He broke off and stared moodily at his cheroot for a while, and then threw it away. "Maybe I should give up smoking too, Senhor Cain, what do you think?"

I said: "I think I want to know all about Fuerte Quemado."

"Well, there's no other way in. No, that can't be quite true, there must be a road of some sort, because people do come and go in the area. All around there, it's...it must be rather like the wild west of your own country, in the old days. The whole district is so remote and inaccessible that it has attracted all the riff-raff of the continent. There's still overt banditry up there, a lot of smuggling, and almost no police control; no law and order. A certain amount of trade: rubber, nuts, semi-precious stones, that sort of thing. Some castor beans and a trade in dried fish for the native villages. The traders go in there quite often, but they have a happy sort of relationship with the local people; in exchange for tribute, the locals take very good care of them. And in the center of this wild and lawless territory, Fuerte Quemado stands on a very forbidding mountain, and even the local people give it a wide berth. The whole of the nut is bad, but its kernel is a very evil place. Moreover, Fuerte Quemado itself is in disputed territory that Bolivia sometimes claims, and sometimes even Peru, though why anybody would want those miserable few thousand square miles I can't imagine. It is terrible country, Mr. Cain. I flew over it once."

"But people still live there."

He was getting more excited by the minute. He said: "Yes, people live there. The local population consists largely of wild-rubber tappers. They send their rubber down the mountain on the backs of mules, or of women where the mules can't go, down to the river, and then on by boat. Even that isn't easy—hostile tribes, deadly insects, and more waterfalls than a man could ever hope to see in a lifetime."

"You said 'the local population,' I believe?"

"Yes." There was great satisfaction on his face now. Fenrek hadn't told him too much, but he knew how to put two and two together. He said: "For the last twenty years, Fuerte Quemado has become a sort of haven for the friends and associates of the late Adolf Hitler."

The little bell stopped ringing in the back of my mind. Fuerte Quemado was on Eichmann's itinerary while the Israelis were trying to flush him out of hiding.

Cunha said: "It's an inaccessible town in disputed territory, with no government but its own. Fifty or sixty of the Nazi war criminals are there, openly daring the whole world to come and get them if it can. The police chief there is—was—the man who succeeded Heydrich in Czechoslovakia and slaughtered eighty-two thousand Czechs in reprisal for Heydrich's assassination. He was. He got caught when he was foolish enough to make a trip down to São Paulo, and we don't know who's taken his place. There's also a man up there who used to rule Papa Doc Duvalier's terror squads, a dreadful man named Luthier Koch, a specialist in everything unpleasant. The town's leading citizen once ran Battista's underground prisons. In short, some of the world's most-wanted men are there, living in open defiance, armed to the teeth and ready for anyone who wants to come and get them. Stengel was there till they got him recently on a visit to his family in Paraguay. Mendel is known to be there, Muller, Horscht, Reichmann, dozens of them. And they even boast—boast, mark you—that Martin Borman is there too."

"And no one has ever tried to get them out?"

Cunha spread his arms eloquently. "Who? The War Crimes Commission? Even an army couldn't get them out. And whose army? Brazil's? For Brazil to mount an attack on territory that Bolivia claims...or for Bolivia to try it either...And even so, what hope would they have? They'd take shelter in the forest, or trickle down to the villages and wait until their little fortress was free again. No, they can't easily be gotten out; as you put it. Their fortress is too strong, they're too well organized. From force, they are safe. The only weapon we have is guile, Senhor Cain. They can be kidnapped, as Eichmann was kidnapped. Or lured out, as Stengel was lured out. But for the rest..." He was frowning suddenly. "But Kolchak, that doesn't sound like a German name. A Nazi?"

"No, a Russian."

"A Communist?"

"Once."

There was a long silence. At last Cunha said: "Then I've been wasting your time, haven't I? The last place for a Communist to hide would be among the Nazis of Fuerte Quemado. Unless he could hide his nationality, his origins, so well that they wouldn't suspect him." The frown deepened. "And that isn't likely. Every newcomer looking for sanctuary in Fuerte Quemado must be screened so well that...No, I've been wasting my time. And yours."

I said: "In a prison, all the prisoners are on one side; the warders are on the other."

"I wonder if that's true? Yes, perhaps it is. Then you think your Kolchak might be there?"

"It's a likelihood, wouldn't you say?"

He beamed. "That's precisely what I'd say."

He took some snapshots from his pocket and handed them to me. "For what they are worth, photographs of Werther and his girlfriend."

Werther was a fragile-looking man, his face lined with care and trouble. His girlfriend, Dorothea, was surprisingly attractive for so insignificant a man to catch. I slipped the photographs into my pocket.

The sun was going down, and the flat-topped mountains across the great valley were wreathed in red and yellow clouds.

Cunha got to his feet quickly and said: "Twilight, we have to watch."

We walked together over to the edge of the bluff and looked to the west. The dark gray of the cloud mass was changing color, the gold that touched it turning to red, and then to purple, and finally to a dark, dark blue. Far, far below us, the shadows were creeping over the town and the lights were beginning to come on. High in the sky, a jet reflected the bright copper sun in silence. The sea was darkening, and the white-topped waves were edging the still yellow sand. It was all unbelievably beautiful. I thought of Leda and wondered if she'd ever been here; I knew how much she'd like to see all this.

Strangely, I felt a nostalgic longing for her company.

Out of deference to Cunha's physique, we took the train down the mountain to Laranjeiro. It had taken us five hours to climb up, and we went down in fifteen minutes.

That damned Volkswagen was still there, and as I squeezed myself into it and tried to find somewhere to put my legs; I asked him: "What's the best way to get to Fuerte Quemado?"

I'd left a letter for Fenrek before I left, and when I got back to the hotel there was already an answer to it. I'd written:

Let me know if anything turns up on Vallence. If you want a lead, there's a burgundy and tan Mercedes 250SL Coupe, not a bad little job, watching Leda's apartment, largely, I suppose, because of my interest in her; soi-disant Interpol interest, of course. License number is 8490SH75. Don't worry about it; it's good; just make sure nothing happens to her. If you ever find the mystery woman, which I doubt, I'd be glad to hear about her, too. And make sure I know at once if any more of the Zrinyi collection turns up on the market. My guess is that if any more pieces are floated out, it will be anywhere but in Paris, and won't be for a while anyway. The price they got for the necklace ought to keep them in clover for the moment. If you use my car, don't forget I'm fussy about greasing it every three thousand miles.

The answer from Fenrek came in the diplomatic bag of the Ambassador, which must have made him mad, and was sent round by special messenger:

Yes, I'm using your car, and I bashed the right front fender this morning, hope you don't mind too much. The Mercedes belongs to Vallence's sister, and what do you mean, not a bad little job, it's a beauty. Strange, the sister looks just like the mystery woman. Took a snapshot and showed it to the hotel clerk, he says that's her, thanks for the tip. Nothing much we can do about it—at least, not at this stage; but I've put the pair of them in my pending tray, except that I'm watching their mail, I'll cable you the code word INDEPENDENCE if and when he follows up his telegram with a letter, which he's almost certain to do. Give my regards to da Cunha, and treat him gently, he's a nice fellow.

Best wishes, Fenrek.

So...Fenrek had got the police working already. He was right, there was nothing he could do at this stage. Mlle. Vallence could shrug off an accusation of visiting the Georges Cinq under the name of Marie Dubois, from Bordeaux. And, of course, there never was a Hungarian passport; that was just a fiction Vallence had invented to give body to his story. Small fry, anyway.

And I'd hardly finished fuming over my bashed front fender when a cable did indeed arrive. It was sent over the special line to Cunha, and he called my room. The connection was pretty lousy, and he said: "Maybe I'd better come round. Only you must promise me we don't go for any long walks."

I said; "How are the legs?"

"I can hardly move them. Shall I read it to you?"

"No, better not. Can I pay you a visit?"

"Mr. Cain, I would be delighted. If you're sure it's not too much trouble? I could send a man with it..."

"I'll be there in half an hour."

He lived in one of the new apartments on Figueroa Magalaes, just round the corner from the place where I used to take my morning coffee when I was here a few years ago: three cents a cup and delicious, but you have to stand poised to strike when the man pours it—the next thing they do is fill the cup to the brim with sugar. Coffee and cotton are the things they produce most of and sugars only sixth on the list, but they still produce a hell of a lot, and somehow they seem to use all of it themselves.

It was an ugly, high-rise apartment house in yellow concrete, and there was a lot of fuss when I arrived because someone had dropped some burning ashes down the garbage chute and the basement was merrily on fire; they said the Fire Department had been called, and they expected it to arrive sometime later in the day, and meanwhile the concierge had recruited the neighborhood kids to slosh buckets of water everywhere. A small crowd had gathered; they turned to stare at me as I went in.

Cunha's wife was a tall, scraggy woman with dark, bony features and intelligent eyes; she must have been very pretty once. She said: "You'll stay to dinner, won't you?" From the noise coming out of the kitchen, I guessed that a sizable gaggle of small children was already at work preparing the meal. I could smell the scent of charcoal burning in the brazier, and she smiled and said: "*Churrasquinho*, if you like that."

Churrasquinho is small pieces of barbecued meat on skewers; if you're lucky, it's prime steak, but it can turn out to be goat, or—at Carnival time, when they make drums out of catskin—even the stray cats unlucky enough to get caught. I said:

"You're very kind. And I'm fond of *churrasquinho*."

"Good, then that's settled." She bustled off to the kitchen, and Cunha poured some *conhaque* before showing me the cable.

FENREK TO CAIN, INDEPENDENCE, SAME ADDRESS AND NAME AS BEFORE, THEY'VE FOUND OUT YOU'RE NOT ME, COPY LETTER FOLLOWS DIPLOMATIC BAG. REGARDS.

Cunha wanted to know what the second sentence meant, but didn't like to ask, so I told him: "Just what I was hoping for. There's a man called Vallence in Paris, who's a front man for getting rid of looted valuables. When I went to see him, I said I was Fenrek. Interpol interest was more likely to spur them into doing something rash." He grinned. I said: "If I questioned Vallence as Cabot Cain, private citizen, he'd have done nothing, assuming that I was a private investigator and quite harmless, But with Interpol on his tail—I guessed it might goose him into doing something desperate."

"Another letter going to Elena da Costa. Shall we pick her up when she collects it?"

I said: "God forbid. As soon as Fenrek's copy gets here we'll know what it's all about anyway. Did you know your building is on fire?"

He shrugged. "It happens all the time. The children block the chute with newspapers and wait for someone upstairs to empty the ashtrays. It provides them with a little excitement."

Before dinner, I was solemnly presented to the somewhat awed children; five of them, all girls, ranging from four years old to eleven, before they were hustled off to bed. The *churrasquinho* turned out to be lamb on long slivers of bamboo, served with a crumbly mixture of beans and flour fried in pork fat and sprinkled with hard-boiled eggs; it was excellent, and when his wife had retired to do the dishes, Cunha said, patting his stomach happily:

"I've found out the best way for you to get to Fuerte Quemado. But it's not going to be easy." He spread an old map, taken from a *National Geographic Magazine*, out on the table, and stubbed at it with his thick fingers. "Commercial airlines most of the way, and it's quite a long haul. First to Guiratinga in the Matto Grosso—that's about eight hundred miles. Another nine hundred to Santo Antonia on the border of Guapore and Amazonas and now you're in the Amazon watershed and cut off, except for the airstrip, from civilization altogether. If you disappear from history, this is where it happens. From there to Fuerte Quemado..." He raised his hands helplessly. "You can get to Urbana, here, fairly easily. There's a charter service at Santo Antonio the traders use, and there's a tiny airstrip at Urbana. But there you've come to the end of the road, into the badlands where honest men aren't very welcome unless they're buying or selling. Maybe you should go up there as a trader? I could fix you up with the necessary cover."

I shook my head, and he shrugged. "In Urbana," he continued, "you're about fifty miles from Fuerte Quemado. That might be the longest fifty miles you've ever traveled." In sudden exasperation, he exploded: "You'll never get in there, Senhor Cain. Never!"

I said: "Well, we don't know that till I try, do we?"

Gloomily: "And if anything happens to you, we'll never even know it. Perhaps I should put a man in Urbana to keep in touch with you, just in case?"

"I have someone." He looked at me strangely, but said nothing. I found a paper and pencil, scribbled a note and gave it to him. "Get this to Fenrek for me, will you? As fast as possible."

He read it carefully, and asked: "Cable? Or Diplomatic pouch?"

"Pouch. I don't want it read by the wrong people."

"All right. By nine o'clock tomorrow morning it will be on the way to Paris."

The message read:

Please ask Leda to take a holiday in Urbana, State of Guapore, Brazil. Use her own passport and travel via northern not, repeat NOT, southern route. The sooner the better. She'll need money.

Regards. Cain.

We got on the phone then to ask about flights to Guiratinga in the Matto Grosso; the day after the next, six o'clock in the morning. It was about right. I told Cunha:

"The morning I leave, I'll have a parcel for you. Just put it away in a safe place and do nothing till you hear from me. Do you have a spare key to your mailbox downstairs?"

"Yes, I do. But I could easily pick up whatever it is."

"I don't want to get you out of bed in the middle of the night. Just lend me the spare key."

A trifle mystified, but not asking any questions, he handed it over. We had a few drinks together, and then Senhora da Cunha came back and sat with us for a while and joked about her husband's unexpected trip up to Corcavado; she seemed to admire him enormously for it, and Curtha beamed and told her:

"Senhor Cain wanted to take the car, but it's not comfortable, you know, for such a big man. So I said: 'Let's walk, Mr. Cain, the exercise will do us good.' And it did, too. I lost nearly three inches round my waistline, in one day, can you imagine that?"

I said: "We must do it again sometime." I caught his quick look of anguish.

It was two in the morning before I got back to the hotel and into bed, and the following afternoon, while I was exercising on the beach in front of the hotel, the clerk found me (bearing a large white card with my name printed in red on it) and told me there was a letter, brought over by a representative from the Swiss Embassy. One of Fenrek's friends, no doubt. I went back to get it.

It was indeed from Fenrek:

Your reasoning is devious, Cain, and one day it's going to get us all into trouble. I understand now why you so glibly took my name in vain with Vallence. The Interpol bit scared them enough to follow you and see what you were up to—which, in turn, indicated to me that I was very wrong in my earlier assessment of Vallence. And then they found out that Fenrek of Interpol is half an inch under six feet, and not the hulking great animal that was presented to them. No doubt, it made them think very carefully, and they seem to have come up with a decision that, no doubt, you foresaw...that they weren't tangling with the law at all, but with some amateur who could probably be scared off. They took the appropriate kind of action, and I'm glad I followed your warning and kept an eye on Leda; someone broke into her apartment in the middle of the night. My man caught him before he could do any damage. He carried a knife, but I don't think he would have used it. Under questioning, he said he'd been told—by whom, we haven't yet found out, a lousy description—to find out exactly what you and she were talking about in the forest of Fontainebleau. Be careful, Cain. We're expendable, you and I, but Leda's not. Your ploy came off well; but it was a trifle near the bone. Now, to better things.

Enclosed is a copy of a letter sent to the elusive (still elusive?) Elena da Costa in Ipanema. Not hard to read between the lines. Vallence wrote it himself, and in spite of his insolent self-assurance, what with one thing and another we've got a case against him—though I don't suppose we want to do anything yet, do we? No, I thought not. Leda sends her love (already?) and hopes you find everything you're looking for.

Best wishes, Fenrek.

P.S. I won't forget to grease the car. The front fender has been repaired. Really is a damn fine car, isn't it? Stay away as long as you like.

The copied letter he had enclosed, intercepted from Vallence, was worded in casual, innocent French. Roughly translated, it read:

It wasn't the Giosil Company after all, but someone using their name to impress us. We're taking action at this end, and you shouldn't be bothered by them. But if you are, it will probably be by a huge American oaf; at least six-feet-eight in height, all muscles and no brains. His name appears to be Cabot Cain, though this is probably merely an alias; could anyone, even an American, really have such a name? He's easily recognizable because of his size. He's about thirty, dark hair, dark eyes, looks like a football player or a boxer, and physically is undoubtedly very dangerous indeed. But I doubt very much his intellectual competence. No indication here as to how or why he got onto us, or if he really is headed for your part of the world. And I think we should consider that he might not be a detective, as I at first supposed, but a criminal himself; he hasn't the brains for the former, and he has the looks of the latter, so let's think about that. There's a good market for item number three, broken up into smaller lots, in Brussels. Perhaps you should have sub-divided the previous property too.

Best regards. Vallence.

I wondered what item three was; the tiara?

But now, things were rolling nicely. I was almost ready to go.

Down by the Ouro Verde Hotel on the Avenida Atlantica that sweeps round Copacabana's glorious beaches, there's a very expensive jewelers named Aaron Filho. Old man Aaron has been in Brazil ever since World War One, and now he's in his eighties and controls millions—one of the best-known and least-loved men on the Continent. Gold mines in Rio Branco, oil in Bahia, carnuba wax in Ceara, as well as coffee, alfalfa, manioc, cotton-seed and sugarcane. As if that weren't enough, he owns huge areas of real estate in every Brazilian city worth the name. I have never met him, but by all reports he's a mean and evil-tempered old bastard. His gems are really a sideline, but they're among the best in the country. The well-stocked window of his Rio store is protected by a heavy grill of expanded metal which is cemented into the concrete walls at either side. There are mostly garnets and zircons on show, but there are quite a lot of diamonds and jade as well.

I went down there at half past three in the morning, when the streets were empty except for a few unfortunates sleeping in doorways and an occasional police patrol prowling around. There were one or two late-night prostitutes still to be seen too; just about right for what I had to do.

I found a broken curbstone and used it to smash the plate glass window, then took hold of the center bar of the grill with both hands and wrenched at it. It was stronger than I expected it to be, so I jumped up and put my two feet on the window ledge, and threw all my two-hundred-and-ten pounds into it, forcing my shoulders back and arching my spine. Even so, it took nearly two minutes before the grill ripped out, and by that time one of the beggars was awake and staring at me in shock, and a couple of girls had taken cover round the corner and were peeking round in astonishment, keeping deathly quiet.

I selected the best of the diamonds and a few good pieces of jade, and stuffed them into my pockets. One of the girls came running up and said: "*Para min tamben*, for me too," holding out her hand. Then someone shouted, and a police whistle blew, and a single shot was fired; I didn't hear where the bullet went, but I judged it time to go. I ran fast up Rua Duvivier, cut through the dark passage to Rudolfo

Dantas, and was back at the hotel ten minutes later.

I wrote a note to Cunha:

Keep these well-hidden, say nothing, and above all, don't stop the police from doing their duty, bless their hearts. I'll apologize to the old man when I get back.

I put the jewels and the note in a heavy manila envelope, walked quickly round to Figueroa Magaloes, and slipped the packet, together with the borrowed key, into Cunha's mailbox. It was four o'clock precisely, and the plane was due out at six. A nice time for a brisk walk out to the airport.

By the time the first cup of coffee was served by the smiling stewardess, we were flying at twenty-eight thousand feet over the bright green carpet that was the forests of the interland. Once you leave the yellow strand of the coast, the gray mountains and the green trees seem to be crowding the cities, sliced through with shimmering, winding rivers and little patches of bright red earth where the coffee grows.

Brazil must be one of the most scenically satisfying countries in the world.

CHAPTER 5

I spent the long haul to Guaratinga, on the Varig Airlines plane, studying those of the Zrinyi sketches that I'd brought along with me.

It's part of the Great Diagonal, the slice through Brazil that the airlines are carving from northwest to southeast in an effort to open up some of that vast and mostly unknown territory. A series of airstrips carved out of the jungles and the marshes and the mountains; and around them nothing but animal-filled forests and the broad waters of the great basin, a life that hasn't changed in a million years, where even evolution seems to have slowed down.

Up here in the aircraft there were smiling hostesses in neat gray uniforms, filet mignon and good French wines, magazines to read in six different languages; but down there, there was an empty land so vast that a man could not imagine its horizons.

I hadn't really expected any trouble at Guaratinga, and there wasn't any; there just hadn't been time in the three hours since we had left Rio. Nobody stirs down there till a sensible hour, not even the police.

At Santo Antonio, I was on my guard. It was now one o'clock in the afternoon, steaming damply, but there was still no sign of any action. I wondered how long it would take them to find out who the burglar was and trace me to the airport; there can't be that many smash-and-grab artists in Rio who are six feet seven inches tall, and dammit, I was seen by at least three people.

But there was nothing,

The airline office directed me to a small hangar where there was a private charter company: two old planes, a Cessna and a Bonanza. A white-haired, toothless old man flew me to Urbana, a bumpy fight over the dense jungle that took an hour and a half, and set the plane down tidily on a strip of cropped dry grass on a small plateau above the river. I watched him take off again in the fading light, and walked down the dirt track to the town, slithering down the steep slope toward the river.

A pretty little town, Cunha had said, and he was right. There was a single main street, running at right-angles to the wide river, with neatly painted houses of adobe and red tile roofs. Two small hotels, three cafés, eight or nine stores, a surprisingly well-kept little park, and a deeply-recessed inlet from the water where the boats were tied up. There was a fairly big launch that looked somehow as though it were at the end of its days, a small canoe with an outboard attached to it, and half a dozen Indian outriggers; there were nets strung along the wharf to dry, with semi-clad men, small and dark and wiry, repairing them carefully.

It was getting dark, and there was not much to see. It was striking that there were no cars in sight; I imagined the problem of getting them here was almost insuperable, and then I saw a beat-up old truck moving clumsily along the dusty street and turning out of my sight. I looked at the men repairing the nets, and wondered what there was to do here besides fish. "They take good care of the traders," Cunha had said. I hoped he was right.

There are always people living in even the remotest places, but you can't help wondering what keeps them there. The river was wide, and a floating island of tangled vines and shrubs had jammed itself into the opposite bank, more than half a mile across. I could hear the chatter of monkeys and the cries of parrots; Urbana was carved out of the jungle, and the jungle was threatening to take it back again and strangle it. Somebody, somewhere, was playing a reed instrument, a thin, softly melodic sound of almost pagan origin. We were in the high mountains here, and it was quite cold.

I walked over to the café that was on the corner across from the wooden wharf, a broken down place of wicker chairs and unsteady tables. I ordered a *pinga*, the crude brandy they make up here, from the heavy-set Indian woman who looked at me in silence. She had been talking to a thick-set, bearded man of indefinable nationality, calling him *proprietario*. I was the only customer, and the thick-set man came over, a stranded adventurer, and said in heavily-accented English: "Americano, eh? We don't get many Americanos up here. You come to trade? You want castor beans? We got a good crop this season."

I said: "No, just looking for peace and quiet, looks like a good place to find it."

He found this a very funny remark, and his evil face wrinkled up with pleasure, giving it a sort of malign charm. He said: "Big man like you not going to find peace no place." I thought that was a friendly bit of homespun philosophy, and he sat down opposite me and helped himself, uninvited, from the *pinga* bottle. He said: "My name Mazlor, Czech. I own this place, own the hotel, own everything. The store, the big launch, the hotel. Everything. Anything you want, I get for you, Senhor...?"

"Cain. Cabot Cain."

"Anything you want, Senhor Cain, I get for you. Don't you go no place else, they steal from you. You stay my hotel, how long you stay?"

"Till I get tired of it. A few days, a few weeks, who knows?"

He grinned broadly. "You don't get tired. What you want, I find for you. Plenty drinks, plenty women, everything."

I said casually: "What's the route like over into Bolivia?"

His chair tipped back, his hands behind his head, he had been staring out across the river; his eyes fixed on a flight of brilliant fireflies that were as bright as a flashlight. Now he tuned to look at me more carefully. He got up and switched on the lights, and said:

"Bolivia? Up the river to Pando, over the mountain to Beni, which way you want to go?"

"Over the mountain, maybe."

"Yes." He grinned. "Is better. On the river, they got army launch."

"I should worry."

"Sure, no need to worry. Honest man don't have to worry." He burst out laughing suddenly, and filled my glass with his brew. He wore baggy blue trousers and a khaki shirt that was torn under the arm, with a thick leather belt heavily decorated with brass studs; his feet were bare. He said: "But you don't get to Bolivia by yourself, not over the mountain, not up the river, is too tough. You need help. River wind this way, that way, you get lost. Mountain is worse, no track anymore."

"No? What about the track that leads up to Fuerte Quemado?"

He leaned forward and dug his elbows into the table, scratching dandruff out of his hair. The smile, the good humor were still there; only now they were false, suspicious, even hostile. He said:

"You want to go to Fuerte Quemado?"

"No, not really. But that's on the old track into Bolivia, isn't it?"

He said: "You speak English pretty good for German. Pretty good."

"And I speak pretty good German for an American."

He thought that was very funny, too. He laughed and said: "Okay, better you forget Fuerte Quemado, my friend. Honest man don't go there no more. Not safe no more." He squinted up at me and said again: "Americano?"

"Uh-huh. Is that bad?"

"Is good, Americano got plenty money, always got plenty money."

"Why isn't Fuerte Quemado safe anymore?"

He laughed. "Germans, nothing but Germans no more, Nazis from war, you remember? Me, I'm Czech, don't like Germans. Last three years, Jewish men come here, from Palestine, you know, agents? Four times, last three years." He began to tick them off on his fingers, not sure he could count correctly. "One, two, three, four—all go Fuerte Quemado, all not come back. First time, one man, second time, two men, third time, one man, all not come back." He drew a finger across his throat and said: "No more coming back now, finished. They look for Bormann, Muller, you know these men? But no good, they get killed. So, better you don't go Fuerte Quemado—you want Bolivia, you take river. Army launch stop you, you pay them little money. What you carrying, eh?"

I jerked a thumb at my light weight, under-the-seat, carry-on flight bag on the floor. I said: "Fifty bars of gold bullion."

He roared with laughter. "Okay, you don't have to tell what you carrying. But friend, you want help, I give it to you. Five percent is all, okay?"

He was still talking to me, but his eyes were wandering, and there was a transparent look of very real anger on his face. I followed his glance. A tall, fair haired man, deeply tanned, was turning the corner and passing by us. He carried a rifle slung in his hand, and he moved like a soldier, though he was dressed in civilian clothes. His eyes were alert, and he looked as though all he wanted was a chance to fire that gun. He moved on, giving me a sharp look as he went by, and when he had gone, Mazlor spat and took some more *pinga* and drank it down in a gulp.

I said: "If I want help, I'll come to you, friend. Now, where's this hotel of yours?"

He insisted on calling a small boy to take my bag across the street while he poured me another drink, on the house. It didn't really matter. All he wanted, I knew, was to give it a good going-over; but there was nothing there to interest the likes of Mazlor.

He was a big man, hard as nails, a rogue from the sewers of time; but I liked him.

The hotel, when I finally got there, was a pleasant surprise. It was Spanish in type, a very old building of thick adobe walls and heavy tile roof. There was a patio with a restaurant in it, and an inner courtyard where an attractive fountain was spouting, with bougainvillaea and honeysuckle all over the walls, and tiny, bright-red hibiscus flowers everywhere. It occurred to me that Mazlor probably kept the grubby joint by the wharf for the benefit of his up-river pals who came in from Bolivia with the police hard on their heels. Here, the atmosphere was quite different; the floors were spotless, the white linen on the tables was gleaming, and the waiters in the restaurant were neatly dressed in white dinner jackets. The room they gave me, on the ground floor, opened off the sheltered patio, and there was a blood-red trumpet-creeper clambering over the portico nearby, with a strongly-smelling *plumeria* in the corner, its bright cream blossoms, yellow-centered, held on bare gray stalks and filling the courtyard with its scent.

There were only six guest rooms in the small hotel. I was in the first of them. My bag was on a stand at the bottom of the big double bed. It had been unpacked, and my spare clothes, the little I was carrying, had been put neatly away in the heavy teak *armoire*. The case is made of very soft, very pliable, very expensive leather, and I consequently never lock it; I'd rather have it opened normally than slit open with a sharp knife.

The maid came in while I was hanging my jacket, carrying a coffee service on a woven rattan tray; an attractive young *cabocla* girl, part white, part Indian. I've always noticed how the mixing of races makes for charming women; a pity were not all better integrated.

She put the coffee tray on the table, and said, smiling: "*O Senhor gusto do cafe*? You like coffee, sir?" Fortunately I could tell her of my passion for it; anything else would have been a gross affront to her nationalist honor. She gestured at the bag and said, a trifle hesitantly: "It was not locked, Senhor, so I unpacked it. Is that all right?"

"Sure, no problems."

"And may I have your passport, Senhor? For the Control?"

I gave it to her, and she made a polite little old fashioned curtsy and went out.

I took a shower, then found the dining room and sat down to dinner. It was hard to believe we were so far away from civilization this was a charming, delightful oasis that contrasted sharply with the grubby aspect of the wharf on the waterfront, This, I thought, this is where they look after the traders so well, in return for the tribute they exact; there's a lot of hard cash in the up-river trade, and a man who knows his way around need want for nothing. I had an excellent dinner of river-crab with *rize a greco*, followed by a pepper steak of venison, hot enough to fry the tongue to a cinder, with three large bottles of beer and some *conhaque* for a nightcap.

I walked down to the wharf after dinner, and saw Mazlor sitting on a wooden chair at the edge of the dock, his feet on the rail and a bottle of beer in his fist. Some naked kids were splashing in the water, though the weather was cool.

Gesturing with the beer, he said cheerfully: "Good dinner? Is good hotel, no? I got good place there."

I said: "Pretty damn good, Mazlor."

He waved a great ham of a hand around him. "Me, I like this better, I keep out of hotel. Hotel is good for traders, traders like you. Me, is better here, don't have to shave." He belched loudly. I wondered what up-river thugs he was waiting for.

Indicating the swimming children, I said: "No piranhas?"

He laughed. "Piranhas? Not here, Senhor. Upstream; plenty. Not here. You drink with me, maybe?"

"When I come back, with pleasure."

"Where you go?"

"Swim."

I took off my trousers and shirt, and dived in. The water was cold and very invigorating. I swam for about five miles against the strong current, fighting it hard, and then turned over on my back and let the stream take me slowly back. I passed an Indian in a small canoe who was paddling furiously upstream. He saw me and stopped paddling, then gaped at me foolishly as I swam quickly back past him and back to the wharf.

Mazlor was standing there, a fresh bottle in his hand, and he threw me a ragged towel as I climbed up out of the river.

"You went a long way, Senhor Cain. I was worried for you."

I said: "You mean that Indian was looking for me?"

He laughed again, showing his strong teeth, his evil old face lighting up: "Maybe I think the piranhas get you up there."

"And maybe you were hoping I wasn't just going for a swim."

He wrenched the top off a beer bottle with his teeth and handed it to me, and said, grinning:

"Why you not tell me what you take to Bolivia, Senhor Cain? We make good partners."

I said: "Believe it or not, I'm not smuggling a goddamn thing. But if you want to make a fast dollar or two, then maybe later on we can talk."

He beamed. "I tell you, Senhor, anything you want, anything at all."

Of course, it's never possible to tell a good man from a bad one; but somehow, I was beginning to like Mazlor very much, I'm not often wrong in these things. I pulled my pants on over my wet shorts, and sat on the rail to drink his beer; it was ice cold. I said:

"Is a woman alone safe up here?"

He squinted at me. "Sure, is safe, what you think, somebody rape her?"

"They'd better not."

"Not to worry, Senhor, is safe." He squinted some more, and said: "Your wife, maybe coming here? You said you look for peace and quiet, I think is not your wife."

"Not my wife. When she comes, can I count on you to take good care of her?"

He made a broad cross on his chest, a dramatic gesture of sincerity. "Cross my heart, Senhor, on my mother's grave, she be okay. Sometimes, pretty rough men come here, down the river; you know? But everybody know, Mazlor don't stand no nonsense. She be safe, safe like my own sister."

"You've got to do better than that."

He roared with laughter and threw his empty bottle into the river; one of the naked kids went swimming after it at once. He went over to an old enameled bathtub that was filled with bottles and broken blocks of ice, took two bottles, opened them with his teeth, and tossed me one. I said:

"I need rope, a small pickax, a compass, a fishing line, Can I get them here?"

He shrugged. "In the morning, I take you my store, we got everything. You need rifle, maybe? Shot gun? I got good ones."

"Nope. Never use them. Can I rent a boat? With a motor?"

He spat in the water and jerked his head at the canoe with the outboard on it. "I got good motor there, go pretty damn fast."

I jerked *my* head at the big launch. In spite of its dilapidated condition, I'd seen a couple of Indian grease monkeys working on it, and somehow I got the idea that this was the special one, the smugglers' boat that could move a lot faster than anyone would expect.

Mazlor grinned. "That one pretty damn good too, only don't go up-river, only down. Too damn shallow. I got no load on board she still hit bottom every place. You want guide? I send one with you, maybe come with you myself, no? We have little bit fun on river."

"Nope."

"How long you go for?"

73

"A few days, maybe."

"Senora come while you gone?"

"Maybe."

"You not worry, I take good care of her. Better like my sister. How you like hotel, is good, no?"

"Is good, yes. Surprisingly good."

He grinned. "Every month boat come here from Manaus, big ship, pick up nuts, wax, rubber...Plenty traders, like good place to stay. Tourists too sometimes. Boat stay two days, go back. Rest of time, nothing, nobody. Keep hotel open just in case, keep it clean, don't cost much money to wash floors. Good business, maybe you want to buy it? Good hotel, plenty money."

"Not this trip, thanks."

"You change your mind, you tell me."

I said: "Who was the guy with the gun this evening?"

He looked a little hesitant. "Guy with the gun?"

"You saw him. You spat at him."

"Oh." He scratched his head, scratched his chin, scratched his belly. Finally, he made up his mind that I was to be trusted. He said: "From Fuerte Quemado."

"Oh? Then what's he doing down here?"

"Better we don't talk about it, Senhor."

"Why? Do they scare you?"

There was a pause. He said at last: "What they do up there, is not my business, I don't care what they do. Sometimes one, two men come down here, take the boat to Crato, or Manicore, stay away three, four, maybe six weeks, come back again, don't tell nobody nothing." He glared at me and said: "And Nazis don't scare me nothing neither. I just mind my own business, better you do that too."

"Sure. How's the beer holding out?" I tossed the bottle away and he grinned and handed me another. We were friends again, and I was glad of it. I said: "Ever hear of a man named Wilhelm Werther? A stonecutter?"

He shook his head. "Names don't mean nothing up here neither."

"He probably came through here eight or nine months ago." I took the photograph Cunha had given me from my hip pocket and showed it to him. He pursed his lips and scratched again, and said:

"Yes, maybe I think I see this man. Yes, September last year, when floods came. He went up-river with man from Fuerte Quemado, come back week later, take launch, come back again after ten, fifteen days maybe." Suddenly suspicious, he said: "You policeman maybe?"

"No. No, I'm not."

He breathed a sigh of relief. "Is good."

It was good too that he believed me; there was no suggestion of doubt in his grin. And he didn't ask any more questions. I said: "Well, see you in the morning. Thanks for the beer."

As I moved away, he called after me: "Senhor Cain!" I turned. He moved in close to me, and peered up and said: "If you looking for this man, Werther, maybe is not good to show me his picture like that."

"Oh? Why not?"

He said: "How you know I not tell him you look for him, pick up ten thousand cruzeiros easy, eh?"

I said pleasantly: "Well, I'm prepared to gamble on my estimate of what kind of a man you are."

"Is very foolish, Mr. Cain."

"Why, are you going to tell him?"

"No, I don't know this man, but..." He sighed and said: "Always, Americano is very simple man. You show that picture in wrong place, maybe you not looking for Werther no more. Maybe he looking for you. With sharp knife up his sleeve, what you think?"

"Then I wouldn't have to look so hard anymore, would I? Good night, friend, you're a good man."

"Sure. Not many of us left."

I could feel his eyes boring into my back as I went.

I slept like a log in a very comfortable bed; kapok mattress, there's nothing like them.

In the morning, the pretty little maid tiptoed in with coffee the moment I opened my eyes, and I wondered how she knew I was awake. When I asked her, she said simply: "I look." There was no key to the door.

I breakfasted off fresh green figs and oven-fresh bread, and wandered off to find Mazlor. He was still wearing the same clothes, and looked as if he hadn't been to bed. He told me cheerfully that one of the boys had come in during the night with a canoe loaded down with refined silver bars, en route to the frontier. Either he didn't care much about security, or had already accepted me as a friend; I rather thought the latter. He was also bubbling over with a sort of repressed amusement, and I soon discovered why. His smuggler friend had brought news from the telegraph post at Santo Antonio. He said happily:

"They looking for big man name Cabot Cain, smash window in store in Rio, steal diamonds worth two, three million cruzeires." He threw back his head and roared with laughter. "In Bolivia, you get pretty good price, I help you."

Now he was sure he knew all about me; it made him a very happy man; and it made us very good friends. Whatever suspicions he may have had, now they'd gone for good.

I said: "A white-haired old man flew me here from Santo Antonio. As soon as he tells the police, they'll be over here looking for me, won't they now?"

He looked shocked. He said: "Carlos? Old man Carlos don't tell police *nothing*. He tell them maybe you fall out of airplane into river, he tell them piranhas eat you, he tell them he fly you down to Manaus. But he don't tell them nothing he brought you here. Then, one day maybe, he meet you again and you pay him little money, is good, no?" He clapped me on the back and said heartily: "Now I *know* you my friend."

I bought some rope in his store, and a small efficient compass, and a hand pick, and some fish hooks and line, and a small tarpaulin and a water bottle, a five-pound bag of shelled Brazil nuts, a machete, binoculars, a bottle of *pinga*, some dried manioc, a few other things. I lashed them securely in the bottom of the small canoe, and then we sat down for a cold beer and a chat.

I could see the distant mountain framed against the blue sky to the north, I said: "When they come down from Fuerte Quemado, do they use the river? Or is there a road?"

He pointed upstream: "River no good for Fuerte Quemado. Is old Indian trail up there, but since mountain fall down, you got cliff in the way, no way to climb it. But road pretty good now, call it Doussa Road, used to be village there called Doussa, fall down into river with mountain. But they got barrier across the road, don't nobody pass it."

"What kind of barrier?"

"Rocks. They move rocks with...what you call it, winch? They make big barrier across road, keep winch there because up in Fuerte Quemado they got cars, plenty cars like we don't have down here. They lift cars over barrier with winch."

"But there's a way round it on foot?"

He shook his head. "Is deep gorge there, nobody don't get past it."

"A gorge? How wide at the narrowest point? And on what side of the road is it?"

"On the right, is maybe thirty, forty feet across."

The broad jump record, as far as I could remember, stood around the twenty-seven foot mark. I said:

"Can you draw a sketch of the river for me? In relation to the Doussa Road?"

He found some paper and a pencil, and made a crude sketch map. I didn't suppose it was very accurate. He said somberly:

"You try to get to Fuerte Quemado, friend, you don't get no closer than twenty miles. They watch that place good."

"So how the hell did the residents get there?"

"Helicopter. They know who come, who go. They don't want, he don't come, he don't go neither."

I said: "Well, I'm not going there anyway, am I? I'm smuggling diamonds over the border into Bolivia, you know that."

He growled: "Like hell I don't know nothing what you do. You just be careful, friend."

"Sure."

We wandered back to the canoe together, and we fastened on the outboard and tested it, and we haggled about prices for a while but came to an amicable agreement in the end, and I said:

"I'll probably be back before then, but if a lady named Leda Zrinyi should arrive before I do, take good care of her. Give her this note for me, okay?"

The note merely told her I was sorry not to welcome her in

person and would she wait. I had no way of knowing when she'd move in. Mazlor said again: "Like my sister," and laughed, and shoved the canoe into midstream for me. I pulled the rope of the starter, the engine caught, and soon I was heading upstream.

Upstream, fast, toward the high cliffs where the mountain had collapsed and dumped into the broad river the track the Spaniards had used to build Fuerte Quemado.

The maps of the area are quite useless. Even the one Cunha had given me was hopelessly inaccurate; but Mazlor's was more helpful than I'd expected.

I followed the course of the winding river, roughly north, for twenty-seven miles before I hit the first obstruction. The motor was laboring against a fast-moving current, and in spite of the high throttle the canoe was slowing down very considerably; waterfall ahead, coming this way. I drove the canoe into the bank, pulled it out, and hefted it. There was a track very close to the edge of the water, which indicated that the Indians did this too, carrying their canoes by portaging to the top of the falls, wherever that might be.

The little boat had a heavy round dowel set aft to brace it against the weight of the outboard, and it was a convenient point for carrying. After roping my supplies firmly to the seat, I simply took hold of it and shoved up, and then held my arms stiffly with the canoe hanging down my back. The whole thing must have weighed about two hundred pounds; not an insufferable weight, but a bit clumsy—it was too high over my head and kept banging into overhanging branches.

I walked for two hours before I found the steep bluff from which the falls came. A track had been cut into the sandstone, reaching to the top, and the bare footprints there told me that Indians sometimes passed this way with their carried canoes; it looked like six men to a canoe, though the prints were old and partly washed away; the track had not been used for some time. It was about two hundred feet high, the bluff, and I climbed it in an hour, steadying the canoe on my back with my shoulders. Once, over a particularly difficult bit, I was forced to drag it up at the end of the long rope.

It was beautiful at the top. The sound of the falls was fierce, and the spray was sliced in two neatly by a rainbow. The dark and light greens of the trees and the ferns were shining wetly. I could see the wide sweep of the river below, winding like a silver ribbon all through the alluvial plain, splashed here and there with a muddy copper. Urbana was faintly visible in the haze, though from this distance it was possible only to see clearly the brilliant green carpet of the castor-bean fields with a few white specks behind them that were the houses. There were brilliant splashes of color where the wild orchids were; I watched a pair of iridescent blue butterflies for a while, fighting each other, their wings more than seven inches across; two males fighting over an unseen female.

I took a swim in a pool to cool off, and then found a cherimoya tree and helped myself to some of the sweet custard-fruit, warm and sticky in the sun, now getting very hot; and then I turned my binoculars on the high mountain to the north. It was some thirty miles away, stark and sheer and imposing. Somewhere up there, though from this angle I could not see it, was Fuerte Quemado.

I hefted the canoe for another couple of miles along the bank until the Indian track petered out and I found that the river divided itself here, one branch swinging round to the east and the other, much narrower, dark and foreboding, going straight on to the north; as straight, that is, as any river winds in this giant watershed. For a while I examined the banks of both branches. There were signs that the eastern tributary was used once in a while—a few footprints in the wet mud, a broken spear shaft, the ant-covered skeleton of a tapir that had a hole (made by the iron head of an arrow) in its skull. But on the northern branch, all I found was a large tree fallen across the river.

Fallen? When I examined it, I saw that it had been expertly cut to fall just so, and effectively block any canoe that might want to use that branch. Close by the water's edge there was a path around it, quite narrow and easy of passage. Too easy.

I left the canoe where it was, cut myself a probing pole, and then tried the path, touching the ground ahead of me as I carefully moved forward. The pole went through the surface at the fourth step, and I dropped to my knees to see what I had found. It was a jaguar trap, a pit about twelve feet deep, carefully covered over with a frame of light bamboo stalks and twigs and leaves; at the bottom of the pit were half a dozen sharpened bamboo stakes. I used the rope and clambered down to examine them. They'd been cut a very long time ago, and were still sharp as needles. They gave me a very uncomfortable feeling.

I climbed out again, rearranged the camouflage as it was before, and thought for a little while about what a hell of a place it was to put a jaguar trap—if you're going to trap a jaguar, you want it alive, not impaled with a bamboo stake through its belly. I judged it time to proceed with more caution.

I returned to the canoe, unfastened the bolts that held the outboard in place, and hid it under some bushes, covering it carefully with palm-fronds and banana leaves and then dragging an exceedingly heavy broken branch across the lot. I cut a way with the machete around the trap, and dragged the canoe through, going back to cover my tracks properly, and then put the boat in the water, broke out the paddle, and paddled my way upstream, keeping close into the shore.

Keeping close in wasn't hard; at some points the river was only a few feet wide, with the trees that met over its top like a canopy hanging down so low over the silent water that sometimes I had to lie down in the canoe to get under them. Once or twice I had to cut trailing vines out of my way; a good sign—the stream had not been used much recently. There was a very fast-running patch of water a little further on where the contour of the land changed. Not a fall, just a weir, with white-capped water rushing over it that made the paddling very hard indeed, almost hard enough to send me ashore again for some more portaging. I looked carefully along the shoreline, and as I expected, I saw a narrow footpath at this point. More traps? I didn't bother to look, but pushed on hard till the deep gorge widened out again and the water was running less swiftly.

Here, I tied up to the bank. My paddle had found some obstructions in the white water, and I wanted to identify them for what I thought they might be. I slipped overboard and waded back, half-walking, half-swimming, fighting the current and being quite sure that it didn't carry me too fast. As soon as I entered the whitecaps, even so, I cut myself badly in the thigh, I grabbed at a rock and steadied myself, then ducked under the water to take a look.

There were a dozen or so long poles there, slanted sharply

upstream and stuck firmly into the rocks and boulders on the riverbed, pointing upstream at an angle of thirty degrees or so from the horizontal I got in between two of them and shoved hard with my feet, and at the second attempt succeeded in loosening one of them. It tumbled over, sank, and rolled over a little, and I grabbed hold of it and surfaced; the water was about five feet deep here. I dragged my pole ashore and took a look at it.

It was a mangrove root, the local ironwood that is impervious to water, or ants, or termites, or anything else—an immensely strong wood that would be fine for construction if only it were easier to cut. The pole was about ten feet long, and one end of it had been sharpened by fire into a sort of heavy spear. It was easy to imagine what would happen to a flimsy dugout canoe riding on the fast water at twenty knots or so back to the main branch of the river. I studied the surface of the water for a while, noting mentally just where the rocks were and how they lay, and selected two big granite boulders as steering points.

Then I went back into the water, and in a couple of hours had cleared the pointed stakes out of that particular piece of water; between the two granite boulders, fast as you like, there was now nothing there. To make sure, I fought the current upstream for a bit, and then swam carefully and slowly back under water, passing between the two markers, with my eyes open and keeping a sharp lookout. The spears all around me were still there—but between the two granite boulders, the passage was clear. I didn't really think I'd ever have to come racing down that river to get the hell out of there fast, but should it become necessary, I wanted to be sure it could be done safely.

I got back into the canoe again, and paddled upstream. Another fifteen miles. The going was getting harder all the time, and finally I just wasn't making any more headway. I pulled the canoe through the sand of the bank, thrust it deep among the bushes, camouflaged it well (again, a very heavy tree trunk over it that no one was going to move in a hurry), took the supplies I needed and threw them over my shoulder.

Using the machete, I went straight north through the jungle, until the darkening of the shadows under the great canopy that was the treetops told me that somewhere out there the sun was going down. The noise of the forest changed; the parrots went to sleep, and the howling monkeys came out—the sunlight hurts their eyes, and they only come out at night. In the darkness the roar of a waterfall close by, somewhere on this or one of the many other rivers, was overpowering. It occurred to me that I was a long, long way from Rio; and from Leda in Paris...

It was time to call it a day. I was soaked to the skin with perspiration, and I found a shallow pool and took a quick dip, then made a small fire of thorn-twigs and roots, building it over three stones, Indian fashion, just in case of any intrusion, though I hardly expected any. I ate a handful of Brazil nuts from my pouch, left the fire burning slowly, and climbed up into the branches of a high *ceibo* tree to sleep. Its trunk was more than thirty feet across, and at the fourth fork I found a comfortable platform smooth enough and wide enough to stretch out on; and then, I was asleep.

I woke once in the night at an alien sound. A twig snapped, and then there was silence.

Now, an animal doesn't do that. If an animal breaks a twig— anything heavy, like a peccary, a tapir, a jaguar—it breaks another and another and another, because it's moving without regard for silence which, in turn, means it's not stalking; if it *is* stalking, you won't hear a thing, A single sound followed by the cover-up of hopeful silence usually means the most careless of all the animals—man. I carefully twisted round on the wide flat branch and peered down. Nothing. I waited.

Soon, two Indians crept forward out of the dense forest. I saw them clearly as a beam of white moonlight cut through the trees and lit up their painted faces. They were naked, and they carried tiny little bows, with small arrows ready fitted, and they were approaching my fire to see who'd made it. I guessed that they'd been close by for a long time, assuring themselves that no one was around before summoning up the courage to approach. They looked around fearfully for my footprints, and began to mutter excitedly when they couldn't find them; I'd made sure there was nothing to see down there. They spoke a dialect I'd never heard before, a guttural, hesitant sort of tongue. I could almost see them trembling.

It's a terrible thing about the forest Indians. They're slowly being wiped out; and everybody is their enemy. They're frightened, and friendless, and everyone seems to take advantage of them. They're tough little bastards, but they're bewildered by the approach, even up here, of civilization.

They heard the sound even before I did. A helicopter was approaching. While it was still no more than a very distant rumble, they chattered excitedly and were gone, hiding once more in their jungle, terrified and sure that the white man was coming to destroy them.

The sound of the helicopter grew louder. It flew north right over my head. I heard it circling round for a while, and then it dropped down somewhere out there and the sound was cut off. I had seen nothing; there's been no lights.

I stretched out once more and went back to sleep.

I caught a fish in the morning and cooked it for breakfast. A long, slender fish the natives call *satarua*, with a rich, oily meat to it. I tossed it in the embers of the fire while I went swimming, and after a mile or two upstream and a comfortable float back again, I found that it was cooked to perfection. I dragged out the supplies from where I'd hidden them, took out the binoculars and compass and climbed back up the tall *ceibo* tree.

High in the uppermost branches, there was a good view of the flat mountaintop where I knew Fuerte Quemado to be. I couldn't see the town, but I had a good view of the old track at the top, covered over with lianas now but still definable; half a mile or so down the slope I could see where it had broken away with the earthquake, a sheer drop of a thousand feet or more, a very effective barrier. The glasses were quite strong, Bausch & Lomb twelve power, as good a glass as you'll find anywhere on the market, and I examined the cliff very carefully, for a very long time. I could see a few deep cuts in the bright-red sandstone that looked like gorges; I saw a small waterfall dropping down for five hundred feet, and made a mental note of precisely where it was. I saw a few caves in the rock face, a few stunted trees striving for existence. I took a compass bearing on it: seven degrees east.

I climbed down from the tree, slung my supplies on my back, and crawled carefully through the matted jungle for the next six hours;

hands and knees most of the way, and no machete to leave any telltale marks. And by two o'clock in the afternoon I was where I wanted to be—at the bottom of the cliff, directly below the waterfall.

The climb to the top, I must admit, was a bit strenuous. I used the pickax and the rope, and made steps where they'd be helpful, and handhelds wherever there was a scraggly bush to hide them. By six-thirty, it was getting dark, and I still had more than a couple of hundred feet to negotiate. But below and behind me there was now a careful series of steps and handholds, of ropes and guidelines up to the top; a man could almost run up that dammed cliff now, providing he knew exactly where the route lay. To test it, I put my kit carefully out of sight and went down empty-handed, quickly; and then I timed myself making the climb again in a hurry. The handholds first, and then a quick climb up the long rope, and then the footholds and a traverse to where the ropes began again; it took me less than fifteen minutes. I was soaked through to the skin, and—worse—I was panting hard; I wondered if I were getting out of shape, and made a mental note to try and get a bit more exercise.

I looked up at the top, so much closer now, and decided I'd better wait for daylight before finishing the prepared route, I made a careful traverse in the darkness to a narrow shelf I'd seen, waited there for the moon to rise and give me at least a little light, and then swung myself over on the ax to a fissure in the rock, with an adequate overhang for protection and a small cave leading off it, deep into the cliff itself. Some brown, furry animals scuttled past me in the darkness: muskrats; the cave was ripely smelling of them.

I cached my supplies, curled up and slept through the night, quite well considering the discomfort, and the first thing I did when the dawn came was to find a hunk of rock and drop it down the cliff to the water-washed granite at the bottom. I checked the second hand of my watch for accuracy. The sound of the stone striking the bottom was a long time coming: seven and a half seconds. At thirty-two feet per second, D equals 16 times T squared, T being the time in seconds— that made it nine hundred feet precisely, a sheer drop. A nice place for a man to break his neck; no place for even a mountain goat to climb. I examined the drop carefully from my perch, and I would have sworn no one could possibly climb it. The steps and handholds and ropes were quite invisible Good.

The last hundred and eighty measured feet up were easier. By eight o'clock I was at the top, lying flat on my back on some bright green moss in the shade of a tall *casuarina* tree. I'd found some wild mandarin oranges growing nearby, and ate half a dozen of them, carefully burying the peel, and then climbed up into the *casuarina* and stared down on Fuerte Quemado.

It was a small, charming, Spanish-Colonial town of some eighteen or twenty square miles, with wide, paved streets and pleasant gardens, with neat little villas set in their own lush grounds and surrounded by high stone walls; the nearest edge of the town was no more than a mile away, down a gentle slope that led to the green basin in which the town lay. There were two old Spanish churches with high arched entrances; a wide portico-shaded area that looked like an arcade of shops, and over on the other side a surprisingly efficient-looking little airport. I could see three helicopters there, and two medium-range Caravel jets, and I counted eight twin-engine Cessnas, Pipers, and Bonanzas.

On first sight, it was a delightful little resort, well-kept with manicured lawns and small parks, with tall palms and yellow-green ferns, and brilliant purple bougainvillea, the kind of country town you'd choose to spend a lazy month or two in, doing nothing but relaxing and taking it easy. But when I looked closer; the spell was broken. I spotted a tall tower at the corner of one of the villas with a machine-gun pointing out of it; and then another and another. There were three or four dozen people on the streets within my range of vision, and most of them had rifles slung over their backs. And out on the airport there were no less than seven anti-aircraft guns. It looked as though Fuerte Quemado was in a constant state of alert.

I saw a jeep roll slowly by with four armed men aboard, and a Bren-gun mounted above their heads. I tried to distinguish the uniforms, but they weren't Brazilian or Bolivian as far as I could make out; the soldiers were small, dark, thick-set men who could have been from any of the heterogeneous races you'll find in this part of the world. I remembered something Cunha had said: *"the kind of place that nobody wants—and that can take good care of itself if it has to.*"

I studied it for a long, long time, setting the layout firmly in my mind, using the glasses all the time. The sun was behind me; there was no danger of any reflection from the lenses giving away my presence. The space between my point of vantage and the town was dense, dense jungle, tall trees heavily interlaced with climbing vines, with greens of every shade and bright splashes of color which were scarlet orchids, high in the treetops. A flight of pink-winged herons was circling around lazily against the blue sky, and there were little puffs of white clouds, motionless and serene. The picture couldn't have been prettier, except for those guns.

It was midday before I climbed back down. I'd seen all I wanted to see at this stage. If Kolchak were there, and it was a pretty good likelihood, I knew I could walk into the town any time I chose to, in spite of their rock barriers, their guards, their jaguar traps and mangrove spears in the water. I was in here close to them; I knew that it was the first and strongest line of defense, and that in less than thirty hours I'd breached it, that now the cliff could be easily climbed and I could cut that time in two.

The only problem was: what next?

It took me less than half an hour to drop back down the cliff. I retraced my steps fast through the forest, paddled back to where I'd left the outboard, and by three o'clock in the morning, I was tying the canoe up at Mazlor's wharf.

He detached himself from the shadows where his cot was as I climbed up onto the dock, rubbing the sleep out of his eyes and grinning at me. I heard the rattle of the beer bottles in the bath as he fished out a couple and opened them. I took a long, long drink, and heard him say:

"Your friend Carlos came, from Santo Antonio. You know, the old man?"

"Oh?"

"He bring passenger. This afternoon. The Senhora, Leda Zrinyi."

I tossed the empty bottle in the water and helped myself to another. I was tingling with excitement; but there was no use waking her at this hour of the day. I could wait another four or five hours.

Three, anyway. I perched myself up on the railing and drank beer with Mazlor until the first red streaks of dawn began to show, brightening the wide sweep of the silver river with a brilliant, gaudy copper.

He told me, Mazlor, that Carlos had also brought some newspapers from Manaus. There was a report on the robbery of Aaron's store in Rio, and a police communique suggesting that one Cabot Cain, American, six foot seven, two hundred and ten pounds, age thirty-four, was believed to be in the State of Guapore and was wanted for questioning in connection with the robbery. He thought it was a huge joke, and I asked him:

"The police will see my name in your hotel register. Will that get you into trouble if you don't tell them I'm here?"

He shrugged. "They make inspection every three months, if they remember. Three months, six months, is all the same."

"But there are police here in Urbana anyway, aren't there?"

He grinned. "One man, Jose Salvador, he do what I tell him, is all the time drunk, I tell him you don't do nothing, he don't do that too."

I said: "Well, isn't that nice? Everything's working out just the way it should."

We talked about smugglers, and Indians, and castor beans, and precious stones, and about *pinga*, and food, and beer; about almost everything, that is, except Fuerte Quemado.

CHAPTER 6

The pretty young serving girl took for granted a relationship that didn't exist. When I went into the hotel, she put down the broom she was using, fumbled for a key, and shepherded me across the patio. An Indian was lying asleep on the portico, tight up against the door to one of the rooms, but he was instantly awake and alert as she crossed toward it. She said: "*Todo bem, via,*" and he gathered up his blanket and went, and she unlocked the door very quietly and opened it, and peeked in, and moved aside to let me pass. She whispered: "*Trazerei do cafe agora? Ou mais tarde...?* Shall I bring coffee now, or after...?" I said: "Now, please." I heard her soft shoes padding away.

Leda was asleep on the bed, quite naked, with a rumpled sheet pushed down at her feet I lifted it gently and spread it over her, and put it back there again when she stirred in her sleep and kicked it off, and then I patted her wrist gently, and she woke up, and I said: "Welcome to Urbana," and kissed her on the cheek.

She blinked her eyes and stared at me, and shook her pale hair out of her eyes, and then smiled and snuggled in under the sheet and closed her eyes again. She murmured something pleasant-sounding but quite indefinable, and in less than five seconds she was fast asleep again.

I pulled up a chair, sat close to the bed, and waited. In a few moments, I heard the girl coming with the coffee. She knocked and waited discreetly, and came in when I opened the door for her, and set down the tray and went out again, smiling and very happy.

Leda had not stirred, but when I poured the coffee she mumbled again, and opened her eyes and yawned, and stretched her long limbs and suddenly said: "Oh!" and pulled the sheet up closer round her neck.

I said: "You take a long time to wake up. Coffee?"

She rolled over on her side, wrapping the sheet around herself, and looked at the wrist watch on the bedside table. "Six o'clock? Oh, no!" She yawned widely again, stretched herself, sat up, and took the coffee cup I gave her, and looked at me and said: "Well, hello Cabot Cain."

"Good trip?"

"Bumpy. Is it always as hot as this here?"

"Beautifully cool this hour of the morning. How about a swim?"

She said: "Oh, God," and yawned again. She took a sip from her cup and said: "There was a man asleep outside my door all night, did you know that?"

"This is a rough town, in patches. I just wanted to be sure you were safe."

"That's nice."

"How's the coffee?"

They make it properly out there, black and thick and strong enough to melt the spoon; you pour one small cup, and the scent of it ripens the air for a hundred yards around.

"Marvelous." She yawned again, and said: "Where were you?"

"A place called Fuerte Quemado. That's where Kolchak is, I think."

She was suddenly wide awake. "That's very quick work, isn't it?"

"Uh-huh. If he really is there."

"You think he is?"

"It's a likelihood."

She was frowning now, looking a little worried. She said: "But you can't just walk in there and say: I want the Zrinyi jewels that Kolchak stole. Can you?"

"No, probably not."

"So?"

89

"One step at a time. What the next one is, God alone knows."

She put down the cup and yawned again, and lay back on the bed with the sheet up under her chin, and looked at me almost reproachfully. She said: "Can you tell me, Cabot Cain, what in God's name am I doing ten thousand miles from home? At less than half a day's notice I come traipsing halfway across the world, and now I'm here, and..."—she sighed—"and I don't even know what for."

"Neither do I, really. I just thought it would be nice to have you along."

"And I can't even believe it. Here I am, and there you are, and...We're an awfully long way from anywhere, aren't we?"

"Uh-huh."

"Will I ever see Paris again?"

"Probably not. How's Fenrek?"

"Fenrek's fine. He said you were to behave very correctly with me."

"That's only because he's jealous."

Her eyes went wide all of a sudden, and she reached for a newspaper that was supposed to be on the table and had fallen to the floor. I picked it up and handed it to her. "This?"

She was flipping over the pages excitedly: "I can't read Portuguese, but...this!" She flapped the back of her hand dramatically onto a smallish headline that had my name in it, and said: "The man who flew me here from Santo Antonio, a nice, white-haired old man with no teeth..."

"Carlos, he's a smuggler."

"He showed it to me, he couldn't stop laughing. What's it all about, for heaven's sake? You didn't really break a window and...and rob the place, did you? Of course not! Then, why should a thing like this get into the paper?"

I said: "You're consorting with a known criminal, but no one will give you away. Senhor Mazlor has this town in his pocket, including its solitary policeman."

"Senhor Mazlor?"

"The Czech ruffian who owns this place."

"Ah. He was very solicitous."

"He thinks you're his sister. The Indian at the door was one of his men, a guard."

Laughing suddenly, she said: "Some guard. I peeked through the window, he was fast asleep all right."

"With a ten-inch dagger under his wrist, and instantly awake at the slightest sound."

She said gravely: "Is this that kind of a place?"

"It's that kind of a place. On the surface, a pleasant little resort. Underneath all that, the hangout of smugglers, cutthroats, thieves, the riff-raff of half a continent. But we belong to the under half, so we're all very happy here."

"Oh. Like that. I see. But when you get back to Rio?"

"I'll apologize handsomely to Senhor Aaron, pay some handsome damages and a handsome fine, and we'll all be friends again. One of Fenrek's men is there, there'll be no trouble with the police. Meanwhile, I'm a wanted man. I fit in with the scenery."

She finished her coffee and I poured her another, and at last, she said thoughtfully, very quietly: "And why did you ask me to come, Cabot? Really?"

I was hoping she wouldn't insist about that, but half expecting it anyway, I said slowly:

"I do have reasons, I suppose, but they're not very clear, even to me. I just have an instinct that...somehow or other I'll need help. It might be better if it's feminine help. And somehow...I think the family should be involved, your family, Does that make sense to you?"

"It makes very good sense."

"And finally...when I tried to find reasons why you shouldn't come, I could only find reasons why you should. Personal reasons. Is that an arrogance? I suppose it is."

She leaned forward quickly and kissed me once on the cheek. "If it is, it's the kind of arrogance I like."

"Good. Then that's all right then." I felt strangely at home with her, as though I'd known her for a very long time. This was only our second meeting. Had it taken place in Paris, we would have been good friends; but here, so far away from everything, just the two of us together in a strange and distant land, there was a potent intimacy between us. Making a point of it, I said: "And I don't even know what you like for breakfast."

91

"Fruit? Juice?"

"Plenty, all kinds."

"Cold?"

"Well iced."

"Then give me ten minutes to dress, and I'll look for you wherever the breakfast is served."

"Right outside the door, on the patio."

"Ten minutes."

I turned at the door and looked at her. She was watching me with a strange, half-surprised, half-amused look on her face; she looked extremely happy, and very beautiful, and I was glad she was there.

I found a shady corner of the patio where the cream-colored *plumeria* was growing, and the purple verbena was crowding the stone wall. A white-coated waiter came out and said: "*Bom dia, Senhor*," and I ordered papaya juice and fresh mangoes and more coffee, and by the time he had served them, she was there. She wore a tight white outfit from one of the advanced boutiques, very smart and fashionable and impossibly fragile; and I hoped I'd never have to take her up-river with me.

Now all I had to do was wait, I figured another twenty-four hours would do the trick.

Two men from Fuerte Quemado came in during the day; it was somehow easy to spot them at once; the dour, challenging sort of look about them, and the arrogant way they carried their rifles loosely by the hand, as though they might need them at any moment. I was lunching with Leda in the hotel restaurant when I saw the first one pass the portico on the street outside. I excused myself and went after him, following him but not making anything of it, and I saw that he went into Mazlor's store; I went back and finished my lunch.

The other one turned up in the late afternoon. The heavy boom on the wharf had collapsed, from old age and neglect, and Mazlor was trying to set it up again with block and tackle; four Indians were straining on the rope and not moving it an inch, and Mazlor cursed and said: "Goddamn, I need another heavy pulley, and I sold the last one day before yesterday." The Indians sweated and grunted and groaned, and got nowhere; so I bent double underneath it, got my shoulders into position, and stood up; it was as simple as that, but everyone was mightily impressed. I steadied the boom while they lashed it into position, and then I saw this Fuerte Quemado type, a tall, deeply-tanned, blond-haired man with a Garand rifle. Like the first one, he carried it in his hand rather than having it slung across his shoulder as you might expect, and it somehow gave the impression that he was always ready to use it. He was staring at me and saying nothing. He looked at my feet, my stomach, my chest, and then stared me full in the eyes, unsmiling and hostile, and then turned sharply on his heel and went away.

I said to Mazlor: "One of your Fuerte Quemado friends. There was another one here this morning, in your store. What was he after?"

Mazlor made a rude noise with his tongue. "Cloth. I got good silk, he buy for his girl."

"They do much shopping down here?"

"If they buy everything here, I be rich man. No, most everything come by plane, helicopter, you see them all the time. Bring stores from Manaus, Belem, Quito, Lima, any place. Just stop here sometimes when they go down river, take home present to girl, you know."

He waited, and I waited, and we both knew there was something else. He said at last with a wide grin: "He ask my Indian about you."

"Oh? What did he tell him?"

He shrugged. "Indian got no brains, he say you come here to mind your own business. This fellow punch him in the nose."

"Is that the Indian who was on guard outside Miss Zrinyi's room last night?"

He nodded. "Same one. No brains, plenty guts, good man. Better they don't have too much brain, you know that?"

"How about lending him to me for a few days?"

Mazlor looked at me shrewdly and said: "Maybe better man for what you got to do is me, myself, no?"

"The Indian will be better."

He shrugged. "Okay, I tell him. He don't do like you say, you beat him."

"You bet. Ever hear of a woman named Elena da Costa?"

He looked surprised. "Sure, is nice girl, you know her?"

"If it's the same one, it's a common enough name. Who is she?"

"She live up there too." He jerked his thumb at the mountain where Fuerte Quemado lay. "I don't know what she do, but every month she pass through here, go down to Rio de Janeiro. Take the launch to Santo Antonio, fly from there to Rio, come back four-five days later. She do this every month now for five, six years, maybe more. Sometimes launch two, three days late, she wait in hotel, nice lady."

"A courier?"

"Maybe."

"What does she look like?"

He thought for a minute, and then said: "Portuguese lady." (I noticed that he said *Senhora* instead of *mulher*; in Mazlor's world that spelled quality.) "Is short, little bit skinny, maybe thirty years old, white, white skin, black, black: hair; dress very nice, smart clothes, good clothes cost lot of money. I think she is very tough woman, but nice, you know. Kind of woman she know what she want always, don't stand no nonsense. But pretty. Very pretty."

I said: "I'm setting out for Fuerte Quemado tonight."

There was a long, long silence. He said at last: "You don't come back, what about Senhora Zrinyi?"

"I'll be back. But just see the police don't worry her."

"Police?"

"They'll be after me about that robbery. And by association...You think you can keep them away from her?"

"Jose Salvador do like I tell him. Is good friend, maybe cop, but good friend. Besides, is drunk today, good and drunk last for long time."

"I'm not really thinking of the local police. That store I robbed belongs to old man Aaron; you know him?"

He made a broad, Fenrek-type gesture. "Everybody know Aaron, bad man, too rich."

"He'll have a lot of the police in his pocket. They might just try a little harder for his sake."

"You don't worry about it, I take care of police."

Now came the hard bit. I said carefully: "And there's just a chance someone else might come gunning for the lady. I don't think it's likely, but I want to be sure she's in good hands."

Again, he thought for a very long time. He said at last: "You let me spend little bit money, I get two, three men, good men, my friends."

"All right. Just tell me who they are."

He began to laugh, his wicked old face wrinkling up with pleasure. He said: "You like my friends, you like them good. We got Jao; he run diamonds up over mountain to Bolivia. Then is Michel, is smart boy; he just simple bandit, but good one. Other man is name Slawata, Czech like me, is good man, very tough. You like."

"And what does Slawata do?"

He said earnestly: "What he do, I don't know good. He just make money sometimes, maybe cut throats little bit here and there, I don't know. But is good man. Never talk too much."

"How long to get them here?"

He shrugged. "I send Indians out, they come two, three hours maybe. Cost little bit money. Not much, little bit. But ain't nobody touch your Senhora with those boys around. Nobody. Not police, not men up there on mountain. Nobody."

It's no good respecting your own judgment if you can't trust it. I can trust mine, and I'm prepared to push it all the way home.

I said; "Listen carefully, friend. I don't know just what I'm going to do up there, but there's a chance they'll come gunning for her, at least one of them. I'm going to be here when he does, if he does, but just in case anything goes wrong...From what I hear of that mob, they're an unpleasant bunch, and I'm exposing her to danger, and...You know what I'm saying?"

Mazlor said gruffly: "I know you talk too much. Nobody going to hurt your Senhora, I promise you."

I said: "Well, I've just hired myself an army. Keep them on their toes all the time, from the moment I've turned my back, ready to hit hard and hit quickly if they have to. Okay?"

"Okay." He grinned happily.

95

I said: "You want some money now? I began reaching for the money belt, but he stopped me.

"After, after you make deal, you give me cut, is okay."

I said: "What deal is that, Mazlor?"

He laughed and pointed a finger under my nose. "You think I don't know what you do, Americano, okay? So I tell you what you do."

"Tell then."

He said carefully: "You rob store in Rio, you got plenty good stones. You go Fuerte Quemado, find this man Werther, Werther cut your stones to different shape, make easy to sell. You send this woman Elena da Costa to Rio, Quito, Lima, who cares? And she sell stones for you. You make money, share with me, we good friends." He looked at me shrewdly and said: "Okay, tell the truth, I tell you good, no?"

I said: "You're a good man, Mazlor. Not many of us left."

He roared with laughter.

I went back to the hotel and had a long talk with Leda.

I told her to sit tight, that she was going to be in some danger now, but that the danger would be held at bay by a private gang of cutthroats. I told her she could trust Mazlor completely, and it was at that point that she asked the first question:

"Can you be sure of that, Cabot?"

I said firmly: "Yes. There's nothing can ever be done in this line of business unless you make up your mind at once who can and who can't be trusted. I've learned to rely on my own judgment, to rely on it heavily."

"And if you should be wrong?"

I said: "If I'm wrong—then we're all dead. But I'm not."

I was delighted with the easy way she accepted my word. I said:

"Stick tight to Mazlor, keep to the hotel or near it, eat, sleep, lie in the sun and improve your tan—and wait till you hear from me. There's a private army guarding you. Don't let them out of your sight at any time, all right?"

She nodded gravely. "You make it sound very dangerous."

"It might be. Are you scared?"

"No."

"I want the family to share the difficulties. But not too much of them. And I think you're up to it."

She put her arms round me and reached up to kiss me on the mouth. She said: "I'm more worried about you."

"Don't be."

"You've worked it all out, haven't you?"

"Not really." I said. "I've set the board, and now I'm going to start moving. They'll move their pieces too; but I set the gambit, and I know just where I put the pawns and what they're worth."

"And is that what I am? One of the pawns?"

"The Queen. You'll be under attack, but the Knight is right beside you. And so's that unholy Bishop Mazlor."

We went for a long walk together along the edge of the river, and watched the huge butterflies playing, and I found some porcupine quills for her, saying: "I haven't the vaguest idea what you can do with these, except scratch." We found three giant otters, more than five feet long, diving in and out of the water at the base of a small waterfall, and I showed her how the mimosa leaves curl up and close when anyone approaches them. I said: "The best watchdog there is. Sit under one of these and in a short while the leaves will all uncurl as long as you stay fairly quiet. But if someone comes along, they all start curling up again, even if he's so silent you don't hear a sound." She caught an unwary iguana by the tail and laughed about it for a while before letting it go, and we argued with a foolish toucan that squawked noisily at us from its perch in a castanea tree that was loaded heavily with the big husks full of Brazil nuts. We stripped off our outer clothing and swam for a while in a clear cool pool of the bluest water I have ever seen, and then lay on a patch of green-yellow moss to dry out in the sun.

I found some avocados and some limes, and we had a bite to eat, and we drank from a clear-running stream and sat down in the shade of a thorn tree to old hands for a while. It was as though we'd been lovers for a long time.

And when we got back to the hotel, it was just getting dark, and the private army was there.

It's impossible to describe them.

Never in my life have I seen such a dirty, ill-kept, uncouth, disreputable bunch of bastards. They all looked impossibly evil, and impossibly cheerful and they were all hung about with revolvers and daggers like pirates; one of them, the boy Michel, even toted a hand grenade. Mazlor was grinning there, with the beer all ready, and he found Leda a more or less comfortable chair under the winch I'd helped him with, and we all put our feet up on the railing and drank together like old friends.

Jao was a dark and wiry Brazilian, forty-five years old or so, and he told me he'd just come back from what he called a "bloody money-good trip" into Bolivia, with three Indian porters weighed down with uncut semi-precious stones and a small bag of diamonds in his own pocket. He picked his teeth with his dagger as he told me how terrified all the police were of him.

Michel was not much more than twenty, a very good-looking boy under all the dirt, with flaxen hair and a quick, easy way of moving. He spoke rapid, fluent French and broken Portuguese, and his strong white teeth and dark skin seemed to indicate more than a touch of the Indian somewhere. He told me his father was Belgian and his mother a *curiboca*, part Negro, part Indian; he'd been born in one of the French Missions, and had been to Brussels, but he didn't like it very much; I gathered the police there were not as easy to cope with as they were out here, so he'd come back to his own neck of the woods, and was now a professional bandit, living in the forest and making forays into the traders' settlements whenever he needed something he hadn't got. His revolver had four very ostentatious notches on its butt; I didn't ask him about them.

But Slawata was something else again. He grinned easily, said nothing, and his eyes were always watchful. Of the three, I thought perhaps Slawata would be the most dangerous—dangerous to whomever was his enemy of the moment. He was a big man, even by my standards, well over six foot three, with the kind of stoop a tall man can develop if he's not careful. He wore a khaki shirt with the sleeves torn off at the shoulders, and his muscles were good. He must have been getting on to sixty, but he was as hard and sharp as a barrel full of shrapnel fragments. They all had one thing in common—they all had that desperado look of unshaven toughness that seems to say: *keep off, brother, don't crowd me, don't try to tangle...*

We talked for a while, and at last I overcame a certain natural trepidation and made up my mind that I'd done the right thing; it was a pretty good likelihood, anyway; and that's all we can really deal in. Nobody even mentioned money. I thought that was very charming of them.

When Leda and I made a move to go back to the hotel, they all got to their feet with a sort of clumsy grace. Michel kissed her hand, Jao patted her behind (much to her astonishment), and Slawata surprised us all by making what for him must have been a very long speech.

He said: "Madame, when your man goes, we take good care of you. For these three, I will not speak. For me, I say this: anyone make you trouble, I kill him, or he kill me. My arms very strong; they your arms now." He made a clumsy little bow, threw me a quick glance, and kissed her hand, too.

I thought: well, if I really can trust them, nobody's going to get near my Leda while I'm away. All sorts of things were about to happen, but they were going to happen to me, not to her.

Mazlor walked back to the hotel with us, and whistled up the Indian, and spoke with him for a while in dialect. His name was Jesus, a short, stubby, barrel-chested tribesman from one of the Missions; I'd liked the looks of him the moment I'd seen him. He spoke good. Portuguese and a little Spanish as well. It was still pretty hot, but he wore a heavy overcoat of dark khaki wool—the kind of thing army surplus dealers push around in the most unlikely places, and a floppy black felt hat. He showed me, unsmiling, that he carried a gun—an ancient, rusted Bayard six-shot revolver; he also told me he had no ammunition for it. He had a long, very sharp knife as well, and the stick he used had a three-inch sharpened iron point on the end of it. Most of all, he was well-armed with an air of extraordinarily casual competence, as though nothing in this world or the next would ever worry him.

Mazlor went off, and Jesus waited, and inside Leda's room I said goodbye and told her again all she had to do. I kissed her, and she kissed me, and I wanted to make love to her there and then, knowing that she would accept it, I remembered her long slim naked body the first time I had seen it, when she didn't even know that I was there, and it was only the second time I'd ever seen her, I held her tight, and she kissed me again, and said: "Be careful, Cabot darling," It was hard to part from her then.

When I closed the door behind me and crossed the moonlit patio, I saw a dark figure squatting under the plumeria tree in the corner; it was Slawata. He was a darker part of a dark shadow, no more.

The moon was down and the night was black as pitch.

The sounds of the night forest were astounding. The cries of the animals and the birds and the frogs were deafening, a cacophony against which the roar of the outboard motor seemed almost a whisper.

We moved fast, with the throttle full open, and after we had stashed the motor and taken to the paddles, there were two of us now to send the little canoe along at a hell of a lick, two to carry it up the portage track to the top of the falls. And we were traveling lighter now; my stores were already in position, where I wanted them to be.

I had carefully pointed out the jaguar trap to Jesus, and although he had nothing more than a grunt to offer, the expression on his face told me that he was thinking the same thing I was—this was no place to catch jaguars. At the whitecapped weir, I took him under the water and guided him carefully to show him where the mangrove spears were, though the darkness made it an almost impossible task, I explained that they were only lethal against a craft, or a swimmer, coming at speed downstream because of the way they were pointed, and showed him the two granite boulders that marked the passage I had cleared. He only grunted; but now there was an amused light in his eyes and once, when we continued paddling, he actually laughed.

I said to him: "They keep the Indians up there in a state of terror, like slaves. If one of them should try to escape, there'll be traps like this all over the place to make sure they don't get out alive." He stopped laughing, and I could feel the added force to his paddle that his anger gave him.

When the river got too fast to fight, even with two of us paddling now, we'd traveled a little further than I had when I was alone—and we'd dome it in nine hours instead of the fourteen I'd taken the first time.

It was ten o'clock in the morning, and we stopped to eat. I gathered a few twigs together and prepared the fire, while Jesus strolled over to the nearest water and speared a fish in two minutes flat with his iron-tipped stick. I flicked my lighter, but the flint was finished, and while I was replacing it, he cut a notch in a piece of dried bamboo, took from his waist the rope he wore as a belt, slipped the rope through the notch and pulled on it fast, holding the bamboo down flat on the ground with a great splayed, naked foot, and at the second pull, before I'd even got the lighter working, the grasses he had placed there caught, and the fire was under way. He held out his hand for the lighter, looked at it when I gave it to him, grunted, and tossed it away. Not to hurt his feelings, I didn't retrieve it till he was busy barbecuing the fish.

I asked him if he was tired, because the going had been pretty hard; I'd pushed along at a good pace. All the answer I got was another grunt, and a cold look that would have been indignant if he'd known what indignation was.

Three hours later, we passed the casuarina tree where I'd spent the night. Jesus touched me on the shoulder, and quick as a flash disappeared from sight. I found him crouching in the bushes, well hidden, and he pointed silently at the ground just ahead of us. It was the fire I'd left. He put his lips close to my ear and whispered: "Arasuyu tribe. Bad men." I shook my head and told him I'd made the fire myself. He scratched at his lip for a while, examined the stones carefully, felt the ashes, decided I was telling the truth, and grunted.

He was following close behind me, and when we came to the very dense place where it was necessary to get onto hands and knees and crawl, he made no complaint, nor even asked why; one look at the track we were leaving would have told him that to a casual glance it wasn't a human track. Six and a half hours later, we were at the base of the cliff. I told him we were going up to the top, and for the first time, he protested. He said quietly: "No man climb up there, Senhor. Impossible."

I pulled away a bush and showed him the first of the dangling ropes. I pulled myself up it, put my foot firmly in one of the steps, reached out to a handhold, pulled myself up, turned and looked back at him. His body was shaking now with silent mirth. Saying nothing, he followed me. He climbed easily, gracefully, like an animal. And we reached the cave near the top just as the sun was setting. We'd made pretty good time. I showed him the stores I'd left there, and said: "Take it easy on the *pinga*, I want you all in one piece. In the morning, I go. You stay here. You stay here till I come, okay?"

Unsmiling, he nodded. "I stay."

I shared some of his dried fish with him for dinner. It had a strong, sour taste to it, but it was a pleasant change of diet. We drank some *pinga* and some water, and when it was quite dark he crawled like a leech along the ledge to a spot where his sharp eyes had caught the movement of a fragile mauve blossom earlier in the evening; he came back soon with his overcoat pockets full of passionfruit, and we ate those too.

I tried to draw him out into conversation; but all he would do was grunt. But he did offer me a spell at his noisome clay pipe. Not wanting to hurt his feelings, I smoked it for a while, then handed it back to him in silence. I told him. I'd be moving out at first light. I jerked a thumb at the dried fish, the water, the brandy, and said: "I don't know how long I'll be gone, but you won't starve to death for a few days, will you?"

He grunted. He took off his overcoat, spread it out neatly on the ground, found a rock for a pillow, lay down without a word, and in a couple of minutes he was fast asleep.

I explored the ledge outside as soon as the moon came up, found the handholds to the top that I'd prepared, and made sure no one had touched the camouflage; I didn't think it was very likely, and no one had.

I sat in the silence and the darkness out there on the ledge for a while, and looked down at the moonlit river and the black valley, listening to the friendly night sounds of the jungle. I'm never more at peace than when I'm in a place like this, when a man lives or dies by his own efforts, where there's nothing to depend on and no one to depend on him. Here, there were just the two of us, Jesus and I, and each of us could have lived alone there forever, with just our bare hands to sustain us, and all the satisfactions of a rich and bountiful and peaceful land.

And down there, there was Leda...I thought about her for a long, long time, enjoying the remembrances, knowing that she had fast become an essential part of my life. I could feel the touch of her embrace, smell the scent of her body, hear the sound of her voice in my ear. I was alone up there, perched on a cliff a thousand feet in a lonely sky; and she was with me.

When I crawled back into the cave and lay down to sleep, one beady Indian eye opened itself and looked at me, and then closed itself again, and all was silence.

CHAPTER 7

The little town was even prettier close up than it had appeared from the top of the distant tree. The streets were clean and tidy, with neat green verges of chamomile that gave out a pleasant scent; they were still wet with dew, and the sun was just coming over the top of the whitewashed church spire. There were colorful tropical gardens everywhere, well-tended, well-watered, cool and delightful.

I sat for a while on a green-painted bench, watching the passers-by. At first there were very few, but they all stared at me curiously, as though it were a very unusual thing for anyone to be taking his ease on a park bench at this hour of the morning, And then there were more people, walking or bicycling to work, and an occasional car went by; and except for the constant stares, to which I'm pretty well inured, no one seemed more than casually aware of my presence.

But the particular character of the place, in spite of its charm, was slowly printing itself quite indelibly on my consciousness. A dozen Indians went to work in the gardens across the road, with rakes and shovels and hedge-clippers; they wore rags, and the well-dressed European with them was carrying a whip. A guard took up his position nearby, squatting casually on a stone bench with a rifle over his shoulder while he munched on a piece of hard cheese.

Some more Indians passed me by, bowed under heavy loads, like animals, and three of them were dragging a heavy barrow that was loaded down with watermelons; a European was driving them too, and he also carried a long whip. There was a sharp division of population here, a cruel and wicked division. I saw a half-caste stumble across the path of a sauntering policeman, and the policeman lashed out with his foot and sent the old man sprawling in the gutter.

There were more cars now, and almost no trucks, and I noticed that nearly all of the cars were the good ones; there were no little Volkswagens or Austins or Renaults; there were plenty of the luxury European cars, and I wondered how much it must have cost to fly them in here.

Here, the rich man drove a Mercedes, or a Rolls, or a Ferrari; the forlorn delights of fine cars, with only ten or twenty miles of road to drive them on. The poor man went on foot and was whipped for his pains; and in between these two extremes, there was nothing, nothing at all.

I was an intruder, sitting there alone and absorbing all that there was to be absorbed. Sooner or later, I'd be in trouble, but for all their vaunted security I was right in among them, past the first line of their defenses. There was an enemy in their midst, and they didn't even know it; yet.

A small and pleasant looking café across the road was just opening up, and a *mestizo* was swilling away any dust that might have been on the pavement with a long black rubber hose. I crossed the road and sat there, and soon became aware that a waiter was peering at me round the corner of the kitchen door; he disappeared as soon as I saw him, and then he came bustling out and stood there to take my order. I said:

"Coffee, please, lots of it."

"*Si, Senhor*"—he said again, questioningly, as though he ought to know my name—"Senhor...?"

I said: "Cabot Cain, does it matter?"

He nodded quickly, nervously, and hurried off, and when he brought the coffee, another man was with him, a thin, good-looking Bolivian in a neat silk suit and smoking an early-morning black cheroot. He made a polite little bow, and gestured to the waiter to set out the coffee. He said:

"Senhor—Cain, was it?"

"That's right. Cabot Cain."

He smiled: "But you didn't come in on the helicopter last night."

"No. I didn't."

He hesitated, the smile was still there, fixed and glassy. "Then may I ask how you got here?"

"Are you the headwaiter?"

Still the smile. "*O proprietario*. You come from...from where, Senhor Cain?"

"San Francisco." That wasn't what he wanted to know, but I thought it would do for the moment.

He bowed again; and said: "I hope the coffee is good."

It was, it was excellent. One thing that's hard to find in this part of the world is dull coffee. When he had gone back to his hiding place, I sat and sipped in peace and comfort, and watched the people on the street; bowed backs everywhere, bowed under loads of hemp, or coffee beans, or sacks of flour; the draft animals here were men, or they were women, or children. Far in the distance, I heard the sound of a ragged volley of rifle fire, just a short sharp burst from half a dozen rifles; it sounded like an execution.

And then, a policeman came up on a bicycle, leaned his machine against the wall, and stood in the doorway watching me for a long time. He turned abruptly, got on his bicycle, cycled off, and five minutes later there was the sound of screeching tires and a jeep pulled up outside.

It was like the jeeps I'd seen through my binoculars; four men and a Bren gun. One of the men was an officer, a thickset, swarthy man with short-cut iron gray hair, and a khaki uniform with scarlet epaulettes and the word *Policia* across the shoulders. He also had three stars on his epaulettes, which I assumed made him a Captain. He strode quickly into the café, stopped at the door to light a cheroot, then moved fast over to my table and saluted.

His manner was correct and cautious; they were so sure that no one could be there who had no right to be there—if you came home one night and found a burglar prowling in the dark, you'd probably start some action; but if you found the same man in your favorite armchair, with his feet up, a book on his knee, a glass in his hand and a smile on his face...well, at least you'd make sure that it all wasn't just a mistake. And so, the officer was formal and well mannered. He said: "Senhor Cain?"

It was the owner, then, who had called them.

I said: "Cabot Cain. Captain..."

"Captain Alonzo Alvarado, Policia da Fuerte Quemado. Your papers, please, Senhor."

I gave him my passport, and he looked at it briefly and slipped it into his pocket. He said: "You will tell where you came from, Mr. Cain? And how you came to this place?"

I said: "I came here from Rio, walked up the side of the mountain from Urbana."

"That is more than eighty kilometers. And they did not see you at the checkpoint."

"Eighty eight, roughly. And I walked round the checkpoint."

He stared at me, disbelieving. "There is no way round the checkpoint."

"Up over the mountain a little, across the gorge. It's not hard."

He was puzzled, unsure of himself. I could see the wheels turning; he was trying to picture the barrier, the rocks and the gorge, and to pinpoint the place where a man could cross it. Then he made up his mind that it couldn't be done. He said:

"You will forgive me if I do not believe you."

"Have you got a better story?"

He looked at me with a certain unpleasant relish. He was still very formal. "If you will come with me, please."

"Am I under arrest? If so, for what?"

He permitted himself a thin smile. "You are a long way from San Francisco here, Senhor Cain. Come with me."

I got up to go, and he smiled and said: "First, there is the coffee to pay for."

I threw some cruzeiro notes on the table and followed him out. The policemen in the jeep moved over to make way for me; one of them looked me up and down a little fearfully, wondering if there was going to be any trouble and knowing that between them they probably couldn't handle it.

We drove off fast, speeding along the pretty, tree-lined streets, and pulled up at a fine old building of heavy white stone that had once been a splendid mansion, the sort of place the rubber barons put up before they all went broke when their precious, secretive seeds had been smuggled out of the country and planted in Southeast Asia. A two-and-a-half-story building with a wide, sweeping staircase leading up from the teak-paneled hall. The furnishings inside were good, but it was no longer a house; it was an office, and a small brass plaque at the entrance bore the legend: *Policia Segreta, Comunidade de Fuerte Quemado.*

I think it was the first time I had ever come across a small town that had its own secret police.

We went into a large and airy room, with a highly-polished red tile floor that had three excellent Eastern carpets spread on it: a Ghiordes-knot Persian, from Kerman, and two Turkish Ushaks, one of which I would have given my soul for. There was a gilt chandelier over a bronze-mounted desk of carefully matched sycamore that had been made, I would say, probably by Caffieri or Oeben in the seventeen hundreds. There was a splendid court cupboard of carved oak which was considerably older, and a long, low draw-table of inlaid ebony; there was nothing in the room that wasn't immensely valuable, but the net effect was of a badly-laid-out museum, with types and periods juxtaposed in no sort of order at all.

And at the bronze-mounted desk, a man was sitting whose photograph had been plastered all over the world's newspapers less than two years ago. The plaque on the desktop said simply: Colonel von Brubeck. But the papers had called him, then, Anton Hans Ullman.

Well, it was none of my business; at least, not for the moment.

Major Anton Hans Ullman, 1st S.S. Regiment, Gauleiter of the Kassa Command, wanted by half the countries of Europe. He'd been seen, quite briefly and by the purest chance, on the streets of Asuncion in Paraguay during a short visit there for some unknown purpose. A visit of a day or two, no more, and his face had changed a lot in the last twenty years; but he'd been seen by quite the wrong people. I remember that two Israeli agents, searching for Stengel, happened to be staying in the same hotel that Ullman had used. There'd been a flurry of startled activity; someone had been shot, someone else had been wounded, and Ullman had suddenly gone. There'd been apologies, and demands for more apologies, a couple of innocent tourists had been declared *non grata* and deported, a police official had been fired, a few half-hearted inquiries made, and then everything had blown over, and that was the end of that.

Ullman had disappeared again; but where?

Well, here he was now, sitting at a highly-polished desk that was worth a hundred thousand dollars, in a tight-fitting steel gray uniform and a Colonel's badges of rank. A tall, thin man with a highly-polished face to match the desk, and short-cropped white hair and very black eyebrows. He sat at the far end of the room as we walked in, and he never once took his eyes off me; black, bright, alert eyes. He dismissed the Captain with a nod, and we were alone; I heard the door close heavily behind me.

I'd even talked to Fenrek about him, I remembered, when we'd been discussing the apparent ease with which some of the old-time Nazis had faded out into oblivion. Fenrek had said: "Take Ullman, for example. He was never the brute that turned up in the extermination camps. He was never the man who took pleasure in what was going on. But he quietly profited by it to put himself in a position of power and wealth. He's got a shrewd, cunning mind, and while he didn't really approve of the terror, he knew that it all helped serve his purpose and so he wouldn't fight it either. Some of them were animals; but Ullman wasn't. Ullman was a cultivated, even a kindly man, who put his better instincts behind him because they stood in the way of what he wanted. And a good brain, make no mistake about that. He knew what he wanted, and quietly, ruthlessly, set out to acquire it. Not really very unpleasant characteristics, when you come to think of it; the kind of man you and I could enjoy a pleasant evening with. But he used the animals, and he let the animals use him. And that made him dangerous. Not a mass murderer himself, in the simplest sense of the word, but he used his considerable talents to help the murderers merrily on their way because he could profit from what they were doing."

I'd said: "This is the man you and could enjoy a pleasant evening with?" But Fenrek had only laughed. "At the end of which either of us would be happy to cut his throat."

Now, here he was; the man who could use the animals and be

used by them. Von Brubeck now, not Ullman any more. I wondered how many other names he could call upon when needed.

He indicated a carved walnut chair, high-backed and hard and ornate. He said:

"You are Mister Cabot Cain, and I am Colonel von Brubeck. Sit down please."

He leaned back in his chair and looked at me, very thoughtfully, and then leaned forward and pushed a silver box of cigarettes toward me. "Please help yourself, you have a lot to tell me."

I said: "I've always thought smoking a foolish pastime. Bad for the health, too."

"Ah yes, the health of the body is a mania with the Americans, isn't it, Mr. Cain? What about the mind? Do you have a mind too?"

"Uh-huh."

"Well, I'm glad to hear it. So tell me first of all why you came here, and secondly how you came here. Perhaps the second question is more important than the first."

I said: "Well, in that case...I came up the Doussa road, on foot, and when I came to your barrier, I simply went round it."

"To the left, or to the right?"

"To the right, across the gorge."

"And how did you cross the gorge?"

"I pole-vaulted it."

He had the grace to look astonished. He said at last: "Yes, I suppose an athlete could do that, a good athlete. That's very interesting. We rather pride ourselves on our tight security here." His English was faultless, immaculate, the English of the country squire, with no trace whatsoever of any German accent, He said: "I'm still rather surprised the guards didn't see you."

"At night?"

"I see." He paused. "All right, now the first question. What are you doing here?"

"You mean a man can't come and go here as he pleases?"

"I mean precisely that."

"According to the Brazilian government, this town is part of the State of Guapore, and not a restricted area."

"According to the Bolivian government, it is nothing of the

sort. Let's pretend that we're on Bolivian territory for the moment."

"Then you carry Bolivian government authority, Colonel?"

He smiled easily. "Only when we're threatened with *Brazilian* governmental authority. At other times..." He gestured vaguely. "Now, your explanation please."

Well, it was time to take a deep breath and plunge in. I said: "I'm looking for a man named Kolchak."

He did not hesitate. "And you expect to find him here?"

"I think it's a likelihood he's here, yes."

He got up and wandered around the room, moving in behind me and talking softly. He said:

"One of the great disadvantages of being cut off like this from the rest of the world is that it takes time to find out all we really ought to know about people who come here uninvited. And that in itself is sufficiently startling. We're in disputed territory, there's no easy road in or out, and we're a tight little self-supporting community, so we don't often get visitors unless we're expecting them. An uninvited stranger suddenly among us...it's quite disconcerting, Mr. Cain. How did you even know of the existence of this happy little town?"

I shrugged. "Among those of us who are interested in it, it does have a reputation, you know."

"Yes, I suppose that's perfectly true."

"And if you want to know more about me a phone call to Urbana, where I've been staying, will indicate that I'm a perfectly harmless passer-by."

"Only we have no telephone to Urbana. Their wishes, not ours. We have to look further afield. To La Paz, or Lima. Or even to Rio de Janeiro."

"Oh. I see."

"And all our friends in Rio can tell us is that you're a rather arrogant and impetuous jewel thief."

"I didn't expect that little episode to catch up with me quite so fast," I said blandly. "But you say we're on Bolivian soil now, so I'm in the clear, aren't I? There's been no time for a formal application for extradition, even if there were an extradition treaty between the two countries, which there's not."

He was just as bland. "When it suits us, this is Brazil, not

Bolivia,"

"I am still hoping for sanctuary here."

"Then you must have heard quite a lot about us. Well, we really make no great effort to hide our little freedoms."

"Then I may stay and continue my search?"

He laughed shortly. "I still don't think you have any brains, Cain, that's pretty apparent, isn't it? But I've always had a sneaking regard for your kind of arrogance." He changed tacks. "My information is that you're carrying a valuable parcel of diamonds and jade. Where are they?"

I said: "Hidden in a tree, three and a half miles outside Urbana, in the middle of a damn great forest. Am I under arrest?"

He chose to ignore my question. "And what do you want with this...what did you say his name was?"

"Kolchak? He has something I want to buy."

"Oh? What's that?"

"If you don't mind, Colonel, I'd rather talk to him. It's rather a delicate matter."

"As far as I know, there's no man of that name here. We have a population of four hundred and eighty Europeans, and I know every one of them personally." He sounded amused. "I have to. We examine our residents very carefully, a matter of prudence."

I heard the door open, and when I looked round there were three soldiers coming in. They took up their positions near the door; two of them were armed with Schmeisser machine-pistols, and the third, a Sergeant, carried a pair of handcuffs. The Colonel said again:

"What is it you want with Kolchak?"

"A deal. A deal that involves a lot of money."

"You want to sell him your little parcel of valuables?"

"No. I told you, I want to buy, not sell."

"And what is it that you want to buy from...Kolchak? An unusual name, that."

"I'm afraid I can't tell you what it is, Colonel. If you'll tell me where I can find him...?"

He came round and sat on the edge of that beautiful desk, looking impossibly suave and elegant in his well-pressed uniform, and alligator-skin shoes. He said:

"Well, there's no one here of that name, so you must give me leave to doubt your story. And that means, I'm afraid, that we'll have to detain you for a while. Not for long, just till we can find out more about you." He gestured to the Sergeant behind me. "Cell four."

Suddenly, there was a Schmeisser under my nose, and the Sergeant was gesturing for me to hold out my wrists. I wasn't worried about the gun; I represented a problem to them, and they would obviously want me in fairly good health until it was all cleared up. The Sergeant fastened the handcuffs on me and stood back with admirable discretion, and the soldier jerked his machine-pistol and shepherded me to the door. As we went out, the Colonel said pleasantly:

"I have a lot of work to do, Cain, but I'll try and come and see you this evening."

The door closed behind me, and the Sergeant shoved me once only and didn't do it again when he met a fairly solid wall of resistance, and they led me to a small door off the hall and down a flight of stairs into a cellar.

No antiques here. The walls were bare stone, and the lighting came from purely functional lamps set in small grills. We went along a short, narrow corridor, the guard threw open an iron-barred door and then a heavy wooden one, and I went into a good sized cell that was lit only from the lamps in the corridor. The doors closed, and I was in darkness. I'd seen a wooden bench, so I sat down to think things out a bit.

So far, they were going very well, I wasn't looking forward to the next episode, but I knew that it was inevitable, They'd left me my watch, my money-belt, everything; they hadn't even bothered to search me. I knew that they soon would.

The door opened less than an hour later. A blinding light was flashed in my eyes, and I heard the swish of the weapon, and then something hit me hard in the back of the head. I'd wondered if they were worried about my obvious physical capabilities; now I knew, they weren't taking any chances, and when I came back to my senses I was sitting in a chair in a darkened room with my hands handcuffed behind me and my feet strapped to the chair legs. I had no idea how long I'd been unconscious. I could smell cigar smoke, and when I looked around in the dim light, I could see someone sitting in a corner on a wooden chair, smoking. Not much to see; a thin man with glasses, a European by the looks of him. He had an annoying cough, and kept clearing his throat as though the cigars were giving him trouble. I heard someone say, in Spanish: "He's come round," and the European said in a thickly-accented voice: "All right, you may begin."

I won't go into the details. There were four of them, and they took it in turn to use the lead-weighted rubber hoses, working with more skill than passion, and just putting me in a receptive frame of mind for the questions that were to follow.

I started yelling after five minutes, and after a few more I said: "All right, all right, for God's sake, I'll tell you whatever you want to know." It was hard to talk; my lips were bruised, an eye was puffing up, and I could see a fearful cut on the swollen flesh of my cheekbone when I tried to squint down at the lump that was swelling up to blind me.

The man in the corner said briefly: "*Bastante, bastante ate agora*, enough for now." He didn't move from his chair, and he didn't stop his nervous cough. I was aware that he was sitting back and stretching out his legs, and he said in English:

"A simple beating, Cain, requires no preparation, no trouble on our part, no difficulties at all. It's merely a matter of finding out just where a man's threshold of pain is, and of showing him that we are prepared to treat him as brutally as we think fit. Is that understood? If not, there are several more steps we can take. If we're prepared to go to a little trouble, which we are if necessary, we can reduce you to a sniveling wreck of what you once were in less than an hour. If you're ready to answer a few questions, then perhaps it won't be necessary." He paused a little, and then said: "Now, why do you believe that this man Kolchak is here? What led you to this place?"

My mouth seemed full of red-hot bricks. I said: "I have a friend in Interpol, he told me he might be here."

"A friend in the police? You, a jewel thief?"

"If you know where to spend your money...there aren't many people can't be bought." I thought of friend Fenrek, driving around in Paris in my beautiful car; bashing the front fender every once in a while.

My questioner seemed to find that very interesting. He said:

"The Interpol people are supposed to be incorruptible."

I wished Fenrek could hear me now. I said: "It just costs a lot more money, that's all."

"What is his name, your friend?"

They knew, of course. I said: "Fenrek, a Colonel who works in Paris. The War Crimes Commission located Kolchak, Interpol heard about it, Fenrek told me."

"And the information cost you...how much?"

I said: "I gave him a fifteen-thousand dollar automobile."

He thought about that for a long time, and said at last: "Yes, that would be more discreet than cash, wouldn't it? So this deal you spoke of, with Kolchak. There must be quite a large sum at stake."

"Half a million, give or take a few bucks."

"And its precise nature?"

I said: "Go to hell."

They started over again, and I stuck it for another few minutes before I yelled Uncle; I figured they'd done enough truth-pulling. And, while we're on the subject of truth, there is a point worth making; I'd been scared stiff they might use Sodium Pentothal, though the likelihood was that the old-fashioned methods would be easier, would come more naturally to them.

He said, the man in the comer: "I will ask you only once more. What is the nature of your deal?"

I could hardly hear myself speak; my voice was a very hoarse croak. I said: "According to the Commission, Kolchak has some Hungarian jewels. Among them, there's a diamond and ruby bracelet, all hung about...hung about with pendants. Two of the pendants are missing, very large rubies. I have them. I want to put them back on the bracelet where they belong, then sell. Split the profits, which should be considerable."

"And where are these rubies now?"

I waited a long time before answering, I said at last: "No need to get your bully-boys working again. You must know I'd hardly bring them with me."

"Where are they now?"

"In Manaus, in a safe-deposit box. I have sketches of them in Urbana, hidden in a tree with...with a lot of other stuff."

There was a long, long silence. The air was heavy with the stink of that damned cigar, and the silence was broken only by his coughing. I knew what he was thinking—or at least, I thought I did—and figured I'd better set him on his predestined track once more. I said:

"Okay, you can take me down there under guard and force me to produce a handful of diamonds and a few lousy sketches. But what you really want is in Manaus, and you can't get that without my goodwill, can you?"

He said, sounding quite astonished: "What we really want? You're in police custody, Cain, not among your fellow criminals."

I thought it wise to keep silent. He didn't say another word. I heard his cough receding down the corridor, and the four men took me back to my cell. It wasn't far, just around the corner of the corridor. When they shut the heavy wooden door, one of them opened the peephole, glanced back over his shoulder, and then slipped me a cigarette and a single match. It was a nice gesture, and I waited till the tiny trap was shut again before crumbling it up and dropping it in the stinking bucket. I checked over my pockets; everything had gone. Everything.

They came back an hour later and took me to Colonel von Brubeck; late Major Ullman. He looked up and clicked his tongue in sympathy when he saw my face, and he said solicitously:

"I really didn't want them to be quite so brutal, but it was necessary that we know just what you're up to. And you are, after all, a pretty hard case, aren't you? A professional criminal can't really expect much sympathy from the police, can he?"

I said: "Depends who the police are."

He sighed. "Yes, you've obviously gone to quite a lot of trouble, so I can only presume that you know what sort of a place Fuerte Quemado really is." He sounded almost sorry about it. "But we try and keep a semblance of order here, though it isn't easy. Disputed territory, you know, a lot of undesirables find their way here, but as long as they keep the peace and do us no harm we leave them alone. The spirit of sanctuary. Some of them are men who have been grossly misunderstood." He was so earnest about it that I began to wonder, did he really believe what he was saying?

I thought it more likely that he found it attractive to maintain a polite facade to hide all the villainy, like the unethical politician who's convinced that the means don't matter as long as the end works out the way he wants it.

He said smoothly: "As far as you are concerned, we've had no request for your person from the Brazilian authorities, and so..." He handed me a flat canvas sack of the kind bankers use. "If you'd like to check over your property?"

Everything was there except my passport. I'd just over four thousand dollars in my money-belt; it was all there. I said: "Only the passport is missing."

"When you are ready to leave us, it will be given you. You have somewhere to stay?"

"I assume there's a hotel here?"

"Of course. Several. I can recommend the Sumidade. But you brought no clothes for a prolonged stay, did you? Well, never mind, as long as you have money." He said pleasantly: "That's the crux of the whole matter, Mr. Cain. As long as a man has money, Fuerte Quemado can be a home away from home for him. With nothing but the best of everything."

A home away from home...it was indeed.

The Sumidade was a pleasant and comfortable place, with good service and a splendid restaurant; it was also extremely expensive. As Ullman, or von Brubeck had said, nothing but the best was good enough. The furnishings and the decor were excellent, and we might have been on the French Riviera or in Acapulco.

There were five or six pretty young girls sitting in the lobby, and as I came in they lost their sad and distant looks and smiled brightly at me, all of them. I went on through to my room, and took a shower, and a very efficient young woman came in, unasked, with a medical kit and fixed up my face; she felt my chest very carefully and said, with a great deal of solicitous sympathy: "Two broken ribs, Senhor Cain, you'd better see the doctor." I shook my head and made a joke about it, and she laughed the professional laugh of the courtesan and asked what she could do to make me happy and comfortable.

There was blood all over my shirt, and I said: "Take me outside and point me in the direction of the stores, I want to do some shopping," She shrugged, and told me where the arcade was.

I bought some slacks by Simpson of Piccadilly, some Hathaway shirts, some Florsheim Royal Imperial shoes, fifty dollars a pair in the States and eighty-five here. I bought a couple of Jantzen swimsuits, and a couple of Rogers Peet suits. I chatted with a salesman about renting a house too; when the word got back, at least they'd know that my plan, hopefully, was to stay for a while.

There was a good pool set in the green gardens of the hotel, sixty feet long and sparklingly well-kept, so I spent the next two hours doing the crawl back and forth as fast as I could, getting the smell of that stinking jail out of my nostrils and the stiffness out of my muscles. I had to put up with a lot of staring too; not the accustomed surprise because of my size, but because my face looked as though it had been put through a coffee grinder; I hoped that the sun and liberal doses of cold water would get rid of most of the swelling. And it was quite tolerable to be looked over so thoroughly, anyway; there were some very attractive people by the pool, a dozen or so women of varying ages and nationalities who seemed to have only one thing in common—strikingly good looks.

I stopped to think about this for a while. Fuerte Quemado was like one of the old frontier towns of the West in many ways—except for the high degree of modern comfort and luxury, of course. But it housed a lot of desperados, just as the Old West did, and they were almost exclusively men. The "natural" inhabitants of the town, therefore, would have to import their women, because the local population, such as it was, was mostly Indian and would surely not satisfy the hedonistic tastes of men who were beyond the law and had plenty of money. And this meant importing their women too; the best of everything again.

The more I thought about it, the more I realized that from this point of view at least, Fuerte Quemado was one gigantic luxury brothel. All that money could buy, with no law except that laid down by the criminals who had taken over the town. What a setup, I thought; I'd made a bad comparison while I was thinking of Dodge City and the Badlands of Oklahoma. A better analogy would be Ferrara under the

Borgias.

But on the surface, I found myself in a luxury resort that seemed to offer complete relaxation and the satisfaction of all the little passions: good food, cold drinks, splendid scenery, lovely women. I finished my long swim, put on a shirt and a pair of slacks, and went for a brisk walk through the town, round the huge patch of mango trees, over the gorge where the bananas were, down the slope into the coffee field, and across to the small airfield. I've always been interested in aircraft; there was a Bellanca 960c that caught my eye, a pretty little craft; sparkling new, with a top speed of well over two hundred miles an hour and a very short takeoff; fast, maneuverable, comfortable. I wondered who it belonged to, and thought I'd like to get my hands on the controls for a while. It's a good flying country up in the mountains there. I walked briskly back into town, and up toward the forest.

All the way there'd been a soldier following me, sweating hard with the pace and not trying in the least to hide his presence. Now, it was time to tell him where to get off. I began to run, just running easily around the blocks; he couldn't keep up with me, and as I passed him for the second time, I clapped him on the shoulder and grinned at him and said in Portuguese: "Got to keep fit." He was nearly dropping from exhaustion. I slowed down to a walk then, and let him catch up with me, and guided him to the edge of the town. I ran into the forest, doubled back again, let him see that I was still merely exercising, was making use of the forest just as a pleasant place to run in.

He gave up at last. He sat on a fallen tree trunk, the sweat soaking his uniform and pouring down off his forehead, panting and gasping for air. I let him hear me crashing through the undergrowth for a while, and then came back and sat beside him. I said very earnestly: "I've got to keep in shape, it's a mania." I flexed my muscles at him shamelessly, and said: "You see? You don't get like this without a lot of exercise, constant exercise, all the time." He was too exhausted to answer, and I patted his shoulder and said: "Don't worry, friend, I'm just working out, I'm not going anywhere."

I ran around for an hour, keeping always within sound of him, and when I came back I was quite sure that now the word would be passed around the guardhouse: *that mad Americano likes to run in the forest.* I was also sure I'd shown him what a nice, friendly fellow he was following around. I waited a while; and then stood up and asked: "*Esta bem*, everything all right?" He nodded, and as I turned away, he said: "Senhor!" I turned back. He looked worried. He said slowly: "Senhor, if I do not know where you go...they will kill me."

I said gently: "Just tell them I'm a nut for physical exercise. But harmless."

I walked back to the hotel, and he kept a discreet hundred yards or so behind me. The darkness was setting in.

And when I reached the hotel, Colonel von Brubeck was there, sitting, waiting in the lobby, with a glass of Cinzano on the rocks with a twist of lemon, at his elbow. He stood up when I approached, and smiled and said: "Mr. Cain, are you doing anything tonight?"

I said: "Well, hardly."

"Splendid. I'd like you to meet some friends of mine. Suppose I send a car for you in a couple of hours?"

"That would be delightful. Who are the friends?"

He gestured vaguely: "Oh, just some of our local residents. They're very anxious to meet you."

"Kolchak?"

He smiled. "Stubborn sort of fellow, aren't you? No, not Kolchak. I assure you, no one here has ever heard of him. But just...some friends." He made a formal little bow and repeated: "In two hours from now. Informal." And then he was gone.

I went on up to my room, showered and changed, and called room service for a glass of Brazilian *pastis* with a lot of ice, and when I went down to the lobby at nine o'clock, there was a delightful surprise waiting for me.

The timing was just right.

She came in through the door as I stepped off the last carpeted stair, and she came straight across to me with her hand held out, moving briskly and smiling, a small, wonderfully attractive woman with very creamy skin and huge dark eyes, and black, black hair that curled up just above the shoulders and swung to and fro as she walked. She wore a tight-fitting black cocktail dress with a single diamond clip on it, a diamond big enough to pay off the national debt. The dress was split up one side almost to her waist, and her legs were marvelous.

She took my band and said: "Mr. Cain, I'm Elena da Costa."

She showed her white, even teeth and said: "I'm your date for the party. Shall we go?" Her English was fluent enough, touched with a pleasant Portuguese lilt, more of an intonation than an accent. She looked up at me and laughed, and said: "And we should not stand here together, should we? I really must look quite ridiculous."

She wasn't really as small as all that, but I said ruefully: "Well, one of us might."

We crossed the hall and went outside. A Lotus Elan was waiting for us, 82-55mm bore, 72-75mm stroke, with a twin-choke Weber carburetor; a little bomb of a car with a torque of a hundred and eight pound feet, Girling disk brakes, and rack and pinion steering, a pretty little bomb you could really take off in.

Thank God the top was down, or I'd never have fitted myself into it.

We didn't have far to go, but she drove fast and well and skillfully, using the gears and taking the corners at very decent speeds indeed. We drove past the café where I'd been picked up, down a wide boulevard lined with flowering magnolia trees and jacarandas, and we pulled up outside a high, white-washed wall of brick and bleeding mortar. She tooted the horn, and the iron gates swung open. There was a long driveway lined with oleander bushes and poinsettias growing under tall flame trees, and then the house was there—a long low villa in the Spanish style. It was one of the houses I'd examined through the glasses from the tree at the top of the hill; as we drove along the driveway, there was plenty of time to see two of the corner towers, smaller than they'd seemed, but just as deadly with the machine-guns poking out of them.

We pulled up outside a very stately front door. As I opened the car door for Elena, she smiled up at me and said: "You are going to like my friends, Cabot. You'll like everything about them."

I said: "Let's hope they like me too." It seemed necessary to be accepted as one of them; for just long enough.

CHAPTER 8

Although I'd half-expected it, it was impossible not to be astonished. I had to keep reminding myself that this place was a prison, not merely for me, but also for those who enjoyed its hedonistic intemperance.

They were here, and they couldn't get out, not for long. If they showed their faces, the predators were ready to pounce, full of a remembered vengeance, with the pictures of uncounted atrocities never forgotten. Here, they were safe, at least as long as the very peculiar characteristics of Fuerte Quemado might last; and I expected they'd last a long time. No extradition, no law, no access except by the routes they controlled.

There were fortress states like these all over Italy in the Middle Ages and the Renaissance; but there, the tides of progress were too fast, the communications too easy; and the fortresses could not hold out long against the advent of a wider culture—or the onslaught of the barbarians.

Here, it was different. Even the relatively normal town of Urbana was cut off from the rest of the world because of communications that were long and arduous. And up here, at Fuerte Quemado, we were a million miles from anywhere because those communications had abruptly ceased, or were rigidly controlled. Here, the great mountain was its own protection; and the protection had been more than adequately bolstered with guards and guns and an arrogant defiance. The governments of both Brazil and Bolivia were wise to wash their hands of if all, to leave Fuerte Quemado to its own devices, like an out-of-control fire that's too far away to do any damage to our own surroundings and will sooner or later, perhaps, burn itself out; or a hurricane that's flexing its muscles out there in the ocean, far from any habitation; leave it alone, it might go away one day.

But, prison or not, everything—almost everything—a man could possibly want was here; the only thing missing was freedom. The presence of great wealth was apparent everywhere. A party, Elena had said.

There were about two hundred and fifty people here, spreading over three or four rooms, the men neatly dressed in well-tailored silk suits with a tuxedo here and there; and the women in cocktail dresses or long gowns, all looking very elegant and expensive. There was a long buffet table set up in one of the rooms, well loaded down with canapes, cold meats, beautifully dressed seafoods and salads, and waiters were circulating with champagne on silver trays. They had Moet Chandon, Veuve Cliguot, and a very good Bolinger 59 that Elena and I settled on. They even had it served in tulip-shaped glasses, a thing that always meets with my heartiest approval. There was Haig and Haig Scotch, Old Granddad bourbon, Booths and Gordon's gin, and a vodka I'd never heard of but which was bottled and distilled in Russia. The cognacs were Courvoisier and Remy Martin Fine Champagne, and lined up on the glass-topped bar was the best array of red wines I'd ever seen assembled in one place. There was Gevrey-Chaimbertin, Clos Vougeot, and Chambolle-Musigny from Burgumndy; Chateau Margaux and Lafite-Rothschild from Bordeaux, a Sang de Bueuf from Anjou, and a Mene-tru-le-Vignoble from the mountains of Franche-Comte. The whites were in silver ice buckets, and I saw Pouilly-Fuisse and Puligny-Montrachet, and it occurred to me that whatever the future might hold for me personally, I was going to enjoy at least part of the evening.

Elena took me round and introduced me to some of the men. Ninety percent of them were Europeans. "Mr. Cabot Cain, Herr Wolkmann-Schlessinger...Captain Vicek...Mr. Gosporra... Colonel Heinrich Geste...Mr. Cain, Mr. and Mrs. Onspadder, Captain and Mrs. Jules Schlect..." Everyone was incredibly courteous and polite, with just the right touch of formality, and a little too much friendliness.

They were all sizing me up, unobtrusively perhaps, but none the less with a great deal of interest. Someone had said: bring him along and let's take a look at him. And that's what they were all doing, taking a good hard look, and masking it all with formality just in case I was to be one of them, a new member of the club who might serve their purpose too.

A professional jewel thief among all the enthusiastic amateurs whose success was merely the result of circumstances? What a blessing that could be to them. Someone who knew the ropes, the markets, the times and the places to sell...

Elena whispered to me when we were a little clear of the crowd: "You don't really want to meet all these people, do you?"

I said: "Hell, no. I thought they wanted to meet me."

We found Colonel von Brubeck at the piano, playing a Chopin Valse, quite expertly though somewhat absently. He stopped as we approached, and shot out his hand to take mine, and said with an amused smile: "I hope you find this place better than the other, Mr. Cain."

I said: "Well, I'd rather stay here than there. What's the party for?"

He shrugged. "We get bored. We throw these little parties once in a while."

"Is Kolchak here?"

He sighed. "Not here, not in Fuerte Quemado, Mr. Cain." He went back to his playing, looked up at once, and said, breaking off again: "Enjoy yourself while you can. The food's good, the wines good, and I'm sure you'll find that Elena is a stimulating companion."

I said: "Nothing but the best."

He went on with his Chopin as we moved away, I was very conscious of those careful, guarded appraisals. I murmured to Elena: "They really want to take a good look at me, don't they?"

She laughed. "Of course. But don't let it bother you. They could have come to inspect you in that dreadful cell, couldn't they?"

We helped ourselves to some crayfish tails and some shrimps in avocados, and I nodded at one of the ice buckets and said: "I've got my eye on a Montrachet there." The waiter opened the bottle for us; it was almost colorless, with a fine, dry, almond flavor to it, and I said:

"Who's the man who buys the wines for Fuerte Quemado?"

She thought that was very amusing, though I couldn't think why.

We had some paper-thin slices of rare roast venison stuffed with duxelles, and switched from the Montrachet to a Clos de Beze, and we circulated among the guests and made some small talk, and listened for a while to a recital of Sibelius Humoresques played by a gorgeous Spanish woman whose violin was a Guarnerius del Gesu, made somewhere around 1740 or so; I remembered that one of these very rare instruments had been looted during the War from the Charlottenburg Museum.

There was a little break, and then von Brubeck felt the need to play some German marching songs, thumping at the piano as though he'd never heard of Chopin, and some of them started singing, so Elena and I went out onto the balcony and sat together for a while, sipping Armagnac instead of cognac, because while good cognacs are relatively easy to find, our host had some Grand-Bas from Monlezun; I found it refreshing to recall that this fine old eau-de-vie had been distilled by a direct descendant of that Count of Artagnan who was one of Dumas' Musketeers. The smiling waiter came out a little later on and left the bottle with us, which I thought was a nice gesture. It was Very Special Old Pale, dated 1928, and I was quite ready to drink more of it than was good for me.

Not too much—I had a job to do that night, after the lovely Elena had made her farewells.

The party started breaking up at three in the morning. I yawned a little rudely, and told her I'd drunk far too much, and put a little slur into my speech though, to tell the truth, I can hold a lot of liquor provided I stick to the rule, which wasn't hard here, of drinking only what is good. I said: "Do you think I can go home to bed, or am I still under surveillance? Have they seen enough of me?"

She said happily: "I think so. Any time you want, I'll run you back in the Lotus."

"All right. Unless you'd rather stay."

"No. I'll take you back. It's not far, but you might get lost." I detected a slightly sardonic note there.

Outside, she took a deep, deep breath of the cool night air and said: "You know the Lotus? Would you like to try it?"

I said gravely: "Better not, not tonight, That Armagnac goes to the head a little too easily." It doesn't, of course, and I was as sober as a judge.

She laughed and got in, and took me round to the airstrip and across it, and up a long slow rise in the road that ended nowhere, and got out to show me the view. The moon was high, and the whole of the valley of the Marmore was spread out there below us, the river shining brightly, and the greens of the trees black as the ace of spades, with a bright night sky hanging over them. We could hear the cries of the night birds coming up, and the air was cool and fresh, and it was indescribably beautiful. I noticed she looked once, a trifle surreptitiously, at her watch, and I wondered what she was waiting for.

She said: "Well, shall we go?" and when I bent down to open the car door for her, she leaned over and put an arm round me and kissed me, and said: "A good party?"

"Excellent. Let's hope we have a lot more of them."

She drove fast back to the hotel, and I said politely: "Why don't you come in for a nightcap?"

She said: "Oh, yes, I'm coming in. There's someone waiting to see you." I said nothing.

We went up to my room together, and there was indeed someone waiting to see me. It was the man with the cough, the man from the prison cell. Now that I could see him more clearly, I judged he was from somewhere in Central Europe; his accent was more noticeable now.

Unsmiling, he said: "Mr. Cain."

Elena sat in the little velvet-covered chair by the window and waited, and I said:

"Well, at least let me know your name. I just might have to beat the hell out of you one day."

He smiled thinly. "The past is behind us, Mr. Cain. And let me remind you that you yourself may one day need my similar services."

Well, that was laying it on the line.

He said: "I'm here on a different kind of business. Someone is interested in the two ruby pendants you spoke of. The question seems to be, just how to get them here from...Manaus, I think you said? So that my principal could inspect them. It's not an easy one, is it, and I wondered if perhaps you had any suggestions?"

I said: "Sure. You want to make a deal, I'll fly back and get them."

"No."

"There's no other way. The key to the safe deposit box is being held by a friend. He won't easily part with it, except to me."

"Yes, that's what I was afraid of. How much do you want for them? We will assume for the moment that they're genuine, though perhaps you'd better tell me too how you managed to acquire them?"

I said: "They're genuine all right. And how I got them? Well, there was a Cardinal named Bakose who broke the bracelet up to distribute the pieces among his girlfriends. Two of the fragments disappeared, but they turned up several hundred years later in the storeroom of a small Turkish museum. That's where I found them. I bought them."

"A jewel thief buying jewels, Mr. Cain?"

"You'll forgive the euphemism. We all like to put up an honest front, don't we? And you still didn't tell me your name."

"My name is Luther, Mr. Cain. Luther Koch. And you are sure they're genuine"

"They are genuine."

"Then they must be worth...what sort of price would you put on them?"

I shrugged. "A couple of ruby pendants that could be made into earrings, perhaps. The gold mounting is filigree, of a very high standard, and their historical value is fairly high. But in the open market—between fifteen and twenty thousand dollars apiece. If the bracelet is anything like the sketches I have, it's worth a rough hundred thousand dollars as is, with the two pieces missing; it would have to be broken up. But put the two together, and I've got a buyer waiting for it. Two hundred and twenty thousand bucks, provided it's complete. I'm prepared to split with Kolchak—twenty-five percent to me, seventy-five to him. That gives me fifty-five thousand, and gives him a hundred and sixty-five. That's a hell of a lot more to each of us than either of us would get for the broken pieces."

"A ready buyer, you say? Who is he?"

"You can put your thugs to work on me again for as long as you like, but that's something you'll never find out. And if you did, it wouldn't do you a bit of good. He knows about the deal, and if I'm not there to make the sale, he'll be scared off. Granted, you could find another buyer—if you succeeded in getting your grubby hands on my pieces of the bracelet. But you wouldn't get so good a price. So, it's hardly worth your while to try any monkey business, is it? The easiest thing all round, and the most profitable, is to play it the way I want it played."

There was a little pause. Then he said: "Of course, we'd have to see your fragments."

"And I'd have to see the bracelet they belong to. You don't have to trust me, and I'm not going to trust you. Let's just be very cautious friends, what do you say?"

He said: "Well, I think that could be arranged. There would be a certain amount of detail to be attended to."

"A considerable amount."

He thought for a while, clearing his abominable throat every ten seconds, and at last he stood up and went to the door. He said: "I'll see you again, Mr. Cain. Good night."

I said: "Are you admitting now that Kolchak is here? He's the one with the bracelet."

"We're admitting nothing, Mr. Cain. We're just trying to make a deal that will be profitable to everybody concerned, yourself included."

He moved off again, and I said: "And you forgot your case, Mr. Koch."

There was a small leather bag on the bed. He said, smiling a little now: "It's not mine, Mr. Cain. Good night."

I closed the door behind him, and when I turned round, Elena was unzipping the case and taking out a negligee and a small toilet set. She said sweetly: "Do you want the bathroom first, or shall I take it?"

I had planned to spend the rest of the night in a rapid dash to the cave in the cliff and back again; but they obviously weren't going to let me out of their sight; not yet awhile, anyway.

Well, I suppose it could have been a lot worse; most jailers are not as accommodating as Elena was obviously going to be, nor half so seductive.

I did push-ups on the floor till she finished her bath—four hundred and eighty-seven of them—and then took a shower and shaved, and when I came back into the room she was lying on the bed in her flimsy, feminine pink negligee; and waiting for me. Under the circumstances, I'd have expected the negligee to be black or red, and all covered with lace; the pink gave her a charming look of unexpected innocence instead. She was incredibly lovely, and it wasn't at all hard to play the part that was expected of me. We kissed, and made love, and slept, and made love again, and I held her tight in my arms and stroked her lovely neck, and she said, grimacing: "Ouch, you're hurting me..." She didn't really mind the pressure of my fingers—one at the superficial cervical nerve at the side of her neck, one on the sternal nerve just above her high breast (and what a marvelous breast it was!), one finger on the posterior scapular, and a thumb very lightly indeed (I didn't want to kill her, Heaven save us) on the acromial clavicular. My other hand left her hip and went round behind her ear to the small occipital, and that was that; without even knowing what was happening, she was out like a light, with the smile still on her lovely lips. She'd wake up with a splitting headache in an hour or so, but nothing that a handful of aspirins wouldn't put right. The likelihood was that she'd fall asleep immediately, without even knowing I'd gone. But I didn't want to count on it, so I thought I'd better run, and run hard.

I scribbled a note, put on a pair of slacks and slipped out the window. As I'd expected, there was no guard (who was going to try to escape from such an efficient warder) and the night was still cloudy and dark though the moon was high.

I ran through the forest and up to the lip of the cliff, found the first of the camouflaged rope-holds, clambered down over the edge, and ten minutes later, I was crawling into the cave where Jesus was.

Or rather, where he wasn't.

I looked round in surprise, and flicked my lighter in the darkness; and then I heard him behind me. I'd made very little noise, I was sure, but he'd slipped out quickly along the ledge to where the passion-vine was, and had been clinging there till he knew who was calling; a good man, and no fool. I gave him the note I'd written, and said: "Take this back to Senhor Mazlor. Come back as fast as you can, and be here by tomorrow night. It took us longer than that to get here, but make it as fast as you can—you know where the boat is, where the motor is... Just as fast as you can, Okay?"

He grunted. And then, like a shadow in the dark, he was gone.

I felt a little ashamed of putting him to all that trouble. The note simply said: "I just want to make sure that Leda's all right, and test our communications. Please send Jesus back posthaste with word. Everything fine here, getting somewhere slowly but surely." I had also written, taking more for granted perhaps than I should have done: "Chances are the maximum of danger for Leda is approaching now. The man I'm after is here, definitely, and he's not likely to sit still for the hit. So action is possibly imminent. Cain."

I'd been worried, desperately worried. I'd dragged her into this thing to share the dangers, and now that they were all around me I was wondering if, even with the best motives, I'd done the right thing. The worry was gnawing at me like a rat biting through my spinal column. But by tomorrow night I'd know. It wasn't really likely that she'd be running into any trouble yet; but in this case, the likelihood just wasn't good enough; I wanted to be sure, very sure.

I ran fast all the way back, looked at my watch as I climbed in the window and saw that it was a quarter of five; I'd been gone almost exactly an hour.

The lovely Elena was lying on her back with the smile gone and a fearful frown on her face. I got into bed beside her, leaned over her, and shook her. It was quite a long time before she came out of her half-coma, and she put a hand to her head and said: "My God, I've got an awful headache, what happened?"

I said: "Serves you right for falling asleep on me, I'll get you some aspirin." There was some in the bathroom. I gave her four tablets and half a glass of water, and she took them and said sleepily: "What time is it?"

"Half-past four. Go to sleep."

She yawned, turned over on her side, put an arm round my middle, and went to sleep. I lay for a while staring up at the darkness that was the ceiling, and soon, I too was fast asleep.

* * *

We slept late that morning, and when she woke up I said: "How's the head?"

She stirred sleepily: "Fine." She sat up suddenly and said: "What do you mean, how's the head?"

"You had a number one hangover during the night. You went right out cold, wide awake one minute, fast asleep the next."

"Oh. Yes, I seem to remember. You gave me some aspirin, didn't you?"

"Twenty grains. All right?"

She smiled and nodded, and we took a shower and got dressed, and then went down to breakfast. Her manner was friendly (as was very proper under the circumstances), and there was no suspicion at all on her part that the night had been anything out of the ordinary. She was smiling, and pleasant, and affable, and a thoroughly nice person to have around. Insidious was the word that came into my mind; the pleasures of Elena could quite easily grow on a man; and then, I knew, he'd arise one day to a very rude awakening indeed.

She put on a tiny black bikini when we went swimming in the pool, and sat around looking lovely while I did my hundred lengths, and then Luther turned up and I came out of the pool to see what he had to say.

He was brief and to the point. He said: "A man will go with you to Manaus, where you can collect the two pendants. He will examine them, and if they are genuine, you will return here with him, and we will fit them to the bracelet."

"Then Kolchak is here."

He said patiently: "A matter of no importance, Mr. Cain. The bracelet is here, that's all that matters." It was all that mattered to me too; it wasn't likely that Kolchak would be far away from his precious collection. He went on: "The man I will send with you is an expert jeweler, a stonecutter we employ here, and he will make the necessary repairs. And then...then you must arrange for your buyer to come within a reasonable distance of this place to make the purchase. Where is he, your buyer?"

I said promptly: "In New York."

"Then, if he could make the trip to Manaus, or Lima, or even Asuncion?"

"He's a very sick man, he can't travel. We'll have to go there. Or I will."

"No, I think not."

I was enjoying making it difficult for them. I said: "And what's more, before I part with my pendants, I want to see the piece Kolchak has."

"We decided, my principals and I, that this would not be necessary."

"Then you can go back to your goddam principals and tell them...tell *him*, that I don't agree. There's a very grave danger he may not be aware of."

His assurance was already coming apart at the seams. "Oh? What might that be?"

I said: "The bracelet was copied in eighteen sixty-five by a French jeweler named, if I remember rightly, Masson. I want to be sure that I don't put my genuine pendants on a phony bracelet."

His mouth was hanging open. He shut it suddenly, but his face still showed the shock. He coughed and said: "Copied?"

"Yes, didn't you know?"

It was obvious he didn't; it wasn't even true. He said thoughtfully:

"I see. Well, perhaps that could be arranged after all. I will speak to you again later in the day."

He got up to go, and I stopped him and said: "I go to Manaus with your stonecutter friend—pick up the pendants, bring them back here. We repair the bracelet, and then...Then?"

He sighed: "If only we could be sure we can *trust* you, Mr. Cain. It would make things so much less complicated."

I said: "You can trust me more than you can trust that dimwit Vallence in Paris. I'd make a hell of a lot better outlet than he'll ever be."

He looked thoroughly disturbed, but he said slowly: "Yes, perhaps you would, Mr. Cain. That's something to think about, too, isn't it?"

"Do that, Luther. Think about it."

He nodded, and was gone.

Elena had been listening, and she said gently: "You just might have upset him very badly. We know, of course, that you'd spoken to Vallence. Why do you call him a dimwit? He's a very good man."

"Is he hell! He put me on the trail that led me here. I told him I was Interpol. If I had been...You see how easy it would be for the cops to get here?"

"To get here, perhaps. But we do have second lines of defense, you know, very substantial ones."

I said scornfully: "Anyone can get in or out of this place any time he chooses."

"No." She shook her head, very sure of herself. "You were lucky, Cabot. There aren't many people who could get across that gorge with only a pole to help them..." She broke off and laughed suddenly. "They had a man down there trying it less than an hour after you'd told them it could be done. A twenty year old muscle-boy who works for Luther Koch. He missed the opposite edge by more than six feet."

I was sick to my stomach. "What happened?"

She shrugged. "He fell. That gorge is a thousand feet deep and more."

"That's a bad business."

"Yes, Luther's going to miss him. He was an expert in the use of the electric rod for persuasion. They were going to use that on you, did you know that? If you hadn't started talking when you did?"

I said sourly: "What nice friends you have." I was already feeling better about the muscle-boy.

Elena went on: "No, Cabot, it isn't easy to get in here, and it's harder still to get out. There's only the one road, well-guarded. Every other approach has been blocked off with...with all kinds of devices."

"Maybe. It would still be better if nobody knew where those gems are, that's why you go to all that trouble, isn't it? You can't be too goddam blatant about it, or sooner or later someone's going to try a frontal attack on this place."

She said scornfully: "We can take care of ourselves. Good care." But she was worried, all the same.

We had lunch and sat around and waited half the afternoon,

133

and I began to get restless because I don't like just sitting around. And then a message came, brought by a young Indian, to the hotel; for Elena. She read it and looked at me and smiled, and said softly: "Cabot, I think this is what you've been waiting for. They want to see you." She said suddenly: "My God, I hope that bracelet isn't an imitation."

"You know about it? You've seen it?"

"Of course." She looked at me and laughed, and said: "Yes, dear Cabot, I'm very much in their confidence. And soon, you will be too. We're all looking forward to a very happy association."

I squeezed her arm. "And us? The two of us? We'll be together too?"

Lying brazenly, she smiled and said earnestly: "Of course, dear Cabot, if that's what you want." She must have thought I was a bloody idiot.

We went to the portico where the Lotus was parked, and we drove out to another of the fine old closely-guarded houses. Again, a high stone wall and a single machine-gun mounted on it, manned by a young Brazilian in gray-green uniform. We drove through iron gates that closed with a clang behind us, and pulled up in front of the massive front door. I was sure that the pages were turning rapidly now, that my words to Luther Koch had made them realize they'd better go along with what I wanted—as far as they thought might be profitable.

A polite and dignified butler showed us in, and again, there was the sense of enormous well-being. The hall was splendidly proportioned, with tall curved windows and dark mahogany paneling. A very pretty serving girl was carrying a basket of fruit into one of the rooms, and another, even lovelier, was dusting the bookshelves that lined one wall; they were both *caboclas*, part white, part Indian, with a remarkably lithe and easy grace.

We walked past the bookshelves, following the butler, and I had time to see that some of the titles were in Russian. And the dark red carpet on the white stone floor was an Ushak, from Asia Minor. There was a fine old painting by the door that caught my eye and sent a quiver of expectation tingling the back of my neck; it was a full length portrait of a Kalmuk fisherman; the Kalmuks were Tartars...

And when the butler threw open the door and we went into the living room...

Kolchak was there, and four other men were with him. There was von Brubeck, and Luther Koch, and another man whom I had not met, but whom I recognized from his photographs as General Konrad Weimar, one of the lesser War Criminals who'd been declared officially dead six years ago; an easy way out, I thought, if you can engineer it. He was the man who was Goering's expert for antiques; he'd helped the Marshal with the selection of paintings for transport out of the Reich, and had lined his own little nest pretty comfortably in the process. Von Brubeck was shrewd and clever; Luther Koch a brutish sadist, and Weimar could be written off as just another one of the hundreds who'd found sanctuary there.

But it was Kolchak, of course, who held my attention. He was fatter than in his photograph, and white-haired now, but still looking solid and powerful, with the Mongolian slant to his eyes much more pronounced than before. He stood, just as I'd always imagined him, with his feet wide spread as though drawing up nourishment from the rich loam of his native fields, his great fists on his hips, and a scowl on his bloated face. He was well dressed, in a light gray linen suit with a rather showy white silk tie; but he still looked like a peasant, with sturdy shoulders and a thick, muscular neck, and wrists of very creditable solidity. His jacket was open and pushed back behind his hips, and I noticed the striking belt he wore, an intricately plaited belt of fine leather thongs with tiny bindings here and there of gold wire.

The fourth man was an Indian. To tell the honest truth, I hardly noticed him at first. He wore a simple khaki shirt and trousers, with bare feet and a cloth band round his head, but somehow he contrived to be almost part of the furnishings, and unnoticeable, unseen, except for one thing—he couldn't keep still; he prowled like a caged animal, in absolute silence, from side to side all the time, with restless movements of his alert and watchful eyes. He was an extraordinary sight; he wore a long knife at his waist, and I could imagine him more easily out there in the jungle, a deadly menace to all his enemies. Nobody bothered to introduce him; I guessed he was a bodyguard, and a very dangerous one at that.

Von Brubeck, sitting by the window, got to his feet, a lithe, easy-moving man still in his uniform. He said, putting out his hand:

"Mr. Cain, I'm glad you could come." He nodded and smiled at Elena, and said, introducing me to the others: "Luther Koch you already know. Cabot Cain, Konrad Leichmann," (this was the man who used to be Weimar), "who is the Mayor of our little community."

The last time Weimar/Leichmann had assumed that sort of position, he'd built, with slave labor, a town that consisted almost entirely of gas ovens. He'd moved up the ladder close to Goering, and there was a spell after the war when he ran the underground prisons in Battista's Cuba, and then someone had said he was dead, and now he'd come to roost at last in a comfortably secure nest of his own choosing.

We moved on, and von Brubeck said, smiling gently: "And this is the man you really want to meet. A different name now, but I don't suppose he'll mind if you call him Colonel General Kolchak. Colonel General Kolchak, Cabot Cain."

The silent Indian, prowling in the background, looked as though he were ready to pounce on me if I even dared to sneeze.

He stared at me hard, Kolchak, for so long a time that the others began to fidget. Neither of us offered to shake hands, and he said at last, speaking tolerable English with an intolerable accent:

"I will tell you this. I do not want to trust you, Cain. But I trust the judgment of my friends, and they tell me that we can do some business together. Business, I am prepared to do. Sit down."

I sat. Kolchak stared at me. The others waited for him to speak. He sat down on a marvelously well-preserved damask sofa, Vienna, seventeen hundred or so, and put his feet up on the inlaid ebony coffee table. He said at last:

"So, you know that I have the Zrinyi bracelet."

I said: "I know you've got a lot more than that. A tiara that's worth quite a lot of hard cash, a Cellini snuffbox that I'd like to get my hands on, a diamond bracelet, some rings...a few other trinkets, if you haven't already disposed of them. And while we're on the subject, I could have got a great deal more for the emerald necklace than Vallence did, and it would never have left a trail right back here, either."

Von Brubeck perched himself on the arm of a Venetian chair and swung a booted leg. He said affably: "Every time you open your mouth, Cain, we find out something more about you."

I shrugged. "I'm a simple, straightforward man. No complications."

"But there's more to your deal that you originally implied."

"There could be. But for openers, I want to talk about a ruby bracelet. I have part of it, Kolchak has the rest. Put the pieces together and the whole is greater than the sum of the parts, what could be more simple than that? Sure, he can sell his piece, and I can sell mine. But we'll both profit better if we get together."

He said gently, watching me: "And then?"

"Then, if we both feel so inclined, we can do some more business. All of us. I'm a useful man for you, I've got the contacts and I know the ropes. And you, all of you, can make my life a hell of a lot richer." In the little silence that followed. I said: "You see what I mean? Simple and straightforward, and everybody profits."

Von Brubeck began to pace up and down again. He said: "I wonder if I underestimated your talents, Cain?"

"I'm damn sure you did. And that's a mistake too, isn't it? All the way down the line, you've played around like a bunch of amateurs. I'm a pro, Colonel. I'm offering you my services."

I could see the idea spreading over them like an octopus, with every tentacle a new opportunity for trickery. Von Brubeck looked at the others and seemed to derive a satisfaction from their faces. He said abruptly:

"Let's talk about that. Perhaps. I'd better tell you precisely what the position is here, vis-a-vis some of our more esteemed colleagues. As you surmised, and it's no use denying it, is it? This place does harbor one or two men who are waiting for the political face of Europe to change its present rather unhappy state. We are, if you like, hiding out and waiting our time. Several of South America's major cities have, over the years, been Hosts to some of us, and now we find that Fuerte Quemiado is as good a place as any to wait for what is, surely, an inevitable awakening of the European political consciousness." He shrugged. "When we escaped the cataclysm that was the end of the war, some of us took the precaution of supplying ourselves with funds or, in some cases, material that could be easily converted into funds. Jewels, tapestries, paintings..." He laughed easily. "The press is always making a great fuss about this, and you must know it, as most people do. From time to time; when we need more money than is immediately available, we send out some little trifle for sale, and the money thus realized keeps the ball rolling till the next time. We employ a number of dealers to make this matter a little simpler than it might be, and we know that they line their own pockets at our expense. But there's not much we can do about it. Although" — that casual shrug again—"there's really enough to last us as long as we're ever likely to live, any of us."

The cover had slipped a little there. But the fiction of a return to Europe was a harmless daydream, and they must have known it; there was just too much lined up against them.

"And, meanwhile, a life of luxury for everybody."

The man who called himself Konrad Leichmann said drily: "Any fool can be uncomfortable." He was a heavily-built man with receding gray hair and an old-fashioned saber scar on his face. He switched to Portuguese and said sharply: "The world has treated us very badly. It behooves us to treat ourselves well, is it not so?"

Von Brubeck said: "Yes, we lead a life of considerable luxury. You're a wanted man in Brazil, Mr. Cain. That robbery of yours in Rio was a foolish, impetuous thing."

I said: "I saw a stone that caught my fancy, and I decided to take it. It was just bad luck that a couple of whores passed by and saw me."

"And is it true that you actually pulled out the steel grill with your bare hands?" He was genuinely curious.

"A matter of leverage. You get your feet just so and shove, that's all there is to it. I am a very strong man."

"And meanwhile, the police are looking for you. In Brazil. Where else, Mr. Cain?"

"No place else. A clean record."

"And friends, I understand, in Interpol. Very useful friends."

"Expensive, but yes, very useful."

"And you can travel in Europe unmolested?"

"Yes, I can."

There was a long silence. Kolchak, I noticed, didn't like the trend of the conversation. Me, I liked it very much. Von Brubeck said at last:

"We were discussing a deal regarding Colonel General Kolchak's Hungarian rubies. If we sell them to your buyer, under the terms you have stipulated, we would almost have to leave you in possession of them for a while before we saw the money resulting from the sale."

He raised a protesting hand when I began to speak, and said: "No, wait." He began to pace up and down the room again, but this time he stayed where I could see him. "The best way to assure ourselves that we would eventually get the money is to treat you just as we treat Vallence and the rest. It's their knowledge of further profitable deals that keeps them—relatively—honest. That, and the fear that they'd soon be liquidated if the tricks they play got out of hand, a fear that is adequately strong in most cases. You might not be so easy to scare or to liquidate, Mr. Cain, once you get out of...our clutches." He smiled. "You do understand what I'm driving at, don't you?"

I nodded. "Very clearly. Suppose you trust me, and suppose it turns out to be a mistake. All right, you've lost your precious bracelet, and I've made a small fortune. But we're not talking about small fortunes, are we? We are talking about big ones. A long-term project."

It was all sinking in very nicely. And they were all leaving it to von Brubeck, and they were all in agreement. Only Kolchak looked as though he was unhappy, and I knew they'd work on him the moment I'd gone.

Von Brubeck asked me: "You have a single buyer? For the bracelet only? Or you have others lined up as well?"

"Several others. In my business, that's a thing you have to study."

"Yes. Yes, of course. Then, in that case, let's assume that we're prepared to trust you with the bracelet, prepared to expect your return here with a hundred and sixty-five thousand dollars—was that the figure?—in, how long would you say to complete the sale?"

"Two days in New York, a day there, two days back. Give me a week. Send your stonecutter with me to Manaus to pick up my portion of it, he can make the repairs down there, isn't that better than bringing them up here?"

"And you have to go to New York yourself to see the buyer?"

I hesitated just the right amount, I said: "Yes, I must go

myself."

"No one else can do this for you?"

"No, I don't think it would be wise. Or even successful. Why, what's the problem?" I hoped a little nervousness was showing.

He said smoothly: "No problem, Mr. Cain."

"And when are you going to let me take a look at this bracelet?"

Von Brubeck said: "Now."

Kolchak had not spoken all this time. Without a word, he got up now and went to a heavy steel wall safe and twisted the dial and flung it open. It was a very large safe, but I couldn't see much of what was in it. He brought out an ordinary brown paper bag and closed the safe, and brought the bag over to the ebony table, He dropped it down carelessly, and said:

"There, there is your bracelet. Take a look if you want."

I said: "That filigree work's very delicate, and that's no way to handle a couple of hundred thousand dollars."

When he grunted, he reminded me of Jesus, running fast through the forest now, just about leaving the river with news that my Leda was safe and sound and waiting patiently for me.

I opened the bag and took out the bracelet. It was beautiful, a glittering brightly-shining mass of deep carmine rubies, and three huge diamonds; the sketches they'd made didn't begin to do it justice. As I examined them carefully, von Brubeck said:

"Spinel rubies, from India."

I said: "God dammit, are you trying to find out if I know my business? They're not spinels, as you must know, and they didn't come from India, as you probably don't know. They came from Upper Burma, probably from somewhere near Mandalay, Mogok at a guess, though it could be Ulasa." He had the grace to laugh, but not in the least uncomfortably. I said: "It's better than I expected. I just might be able to make that two hundred and twenty thousand into the round quarter million. Could I take a look at the tiara?"

I saw Kolchak's head move an imperceptible trifle, and von Brubeck said: "No, not now, Mr. Cain. Let's worry about one thing at a time, shall we?"

"A test?"

"If you like to call it that."

"All right." I put the sparkling gems back in their horrible paper bag. "Shall I take them with me now?"

"No, Mr. Cain, not till you're ready to start out for Manaus."

"And who's the man coming with me?"

Leichmann said: "You haven't met him, a man named Werther. A very good man with gems, but nothing much else to commend him. He will, however, stay with you at all times."

"Well, I'm not going to let him sleep with me." I couldn't resist it; I said sarcastically: "If you want your surveillance as close as all that, let Elena da Costa come too."

She threw me a very sharp look from the window seat, but said nothing. Von Brubeck offered me a cigarette, and lit one himself when I refused.

"No, that won't be necessary, I'm sure Elena will wait quite happily for your return with the money. When can you leave, Mr. Cain?"

I said: "Dammit, you're my jailers, whenever you say. What about first thing tomorrow morning?"

"All right, first thing in the morning. I'll see you get the bracelet by eight o'clock, is that soon enough?"

"Sure."

"A car will take you down the Doussa road. This time, you'll be able to cross the barrier in a more civilized manner."

Elena stood up abruptly. Looking at me brightly, she said: "Well, are we ready to go?"

If someone had signaled her, I hadn't noticed. Or perhaps she had more authority here than I'd given her credit for. We moved to the door and I opened it for her, and then von Brubeck, behind me, said: "Mr. Cain?"

I waited. His voice was deceptively soft. He said: "Why did you bring Leda Zrinyi to Brazil with you?"

Well, there it was, the question I'd been waiting for, for a long, long time. I closed the door carefully, turned to face them, and leaned back with the feel of the smoothly-polished wood against my shoulders. I wanted them to see my face, to read all the lies there; I wanted them to be quite sure that they knew just how much of what I was telling them was true, and how much wasn't. It occurred to me that quite a lot was hanging on their acceptance of what I wanted them to accept and the rejection of all the rest. And most of all, I wanted to see Kolchak's face too; I wanted to see the wheels turning and make sure they were turning in the right direction, and all I had to go on was a carefully-studied file, an Interpol file that was as complete as a dossier can ever be, but still not complete enough. The various agencies had compiled some very thorough material, though it hadn't gotten them very far.

"He doesn't trust a living soul, and where humanly possible he does everything himself. This is at once his weakness and his strength..."

It seemed to me now that perhaps I should also have studied the file on the agent who wrote those words, to make sure he was the kind of man who could make so specific an assessment with at least some kind of plausibility; I was taking it on trust that Fenrek had given me only what was thoroughly reliable.

They were all facing me, waiting, expectant. The question was von Brubeck's; but it was Kolchak who wanted the answer. His stolid, peasants face was impassive; too impassive.

I said carefully: "Her uncle in New York is the buyer." Lie number one, and they didn't believe it; good. I said: "She was to have been my messenger, to take the bracelet to him and bring back the money." Lie number two, not believed either, though I thought I sensed a touch of doubt there. I turned to go, my heart thumping, and the question came faster than it should have done. Von Brubeck—the spokesman—said with a strong flavor of malicious triumph in his voice:

"Or is she really the current possessor of those two pendants, Cain?"

I turned back once more and said abruptly, letting the anger show: "I told you, I have the pendants, I told you how I acquired them."

Von Brubeck looked at Luther, and Luther smiled and nodded wisely. I understood now what Luther's specialty was; any fool can beat a man half to death, but it takes a special kind of mind to know when to start and when to stop.

When to stop...The memories were coming back, more and more of them. I remembered how Luther used to stop; he used to hold his victim's head under water until they were dead. He smiled now at von Brubeck, and von Brubeck said:

"I wonder if I'm right in thinking that you only tell the truth when it's beaten out of you? There's surely a possibility that the Zrinyi family would have kept those broken pieces, isn't there? That Leda Zrinyi would go so far as to bring them here to make sure the rest of the bracelet, which you hope to lay your hands on, really does match her own pieces, and is not the copy you spoke of. Personally, I think this is a much more likely supposition, what do you say?"

I said, shrugging: "I don't care a damn what you think. Wherever the broken pieces are, access to them is mine, isn't it? And mine only. So you're faced with a take-it-or-leave-it situation, and if you want to call the deal off..."

He finished it for me: "You wouldn't mind in the least."

I said promptly: "You are out of your goddam mind if you think that. I stand to pick up an easy fifty-five thousand dollars."

"Out of a total of nearly a quarter of a million."

"That's right. The top price for your pieces, the top price for mine. That's only possible if they go together. Otherwise, we're selling damaged goods, both of us, and we won't get half that." I began to bluster a trifle. "God dammit, you think I'd go to all this trouble if I didn't know what I was doing?"

Luther said, coughing: "No, I don't think you would. There's an easy way to find out, isn't there?"

"Oh? How's that?"

Von Brubeck said, smiling: "Luther tells me that your pain threshold is fairly high, but not insurmountable. Would you care for another session in the cells?"

I said: "What the hell for, for God's sake?" I found it was very easy to sound alarmed; there was still a very painful reminder of the last session throbbing through my chest. I said: "That wouldn't do either of us any good. Either I'm with you, or I'm not, and I thought I'd made it clear; you need me, and I need you."

He said: "Who is the buyer, Mr. Cain?"

"I told you, one of the Zrinyi clan, in New York."

"Yes, but we don't believe that. Who is it?"

More blustering. I said: "It won't do you any good. Without the pieces that I hold, you'll never get a decent price."

"Who, Mr. Cain?"

I threw Luther a look, and waited until someone was about to speak again. And then I took a deep breath and said: "It's old man Aaron. In Rio."

Ha! That threw a spanner in the works!

Von Brubeck stared, disbelieving (which meant he was quite ready to be persuaded), and said: "Aaron?"

"You've heard of his ruby collection. He wants to add the Zrinyi bracelet to it."

"And you broke into his store...?"

I said piously: "This trip has cost me a lot more than I figured. Before I go home, I want to recoup some of those expenses."

Von Brubeck was smiling broadly. Even Luther was amused. Weimar was nodding his head slowly, and mumbling: "Yes, it makes sense, it makes sense." Von Brubeck said affably: "You see, Cain? All you have to do is tell the truth, and everybody's happy. *Trust*," he said, "trust is absolutely essential." He spread his hands broadly in a gesture of complete openness. "Do I try to hide from you the fact that I'm a thorough rogue myself? No, of course I don't." He came over and slapped me on the back with a geniality that was anything but forced; he was a very happy man, with all his nasty little schemes falling neatly into place, with all the lies thrust aside and all the little bits of truths neatly assembled. He laughed and said: "There's only one thing you haven't admitted."

"Oh? What's that?"

"She has the fragments, hasn't she? The Zrinyi woman?"

Careful now; the whole thing could still collapse.

I said: "No."

He kept the broad smile: "And at the back of your mind you know very well that you plan to double-cross her. You really are a Judas, Cain, aren't you?"

The idea didn't seem to displease him in the least.

I said nastily: "Nice guys never make much money, do they?" I turned belligerent and said: "Well, is the deal on, or off?"

He said heartily: "Of course it's on, my dear fellow! First thing in the morning, I think you said?"

Elena was smiling at me, a warm, friendly smile that was completely open and without guile. Von Brubeck held the door open as we went out, and closed it quietly behind us, and Elena said brightly: "Well, except for that foolish threat that Luther made, I thought that went of very nicely, didn't you?"

She took my arm as we walked across the great hall. I didn't answer her; I was too busy enjoying the scene that was going on, no doubt, behind those closed doors. I could imagine every word of it. It would be going something like this:

Von Brubeck:	*There's nothing much to discuss, is there? I assume that we all know what we have to do?*
Weimar:	*We should have thought of Aaron ourselves. That collection of his is legendary.*
Luther:	*We bring the girl up here, I'll find out where those fragments are in no time at all.*
Von Brubeck:	*No, we'd better do that down there. She won't be carrying them on her, they'll be hidden away somewhere. We'll take her out in the forest, and you'll have a chance to exercise your talents on her there. I don't suppose it will take very long.*
Luther:	*They said she's a very attractive young woman.* (He'd be coughing now.)
Von Brubeck:	*You agree, Kolchak?*

There would be a pause, and then:

Kolchak:	*No. No, I do this myself.*

All I had to do now was to get back to Leda before Kolchak

got there, chasing two non-existent fragments of a sixteenth century diamond and ruby bracelet.

And, of course, get my hands on the rest of the collection in the interim.

CHAPTER 9

Mazlor, and Cunha before him, had made it very clear: the Brazilian police could be counted on to pounce if any of the notoriously-wanted men showed their faces on the streets of any half-civilized country town. Given a forewarning, given a little time, given a little luck, they'd act if Ullmann, or Weimar, or Kolchak, or any of the others left their inaccessible refuge on the tip of the mountain.

In Paraguay, in Argentina, even in Bolivia, they were relatively safe, and could usually move around with a certain amount of contemptuous arrogance—but in Brazil, no; the political climate was not so favorable for them. In Brazil, it was a question of the utmost circumspection, but not too worrisome a matter if they were quick and efficient and moved with sufficient force. In Urbana, where the bait was waiting for them, there was only one cop, Mazlor's friend Jose Salvador, and he wouldn't provide much opposition. And while I was safely out of the way, in the lovely Elena's arms, a long and impossible way from the town below, that's when they'd act.

Then how long did I have?

If everything went well for them, there was all the time in the world; they'd go down to Urbana, get their filthy hands on Leda, get from her those non-existent pendants, get back to Fuerte Quemado and then take care of me in whatever way they fancied. But if everything did not go well?

Well, in that case it was necessary for my suspicions to be allayed completely. If something *did* go wrong, if my story were not, after all, true...or if Leda had gone...or if she died before telling them where the pendants were hidden...There were so many imponderables that could upset their horrible apple-cart for them, so very many things they had to take into possible account. And in that case they had to have a second string, and I was it.

Then, at all costs, I had to be kept sweet; no suspicions from Cabot Cain please, keep him happy, let him roam around at will; just make sure he hasn't got something tricky up his sleeve, and if he has, be ready for it.

Time: it was all a question of time.

What they had to do, they had to do during the night. Then, if things went wrong, they'd be smiling there with the bracelet at eight in the morning, handing it over with good grace; there you are, Mr. Cain, go and find the broken pieces, and we'll be right behind you with a knife ready, or a machine-pistol, and thanks for telling us about old man Aaron, who would ever have believed it?

And if I couldn't even *think* the words—if something had happened to Leda? What would I do? What would I do? Why, I'd dash off madly to see they hadn't got the pendants as well, that's the sort of gutless bastard I am, and they'd be there, hard behind me. So, whichever way you cared to look at it, everything was humming along for them nicely, just as it should be.

Pushing my luck, I said to Elena: "You're still keeping an eye on me? Still under orders?"

She had sense enough not to deny it. She grimaced: "It's not too bad for you, is it?"

I said: "I like it. I'm a big man, a strong man, and my appetites take a lot of satisfying." She laughed. I said: "Let's take a walk in the forest. This time of the evening..."

She smiled, too easily: "Wouldn't you rather go for a swim?"

"A swim at midnight. A stroll through the woods before dinner, what do you say?"

She had to agree. I was wondering how she'd contrive to get the message to whoever it was she had to let know, and while I was thinking about it, she told me. She smiled and said: "Let me change my shoes then."

We drove round to the hotel in the Lotus, and she went in for just long enough to write one message or make one phone call, and came out wearing low-heeled sandals and said brightly:

"All right, shall we drive over? Or walk?"

I'd taken the seat behind the wheel for the pleasure of driving the little Lotus, taking her up on her previous offer, and I drove slowly around the town for a while, watching to see if she started to squirm; she didn't, though she couldn't have told them *"we're headed for the forest"* just in case I changed my mind and went over to the airport or down to the river instead. They were behind us somewhere, they had to be, but I didn't see them, not even once. And on Elena's calm and lovely face there was nothing but the sweetest, most contented, most innocent of smiles. She even snuggled up against me and closed her eyes. I kissed the top of her head and thought: if Machiavelli had been a woman, this is what that woman would have been like.

How long before Kolchak would leave the house? Soon after dark? I didn't even have much of a likelihood to go on.

We came to the edge of the town, and I parked the car and opened the door for her, and we wandered off slowly along the track that led to the big casuarina tree. It took us longer than I'd hoped, and she began to grow impatient; the smile was beginning to look a little frayed at the edges when we got there. I walked her over to the edge of the bluff, and we stood there for a while, looking down into the valley; we were standing directly above the cave where Jesus was waiting, two hundred feet above it on the edge of the sheer cliff.

Behind us, at last, I could hear the clumsy sounds of men trying to move silently through the bush, and with admirable composure Elena said: "A lot of animals around, are we safe here?"

I wondered how many of them there were; I judged about three from the noise they made; four, perhaps, a jeep-load, or one man left behind to guard the gun.

I said: "It's only a fable that animals are quiet in the jungle. They're the noisiest things in the world."

We listened to the sounds of the monkeys and the parrots, and she began to get nervous and said: "Well, have you had enough, shall we go back?"

I said: "Not yet, dear Elena." I called out loudly: *"Jesus! Aqui, agora mesmo!"*

149

She looked at me, startled, and it didn't take her long to realize that everything was not as it should be. She opened her mouth to yell, and I had a hand over it long before the first sounds tried to come out. She didn't struggle, but stared up at me with as much venom in her huge black eyes as I've ever seen on a woman's face. The sounds behind us had stopped. I thought, incongruously: *I wonder if one of them is called Jesus too...*But they were waiting, unsure, knowing that they had to keep hidden until she called for them to come out and bring the devil to his knees.

And then, in absolute silence, Jesus was there, slipping lithely over the edge of the cliff, his long knife in the leather belt that fastened his ludicrous overcoat. I told him: "Just keep an eye on her for me, down in the cave, will you do that? Don't hurt her, but watch her like a lynx, she's more dangerous than any woman you've ever seen in your life. And if I'm not back in a reasonable time, take her down to Mazlor, maybe he can find something useful for her to do. Some things, she's very good at."

He wanted to know what "a reasonable time" meant. I said: "If she gets to be too much for you to handle, that's already unreasonable. A couple of days or so."

She was trembling with suppressed fury.

Jesus nodded, and I waited for him to grunt. But he didn't. He pulled an envelope out of his overcoat pocket and handed it to me, and I slipped it into my own pocket with my free hand. Elena had not moved, was not trying to move.

I held her pressed to my chest with one hand over her mouth, and I said, quite gently, because after all she was only doing to me what I was doing to her.

"You'll be all right with him as long as you don't try to be clever. He's a very simple man and he wouldn't understand what you're up to, so he'd just take the easy way out and slit your lovely throat, and that wouldn't do at all, would it? There's a cave just below us in the cliff face, and there are rope handholds all the way down, you understand? I'm going to have to leave you there for a while, but you can ponder all the good times we've had together, and now you can yell your head off."

It was hardly necessary to tell her; her eyes told me just what she was going to do. I took my hand away and her teeth snapped first, but missed, and then she shouted at the top of her voice: "*Venha! Depressa!*"

They came all right, and fast too, with their machine-pistols firing, the noisy animals from the woods. But by then Jesus had swung her in his strong arm over the edge, and I was up in the lower branches of a tree as they ran past below me, firing their guns uselessly at the shadows. The lead man was a Sergeant, and I chose him to drop on, hitting the top of his head with my fist as I came down. I picked up the second man and threw him at the third, hard enough to damage them both more or less permanently, and in less than ten seconds they were all out cold, all three of them. I stripped off their military-style belts and strapped them together by their necks, with their hands around tree trunks, the thumbs tied together with their bootlaces. They made an awkward, untidy bundle; but they were going to stay there until someone came and set them free.

I found the jeep they'd been using, with the machine-gunner peering anxiously toward the forest where the noise had come from and fingering his weapon as though it might give him comfort. I hit him quite lightly, he was only a boy, and took his unconscious form back to join the others and tied him there too. I found a patch of bright moonlight, and took time enough, though time was scarce now, to read what Jesus had handed me.

"*Cabot, my darling, I miss you, come back soon. I'm well, and there's nothing to worry about, Love. Leda*"

There was also a note from Mazlor, written in a surprisingly neat and tidy hand.

"*Everything is good, you don't got nothing to worry about, if anything happen, we waiting for it, all of us. Only trouble is cops, they come from Manaus looking for you, I try pretty hard keep them away, they don't give lady no trouble, only trouble for you maybe when you get back. Good luck, Mazlor.*"

I tore the notes up into tiny pieces and dropped them over the edge of the cliff. And then, I began to run, very fast. And in fifteen minutes I was back at Kolchak's house.

It was surprisingly easy to enter that fortress of a mansion.

I never was a professional burglar, but I have one thing going for me that most men don't have—a physical strength that is almost embarrassingly bountiful. It was just a question of crashing, one by one, the barriers that were meant to keep out the unwelcome.

I threw my jacket up on top of the wall, just in case there was broken glass there (there was), and took a running jump at it and hauled myself up; I ruined a perfectly good jacket, but saved a lot of blood. I toyed with the idea of attacking the watch-tower and incapacitating the guard there; but then I thought it might not be necessary and went instead across the well-kept grounds to the back of the house. There were lights in the kitchen, and through the window— heavily barred—I could see one of the pretty little aids washing some dishes. The other young girl came in while I watched, and she was carrying a small tray with, among other things, a brandy snifter on it.

So he'd finished his dinner, but had he gone yet or not?

I found the garage; two cars. There was a Mercedes-Benz 300Seb sedan, a ton and a half of immaculate luxury. And there was a Land Rover long wheel-base station wagon. The garage was large and airy, open on three sides like a carport, and I could see a fuse box on the wall of the house that looked like the main box; I wondered if I might need it. No room for any other cars, so Kolchak was probably still there.

I moved away, and made a careful inspection of the outside of the house. There were lawns, and flower beds, and bushes, and well-kept driveways; and every window of the house had a wrought-iron cage over it, in the Spanish fashion. I located the big room where I'd seen the safe, and I found what was probably Kolchak's bedroom; the lights were on there, I heard the sound of running water, and soon the lights went off and came on in another part of the house.

Keeping well concealed in the shadows of the shrubbery, I ran back to the garage, and was in time to see Kolchak coming out of the house. He got into the car and backed out, and tooted the horn, and I heard a footstep behind me, over by the front door. I pulled deeper into the bushes, and then Luther was there, moving along the path to the garage and lighting a cigarette as he moved. He passed within three feet of me, and I heard Kolchak say in German: "That was a good meal, I like the new cook." And Luther coughed and said: "And pretty, too." I heard Kolchak laugh; he was in a good humor. The doors of the car slammed, and a moment later I heard the big iron gates open and close, and then the soft, luxurious sound of the car was gone.

The house was mine, I hoped, to do with what I liked. There were two guards patrolling the grounds, but it wasn't yet time to worry about them, so I kept out of their sight; quite easy.

I had already chosen my window. Beyond the iron grill, the window was ajar, and I hate breaking glass; in spite of all the tricks, it can't be done quietly. I took hold of two of the bars, with my fists close to my chest, and pulled, hard. They were stronger than I'd thought, but in less than five minutes I had them pulled wide enough apart for me to get through; and a moment later I was inside the house.

I wondered if there'd be burglar alarms; I decided that the likelihood was that there would be none. After all, a town like this wouldn't really harbor many thieves.

My rubber-soled shoes made no sound at all on the stone-flagged floor. I began a careful examination of the house, room by room, in the darkness, getting my bearings and finding out who was where...There was the noise of dishes being washed in the kitchen, and the chatter of the two girls. To my surprise there were no guards inside the house, no men servants either. In one of the bedrooms, I found a young girl lying fast asleep, with the moonlight streaming across her face, a sheet carelessly pulled across her naked body; she lay on her face, and there were welts across her back. She did not hear me, and I closed the door silently, wondering what her name was and where she'd come from.

I found the cook Kolchak had spoken of, a plump, cheerful woman of thirty or so, with a bright, mischievous, happy sort of face; she came into the kitchen from her room, to check on the girls, just as I was peering through the fanlight over the door. She held an open magazine in her hand, and when she'd satisfied herself that the girls were behaving themselves, she went back to her room and closed the door.

I went into the big room where the safe was, checked that the heavy drapes were closed, put a chair under the door handle, unlocked the steel shutters that were over the patio door and made sure there was a quick way out if I needed it, and switched on a small desk lamp to take a look at the safe.

It was large, and old-fashioned, and well made, and it took me nearly an hour to open. The combination-lock was a good one; but those things need servicing, and this one was too noisy for full efficiency. An hour, much too long...found the bracelet; and the tiara, and some pearls, and some diamonds in a cardboard box, and a paper bag full of really fine pins of gold filigree, and a lot of other stuff that I didn't have the time to examine. There was one huge diamond that must have weighed eighty-two carats, and a smaller, bluish-white stone of unbelievable perfection. Between them, there was a huge fortune by any man's standards, and most of it was in paper bags, or cardboard boxes. One excellent ruby was wrapped in a piece of newspaper. There were some rolled-up canvas paintings, and these too I had no time to examine. A canvas bag held two or three hundred gold Napoleons, which I tipped out onto the carpet as too heavy to carry in comfort, and I used the sack to store my loot in, filling it and drawing tight the leather string that secured it. I tied it round my belt, looked at my watch, and hurried out through the steel shutters that led to the patio. There was one more job to do; I didn't want the guards spotting the bent bars of the window and giving the alarm. I went hunting for them.

They'd left their posts; the boss had gone and they were taking things easy in the kitchen, drinking wine from a bottle and flirting with the girls. I wondered how Kolchak would treat them if he heard some of the things they were saying. The girls were giggling, and I put my foot to the door and thrust it open, and was inside the kitchen before the first of the guards had risen to his feet. I hit him once, and grabbed at the barrel of the other man's machine-pistol and took it from him, and hit him once over the back of the head with it, and then I tried to stop the girls' screaming. The cook came running in, white-faced and still clutching her magazine, and I said: "For God's sake keep these kids quiet, nothing's going to happen to them."

They stared at me, all of them, while I tied up the two guards, and then I said pleasantly to the cook: "Anybody else in the house? You and the two girls and the soldiers, any others?"

She shook her head. "No. Only..." Her voice trailed away.

I said: "Only the girl with the welts on her back. All right, where can I put you to keep you quiet for an hour or two?"

Nobody said anything.

I found a large closet with a substantial lock on it and plenty of air inside, and I opened the door to it and let them huddle in there, scared out of their wits. I found some wine and gave it to them, and said: "Drink this and you won't feel so badly about it."

One of the girls got her voice back, a dark-skinned, black-eyed *cabocla* girl, just recovering from her fright. She said hesitantly: "What...what are you going to do?"

I said: "I'm going to rob the house. I'm going to try and open the safe. I figure that it will take me three or four hours, and if I hear a peep out of any of you during that time I'll come back here and beat the living daylights out of you. But if I don't hear a sound from you, if I know you're behaving yourselves, then nobody's going to get hurt. So, just stay there and get slowly drunk, and keep reasonably quiet, and everything's going to be fine. When I'm through, in three or four hours, I'll check with you again."

I locked the door on them, shoved the bound soldiers out of sight under the table, let myself out, climbed back over the wall, and three minutes later I was revving up the engine of the little Lotus and racing for the airport. Speed was essential now.

I swear that for a while I seriously considered busting into a few more of the Fuerte Quemado houses. A salient fact had just been brought home to me; in a civilized community you need good safes, and burglar alarms; and a cop on the beat just around the corner; but in a place like this, the town itself is the first line of defense against the robber. With a Chief of Police like von Brubeck, and a Mayor like Wiemar, and a few other thorough-going villains in positions of authority—with a blockaded town you couldn't get into or out of, those jewels would have been just as safe lying around on the kitchen table for anyone to see.

It was all part of the picture, of the arrogance that was the town itself: *here we are*, they all seemed to be saying, *come and get us if you think you can.* Cunha had made quite a point of it, and so had Mazlor; and it seemed that their assurance was so strong that they could never believe anyone would dare skip in and find their little weaknesses.

I thought of the huge diamond in my pocket, and where it came from; I rather hoped it was one of those untraceable, undisclosed gems that really don't have an owner any more. If that were so, I wouldn't have to charge Stefan Zrinyi a penny; I knew I couldn't, anyway, not with Leda down there waiting for me.

Leda...I put my foot down and the little bomb shot across the tarmac to the Bellanca I'd had my eye on ever since I'd arrived. A helicopter, of course, would have been better in some ways. But on a plane you can glide in and nobody knows you're there. I climbed aboard and found that the ignition was locked, but there were tools in a box close by, and I soon had the wires stripped and ready. A searchlight went on and lit the scene brightly for me, and a voice boomed out on a loudspeaker, in Portuguese and then in German: "Get your clearance from the tower, please, clearance from the tower," I pushed the button, and the engine roared and then cut, and now a jeep was driving out toward me, not hurrying, just checking to see what was taking off without clearance from the tower. I started up again, and taxied into the wind; I could hear the loudspeaker booming, an angry voice now, though the words were unclear above the sound of the engine. I looked down and saw the jeep speeding forward, cutting across my bows now; I hoped they wouldn't open fire, and assumed, correctly, that they couldn't really be sure that anything was seriously wrong.

I gave her gas and pulled back on the stick, and dipped the wings in a friendly gesture to the tower; I looked down and saw white faces staring up at me, illuminated now by the searchlight. I was low enough to see someone shrug. And then I was wheeling round south and heading for the valley toward Urbana.

It had taken me thirty hours to get up to Fuerte Quemado the first time, and sixteen when I'd used the road I'd prepared; I was approaching Urbana twenty minutes after I'd left the airport. I climbed to eight thousand, cut the motor, and glided. I wasn't at all happy about it, but just in case the Mercedes was ahead of me, I didn't think a plane trying to land in the darkness on the little airstrip would be a very good idea; it might attract just the wrong sort of attention. So I used the broad river as a landing field, and when the wheels went in and she settled on her belly, I threw the fasteners on my seat belt and jumped out quickly. She was just going under, leaving no trace at all, when I hit the shore. I was less than a mile from the wharf, and I dried out by running fast along the riverbank. I looked at my watch when I got there; midnight; it was only six hours ago that I'd dumped the lovely, wicked Elena.

More important, it was three hours since Kolchak had left his house. He'd be just ahead of me, or just behind me, depending on how fast he drove; it was a likelihood that I was ahead of him, but not a very strong one.

I hid the heavy bag of valuables under the wharf; all except one piece; I took cut the beautiful bluish-white diamond and slipped it into my pocket. In the darkness, I wondered why Mazlor had not heard me coming in, why he wasn't there with an outstretched ham-fist full of beer bottle. The old, chipped enamel bath was there, and it was still full of ice and bottles. But Mazlor's chair was empty, and so was his cot.

It did not disturb me too much; there was every reason to believe that he wouldn't be wasting his time sitting around all night after our last little talk. And it was Leda I wanted to see most of all, and soon. There was a bursting emotion inside me that demanded her instant presence. I wanted more than anything in the world to put my arms round her and hold her slim young body tight, to hold her hand, to walk with her along the river, to remember that somehow, in a very short space of time, she had become a very important part of me.

And, most of all, I wanted to tell her how I'd risked her life; and how it was going to pay off.

I ran round to the hotel, moving fast and silently in the darkness. And there, under the portico, was the big black Mercedes; Kolchak's Mercedes, covered in the fine red dust of the mountain.

And there was also one of the jeeps from Fuerte Quemado.

CHAPTER 10

Urbana wasn't exactly jumping at the best of times. A sleepy little country village where everyone—except those who were currently engaged in one of their dubious operations—took a few drinks as soon as it was dark, and then went to bed for want of anything better to do.

At night, there was nothing but silence in the cleared jungle area that was the little town, with the forest noises coming across the river and over the castor fields, and nothing much stirring on the streets except for a few stray cats and an occasional bush animal searching for easy food among the discarded melon skins.

But now, the silence was menacing. It seemed as if even the jungle was quiet. The moon was high, a half-moon that was ringed in yellow, and it cast sharp shadows of the buildings onto the dusty streets. The magnolias glowed whitely, and a huge, rich-scented creeper that blooms only once in seven years was bright with cream-colored blooms that stood out against the dark-green glossy foliage; the scent of it was overpowering, the sickly smell of death. Somewhere, a cat snarled.

The jeep worried me more than anything else, and I couldn't figure out why. It was just one of those strangely unaccountable thoughts that come from the back of the mind to nag, to warn, to tell of something that isn't as it should be. A quartet of Fuerte Quemado's soldiers? They shouldn't cause too much of a problem; but the nagging was still there. Perhaps because I hadn't counted on them? My subconscious told me: no, it's something else...

I was in a hurry to get to Leda's room, fast; but the silence disturbed me; it didn't seem as though silence were the proper thing to expect at this precise moment of time. I crept up on the two cars in the darkness. The jeep was empty, its machine-gun gone, too. But there was a shadow on the back seat of the Mercedes, a man. Bent double, I moved in and flung open the door, and reached in and grabbed and pulled hard, and the man came tumbling out strangely unresisting. He fell on the road with his head back and the blood all over his chest looking black in the moonlight. It was the good-looking Belgian boy, Michel, the self-proclaimed bandit, and he was dead.

The time for silence was gone. I ran fast along the tiled walk under the patio, and I put my shoulder, not stopping, at the wooden jalousies of the window that led to Leda's room, and I felt the wood shatter under the impact. The glass smashed too, and I was falling into the room and on my feet again as fast as a man could move.

There was no sound. I ran to the door and stumbled over a soft, resisting body before I found the light switch, and I turned on the lights and stared at what I was sure must be my Leda; for the first time in my life, almost, I knew the meaning of absolute panic, with all the planning gone wrong and all the dreadful risks coming home to roost.

But it was Mazlor, and I heard him moan. He was clutching at his stomach, and his eyes were glassy, but he reached out at me, trying to grab hold, and saying thickly: "The patio...quick...just a minute ago..."

I felt sick at leaving him, but I ran outside and felt the damp grass under my feet, and almost instantly something hit me across the back of the shoulder, hard enough to send me sprawling, and I thought: thank God...

I was on my feet in a second, and I grabbed at the man who had hit me, knowing that if the blow had landed on my head, where it was meant to land, and would have landed had I not been moving so fast, I would now be as dead as Michel. He was a big man, and I lifted him clear off his feet in the shadows, with one hand grasping the collar of his shirt, and the other gripping a bunched-up handful of his trousers, just above the crotch. I swung him round and up, and was already sending him head first into the brick wall, when he yelled once:

"Cain!"

It was Slawata, the dangerous one. I dropped him, and he wasted no time in recriminations or explanations; he stumbled to his feet and shouted: "This way!" and was running already, very fast and agile for a man of his age and bulk, running across the patio to the corner where the kitchens were. He threw himself at the kitchen door, and it held, and I yelled: "Stand back, damn you!" and put my foot at it and shattered it off its hinges.

We were both inside then, and he switched on the lights and pointed to an open window and went leaping through it onto the gardens outside, and when I followed, he was standing there with a hand on my arm and his head on one side, listening. I pulled him back silently out of the moonlight, and we listened; there was only silence. He said softly: "Two minutes, less than that, where are they?"

I whispered: "How many?"

"I could not see. Five, six, more maybe."

"Stay here, keep your eyes open."

I ran over the vegetable garden, smelling the mint where my feet tore it up, and when I reached the front of the building, the two cars were still there. I tore out the ignition wires of both of them, and threw them away, and ran back to where Slawata was still waiting, and whispered savagely: "They can't get away from Urbana, we'll take them here, on our home ground."

He said: "What time is it?"

"Six hours to daylight, for God's sake, six hours!"

"Is bad."

I said: "For God's sake, you said two minutes, was it really no more than that?"

"Less, maybe."

"Five or six men can't move around in the dark without making some noise. And Leda, what about Leda?"

"They carry her, maybe."

"If she was conscious, she'd be screaming."

"Is true. So they carry her."

"Then they're lying low, nearby, listening to us, waiting...Waiting for what, Slawata?"

Not lowering his voice any more, he said calmly: "They wait

to get us in their line of fire."

The silence was uncanny; was *nobody* on the streets so early in the night? I whispered angrily:

"The cops, what happened to the cops who came here from Manaus, where are they?"

He gestured: "They find out you go to Fuerte Quemado, they give up, they don't try to find you no more."

"And the local man? Salvador? Even he would be better than nothing."

The gesture again: "Like always, dead drunk. We're on our own, friend." I swore.

I said: "For Christ's sake, there's one man I want arrested. Not killed, I want the police to arrest him, to send him back..."

Out there in the black night across the castor fields there was nothing.

I yelled stupidly: "Kolchak! Where are you, Kolchak?" I felt the old man's hand on my arm. I whispered: "Are you all right?"

"Sure, Michel is dead." He had dropped his voice to a whisper again.

"I know. Where's Jao?"

"Jao was here, so was Mazlor, with the lady, when they came. Now, I don't know."

I said: "Mazlor's hurt, hurt badly. Wait here, If you hear anything, yell."

He nodded.

It was going to be a waiting game, a wait for someone to move and six hours to daylight.

I went back very quietly into Leda's room, and closed the door and pulled the drapes over the window, and Mazlor looked up at me off the floor and said, his voice a rasping sound: "I am sorry...they come, too many of them, too fast..."

I lifted him up onto the bed and looked at the great gash in his side, and said: "I'm needed, I haven't much time..."

He interrupted me, grimacing with the pain: "You go...I be okay."

"No. Who can I get to take care of you?"

He shuddered. "Marietta, the girl, she sleep...there, the room at the end..."

I ran out and along the patio, and tried the door; it was locked. I hammered on it and called: "Marietta! Depressa!" She was there in an instant, her eyes wide but sleepy, opening the door and wrapping a slip around her naked brown body. "*O Senhor quer...?*"

I said rapidly: "Mazlor, *ferido*, he's hurt badly, *o quarto da minha dama...*" She stared at me, and yelled: "*Compreende o que estou dizendo*, you understand what I'm saying?"

The sleep went quickly then, and she was already running to Leda's room, quick and lithe and efficient again, and I hurried back to where I'd left Slawata.

He wasn't there.

Silence now once more. I stood stock still in the shadows of the garden, and waited. I heard a bullfrog croaking out of tune and moved toward the sound, and found him crouched in the absolute blackness under a bushy fig tree, crouched on his haunches like an Indian. He took a hard, firm grip of my arm and pointed. I could see his eyes shining. He looked at me once and nodded, sure of himself, and I made a signal meaning: let's go there. He nodded again, tapped me on the chest and pointed, tapped himself and pointed to the side.

We moved off in silence, splitting up now to outflank whatever it was that had alerted his attention.

I moved for fifty feet, a hundred, a hundred and fifty, and then I waited, straining my ears and trying to pick up any alien sound; I couldn't even hear Slawata. And then, just a little way ahead, I thought I heard a sound, a dry, rustling sound that could have been an animal. I lay down on my belly, and there, against the skyline now, I could see the outline of a man's head and shoulders. I saw the head move, looking back toward me, and there was something familiar about it. Flat on my stomach, I inched my way toward him, moving through the wet grass in silence. I looked and saw him again, and then he was gone, and I lay still and waited; I could hear just the faintest sounds, and it was coming nearer. And then I heard a whistle, so quiet that at first I wasn't sure even that it wasn't my imagination. It came again, and then I was certain; I answered it, just as softly, and a zephyr of a whisper came back: "Slawata?"

It was Jao, the diamond smuggler, the man all the police were terrified of. I wriggled over to him and whispered: "Where?"

He put his mouth close to my ear and said, so quietly that I could hardly hear him: "Two men, in front there, seventy, eighty meters, I follow them."

There was hardly enough light to see by. I held up two fingers, raised my eyebrows, frowned, held up the five fingers of one hand. He shook his head vigorously and made a sign: only two.

I said out loud: "They're trying to draw us off..." As I spoke I got to my feet and charged forward blindly, and my likelihood turned up trumps. There was a burst of machine-pistol fire and I heard the bullets spitting among the leaves of the trees. I yelled to Jao: "Go back, for the others!" and then they were there, the two of them, firing blindly into the darkness and quite clearly visible.

I threw myself to one side, ran forward doubled up, rolled over twice, and came up behind them. I hit the first man so hard that I felt his vertebrae snap, and he went down like a log, as dead as a leg of mutton, and before I could grab at the other he'd swung round at me with the gun chattering and I threw myself at his feet. I heard a memorable whistling sound, and a thrown knife hit him in the chest, and then Jao was there to make sure of it before I could get to my feet, driving a heavy boot into his neck as he lay on the ground, and breaking it, and then we were running fast back the way we'd come, yelling: "Here!" for Slawata.

Having called loudly, to indicate my position, I changed direction to fool them, running fast to where I judged Slawata would be. He crossed a patch of moonlight quickly to show himself, and then was in shadow again, and when we reached him, I dropped down on the ground close by him and whispered: "They were drawing us away, just two of them."

He didn't speak. He looked back in the direction we'd come from and pointed and nodded once; and then we were all running, fast and silently, back across the kitchen gardens. We found a dark corner by the brick wall and had a very whispered consultation.

I opened it up: "Did you hear anything back here?"

Slawata said: "Nothing."

"If they'd have moved an inch, would you have heard?"

He nodded. "I hear good. Nothing."

"Me too. Then they're still within a few hundred yards of us, waiting for us to move out of their hearing, over there."

"Behind us then."

"There's only the hotel behind us."

Jao said: "The cars?"

I shook my head in the silence.

A few hundred yards? How far could they have gone between the time they'd left the kitchen window and the time the silence started when I followed them through it? They must have heard me, and they'd have frozen, waiting for the danger to go so that they could move again in safety, sure that sooner or later we'd go crashing off through the bushes after the decoy and they could quietly withdraw in another direction. Unless...

I whispered: "Suppose no one used that kitchen window? Suppose only the two of them used it? My God, they're still in the hotel!"

Slawata nodded slowly, wondering about it. He said at last: "You stay here, I look there, I find, I call out."

I said: "No, wait." It seemed to me that of the three of us, I was the only one they would want to stay alive, and a shot out of the darkness toward the lights of the hotel...I said: "No, you and Jao wait here, split up, if you see or hear anything, call me. I'll take the hotel. They're after something they think I've got, and they won't want me dead. Listen for a sound of any sort..."

Impatiently, wanting the action himself, Slawata growled: "Okay, I know what to do." As I began to move off, he put a hand on my arm, put his mouth close to my ear, and said: "I tell you before, they kill me before they get her. Okay, they get her."

"I know. We'll get her back."

I felt his hand on mine trembling. I knew that he was feeling almost as badly about this as I was. I thought: if there were six of them, there's Kolchak and Luther left, and the bodyguard, no doubt, and one other man; and the deadliest of these is Kolchak. I wasn't happy either about the bodyguard; there had been something in his lithe and silent movements, like a fox in a cage, and in the sharp awareness in his eyes. I wondered, was this the man who killed Michel? Whose knife had ripped a near-mortal wound in Mazlor's side? They'd have sent him in first, I suspected, a silent advance guard to get in there and wreak havoc before the real assault started, to slip in and kill in silence and leave the field clear for the others. The Commandos first, and then the attack. I remembered him in Kolchak's house back there, prowling, restless, constantly on the move, his sharp eyes darting from side to side, his whole body like a coiled spring, tense and immensely resilient; it's strange how even the way a man moves can show him to be dangerous.

I said again: "You listen, listen carefully, anything that doesn't smell right, yell, there'll be no need for silence." I moved off then, making a little noise, but not too much, just like three people trying to keep quiet and not succeeding. For good measure, I spoke to a non-existent Jao when I'd gone a hundred yards or so, keeping my voice low but loud enough for them to hear if they were nearby. I said: "Keep out of sight but close behind me." Only the silence answered, I crept along the portico, keeping to the shadow, and then I heard a sound that started me running, a sudden elation all over me. It was the gentle purr of the big Mercedes starter.

Now, a Mercedes starts when you sneeze at it, and when the motor turned over a couple of times and didn't fire, I knew they'd realize at once that it had been tampered with. I heard the motor growl once more, and then I was there, racing for it as fast as I've ever moved in all my life; and in my decathlon days I was pretty fast. The hell with the sound of it; I *ran*.

The driver's door was open when I got there, and Luther was sitting there with one hand on the door and the other on the starter. He saw me coming, and reached for the gun on the seat beside him, but I went for the opened door and didn't bother to pull up, and hit it hard enough to slam it almost shut; it was only the bones of his wrist that prevented its closing completely. He screamed, and the gun fired and I felt the bullet hit my forearms and burn a furrow along it, and then I had the door open again and a hand round his throat, and he looked up at me with a look of abject terror in his eyes. I held his gun hand, twisting it just enough to release his grip, and I shouted: "I'll give you two seconds to tell me where she is!" I found I could not control my fury, even though I knew, intellectually, that what I needed most now was a calm and ordered process of thought. I heard myself screaming, violently: "Where is she!?"

He said, gasping: "Kolchak...Kolchak's got her."

I yelled: "Where? Where, you bastard?"

I heard him choking, trying to cough and take in some air at the same time, and I took the pressure off his throat and he collapsed to the ground and said: "In the cellar, the cellar under the hotel..." I yanked him to his feet and swung him round heavily and let go, and heard him land thirty feet or so. He lay still, and I didn't care whether or not I'd broken his bloody back.

I ran to the portico and across to the broken kitchen door, and found the door to the cellar bolted on the other side, but it only took two blows with the flat of my foot to burst it open. The lights were on. I thought: now is the time for maximum caution.

Instead, I ran down the stairs like a madman; and there was Kolchak.

He stood in the center of the room, stolid and impassive, with one foot on a heavy wooden stool, his hand on his hips, his great head tilted back, his Mongolian eyes alert and watchful and even showing a touch of unexpected humor.

The Indian stood behind him, a rifle levelled at my belly. And close by, the police officer I'd met on my first day on the mountain, Captain Alonzo Alvarado. He had a Schmeisser machine-pistol steadily held and ready to blow the top of my head off.

Behind me, the door slammed shut, and I looked round to see von Brubeck there. He had a revolver, a Smith and Wesson thirty-eight, and that was aimed in the right direction too. Kolchak, and Luther, and Alvarado, and von Brubeck and the Indian; two men out there lying dead as decoys. Five or six men, Slawata had said: five or six that he'd seen, that is. Four in the jeep and two in the car? Still more to account for? Who could tell? Another jeep-load somewhere? Two more, or three more, or the whole of the Fuerte Quemado police force down here to make a sure go of it?

Again, who could tell?

Von Brubeck said harshly "All right, what are you waiting for? Put your hands up!"

I said as calmly as I could: "Guns or no guns, I can take every one of you in this cellar any time I want. The only way you can stop me is to shoot me now, this very minute, before anything else can happen, and I don't think you want to do that until you've heard what you think I have to say."

I pulled up a wooden chair as casually as I could and sat down; no one had moved, though the Indian had tensed when I stretched out a hand for it. I stared at Kolchak, and said:

"All right, you hold most of the cards. You want to deal for the rest of them?"

Kolchak's eyes flickered behind me, to von Brubeck. He said drily, well in command of the situation: "I told you, an arrogant man." He looked back to me and said: "Deal? You have nothing to deal with."

I said: "I've got your collection, Kolchak."

Now I had the satisfaction, such as it was, of seeing the consternation briefly on his face. Then he scowled and said: "Another lie."

I said: "Can I reach into my pocket without anyone getting too excited?"

I felt von Brubeck moving in, and waited while he searched me. I said: "I don't carry a gun, I never feel I need it." But he found the bluish-white diamond and stared at it, and held it out for Kolchak to see. For a moment there was a little silence, and then Kolchak swore, and in one strong movement picked up the stool from under his feet and smashed it into me. I went over sideways and avoided most of the blow, and picked myself up and sat down again while he glowered at me. Breathing hard, he said to Alvarado: "Get Luther."

Alvarado backed away, with the gun still carefully trained at me, and when he had gone and closed the door, I said: "He's wasting his time, Luther's not in very good shape just now. He's dead." I knew he wasn't; but I knew too that he'd be probably out of commission for quite some time, and the temptation to show them that I wasn't down and out yet was just too strong to resist. But Kolchak only shrugged.

Von Brubeck said: "He's expendable, Cain. We all are. Except you. Yes, we've got to keep you alive until we've all had a friendly little conference. We came for the pendants. And now, it seems, there's the matter of the rest of the collection as well. A good threshold of pain, Luther said you had. But do you really think that with so much at stake we won't break you?"

I said: "And do you really think the Brazilian police are going to let you take this town over? This isn't Fuerte Quemado, for God's sake! You've got three or four more hours till daylight, and by then...Brother, you'd better be gone."

"Three hours will be long enough, plenty long enough. Unless, of course, you want to trade. Your trumps, for ours."

Somehow, on the spur of the moment, it seemed to me that one thing had to be kept hidden from them, at all costs; just how priceless to me that tramp of theirs was. They couldn't know, I was sure of it, just what Leda had come to mean to me in so short a time. I'd told them I was ready to double-cross her, and I was sure they believed it. And this, I thought, was the edge I had over them—provided I made sure they never even suspected what was between us.

I said: "All right, we'll trade. My life is dearer to me than a sackful of diamonds, I don't care what they're worth. We'll trade. Only question is, how do we do it?"

Kolchak said stolidly: "Your life...and what else?"

I shrugged. "A fair trade as is," and von Brubeck said, gently mocking: "What tricks are you trying out on us now, Cain? Surely you must know we have your Zrinyi woman? The woman that Mazlor tried so gallantly to save from the inevitable?"

Kolchak had handed the ball to von Brubeck, the animal using him as he had always been used. It was my wits against his now.

I said carelessly: "Oh, her."

Von Brubeck looked at me sharply.

I said: "Let's get one thing clear, shall we? I didn't want to bring her here, she insisted on coming. She wouldn't part with those rubies, and she insisted on making sure that Kolchak's bracelet wasn't the copy. She wanted to see it herself. Ergo..." I shrugged. "She's only herself to blame. Like Luther, she's expendable as far as I'm concerned."

He was watching me, not too sure.

I thought: as long as they don't know what she is to me, I can still get out of this, and get her out too.

I said: "You went to a lot of trouble to play a card that doesn't mean a damn thing. She's got the fragments, Get them from her, it shouldn't be hard. And if you still want to cut me in..."

The last piece was just for effect, but von Brubeck took me up on my attitude. He said smoothly: "You mean she's nothing to you, a good looking woman like that?"

I said: "Good looking women are a dime a dozen."

"Good. Then that's all right then."

I said sourly: "What's all right about it?"

He was still smiling gently. He lit a cheroot and watched me, and said calmly:

"Leda Zrinyi is dead, Mr. Cain. Someone hit her a little too hard and she died."

I felt the blood drain out of my face; I knew that I had suddenly gone as white as a sheet. I leaped off my chair and threw myself at both of them, von Brubeck and Kolchak, throwing my arms round them both in a bear-hug and smashing their heads together with all the force I could command. But I didn't quite make it; I'd barely touched them both when something smashed onto the back of my head with a brutal force. I went over sideways onto the floor, and saw the Indian raise the rifle again and ram it down into my neck. I still wasn't quite out; but nothing answered the commands of my brain, my muscles wouldn't move, my limbs were made of lead. I saw the gun go up again, saw it come down, saw that the cellar was suddenly filled with stars.

Red, and green, and yellow stars bursting everywhere in the pitch darkness of the coma. My head was splitting open, and a great cavern was opening up to let me lower myself gently into it.

And then, there was only silence.

CHAPTER 11

The darkness was still with me. I heard someone call my name. Was it Elena?

Elena? I'd left her up in a cave in the face of a cliff, with only a bottle of *pinga* and some dried fish to live on, with whatever fruit the Indian could find for her if he felt so inclined.

What was his name? Jesus?

She called out to me again in the darkness, and I tried to say to her: *Elena, she's dead, they killed my girl.* All I could manage was a moan; what else was there to do in the world now?

There was a pain in my left forearm, a pain that was stronger than it was worth, because I knew that Luther's bullet had cut a long furrow from my wrist to my elbow, but had not gone very deep. My head was pounding like a jackhammer, and when I put my hand to it I could feel blood.

No, I couldn't. My hands were tied, I couldn't even move them. Why did I think then...?

My name again, a woman's voice calling my name, miles and miles away up in the cave there, or down by the ocean somewhere, calling my name over and over again.

What did she want with me? Was she saying: Cabot, you made love to me, coldly, and how can you treat me like this? Or was she gloating: it's all over now, and I'm coming for you again, and my name is Elena...

Only it wasn't Elena at all, it was Leda, only Leda was dead and all my careful plotting had not been as careful as I'd thought, just reckless, reckless enough to use a young girl's life as a playing card, not even a Joker.

She said clearly: "Cabot? Cabot? Can you hear me? Are you awake, Cabot?"

The clarity came all of a sudden. One minute the black waves were sweeping over me, pounding my head into the rocks, and the next minute my consciousness was back and fully operative. I sat up fast, and bumped my splitting head on a beam in the darkness, and twisted round and said, with a surge of bewilderment bursting inside me:

"Leda? Is that you, Leda?"

She said: "My God, you're alive, thank God..."

"Leda?" I was groping, my mind still muddled. "Is that you?"

"Yes, my darling, it's me. Are you all right?"

"Yes, yes, I'm all right, where are you?"

"Here, below you, on the ground. I'm tied, I can't move."

I said: "Did they hurt you, my Leda? Did they hurt you?"

Her voice was a whisper, "Only a little. It's over now."

Clarity was coming back now, the focus sharpening.

"Where are we, do you know?"

She said: "In the storeroom that leads off the wine cellar. There's a light somewhere; but..."

"And how long have I been here?"

"Fifteen minutes or so. They brought you in and dumped you, you were unconscious, and then they tied your hands and feet, and they've gone to get Luther."

"Luther?"

"The Indian came in while they were tying you. I didn't understand what he said to them, but I heard one of them say to the other, in German, 'We're going to need Luther now.' Who is he, Cabot?"

I said: "Luther's one of their underlings." I was sick. A dread was coming over me at the mention of his name. A woman like Leda in Luther's hands! I said: "Fifteen minutes? Is that all? And you're sure you're not hurt?"

"I'm not hurt, my darling."

"Thank God. Thank God at least for that."

There was a little silence. I strained at the ropes, testing them, pulling them hard and cutting my wrists to pieces in the process.

She whispered: "The big man is Kolchak, isn't he? The one who looks like a Mongolian?"

"That's Kolchak."

She tried to joke; "Well, you found him."

"I found him all right. I found your collection of jewelry too. So, from one point of view, I guess you could say we're doing all right."

"You found them?" In spite of our predicament there was an excitement, an admiration, in her voice.

I said: "Yes, and they're hidden away safely too."

"And is that...is that what they want now? Why they've got us trussed up like this?"

"That's why. They want their jewels back."

For a long time now, I'd heard breathing; it wasn't hers, and it wasn't mine. The sound was so fragile that at first I'd taken it for the murmur of the breeze outside, over our heads somewhere. But listening carefully, I learned that it was regular, controlled, stifled; a man breathing very carefully and maintaining the utmost silence. Over to the left, somewhere in the darkness...

I said: "And that's not the worst of it. You remember the ruby bracelet?"

"Yes, of course, the one with the two pendants missing."

"I'm afraid they think you may have the two missing pieces."

"But..."

"Yes, I know," I interrupted her, not too quickly. "I still have them hidden away, of course, but somehow, I suspect they got the impression that I gave them to you. I also told them that you'd be taking the bracelet down to Aaron for me. I think that's what gave them the idea that you might have the pieces."

Her voice was strained. "I see." Wisely, she said no more, and I knew that even if she wasn't sure what was going on, she knew I didn't think we were alone, that I was talking for someone else's benefit.

And now...

Now I wasn't sure at all that I'd done the right thing. If I'd said, ostensibly, to her: There are no fragments, I dreamed them up. Would the silent listener have believed me? Would he have thought instead: Aha! He's heard me. If I'd known who it was out there I could have estimated the chances better.

I toyed with the thought for a moment. Von Brubeck, who had so easily tricked me into disproving my lie when I'd said Leda was of no concern to me. He would have taken the whole thing with more than a pinch of salt. Kolchak would have believed the whole thing, sure that I'd never guess at his presence there to eavesdrop. The others? The Indian? Alvarado? I had no idea. I said suddenly:

"They told me you were dead; they told me they'd killed you."

I could hear the surprise in her voice, the fear too. If they said they'd done it, did it mean they were going to? She said: "Why should they do a thing like that?"

"I knew they were holding you, I didn't want them to know...to know what was between us. A man's not much use when the woman he loves is threatened. If she doesn't mean so much to him, it might just give him the edge he needs, and God knows I needed an edge. So I told them I didn't care what happened to you. There was a man named von Brubeck there, and he didn't quite believe me, so he decided to find out for sure. He said you were dead, and...and I lost control. So then, I'm afraid, he knew. He outsmarted me." There were things I wanted the listening man to hear, other things. I said: "And Mazlor, Slawata, the others, they're all dead too. Mazlor was knifed, Michel was knifed, the others were cut down by machine-gun fire out in the castor fields. Now, there's only me left."

I hated doing it; I could hear her catch her breath and start crying. She said at last: "And what...what will happen now?"

Now I had to lay it on the line. The rest of the jewels were of no consequence; it was those two damned imaginary fragments that I was worried about.

I said: "I'm going to demand that they send you to Santo Antonio. And the moment you're on that plane, I'm going to hand over the jewels, the rubies and all, all of it."

There was a little silence; she was thinking about the non-existent fragments. "And then?"

I said casually: "They'll let me go. There's no reason why they shouldn't once they've got what they want. Besides, there's always a chance that I might one day be useful to them. I'm the best jewel thief in the business, I've got the contacts...No, they won't hurt me once they've got what they came for. But I'm not handing a damn thing over till you are safely out of the way."

"I see." What else could she say? She was learning so many things, so fast. But it was necessary that I comfort her as much as I could. And she was thinking fast, too. She said: "Where did you hide the jewels?" It was a good question, one that I could answer as concisely or as vaguely as I chose.

I said: "In the bole of a tree out in the woods. Easy enough to find again in the daylight, though I'd never locate it in the dark. I hope they don't expect me to describe it to them—they'd never find it in a month of Sundays. A big casuarina tree with some purple orchids hanging from its branches."

Now, at last, the man stirred. I heard the scrape of a chair, and the lights went on, three bare bulbs hanging from the ceiling. It was von Brubeck, and somehow the thought gave me pleasure. He stretched himself luxuriously, as though he'd been sitting too still for too long, and lit a black cheroot and came over and inspected the cords that tied my hands behind my back. I noticed he kept his gun very handy all the time. I looked at him with as much astonishment and alarm as I could muster.

Leda was on the stone floor below me, her hands tied together and her ankles as well, and I was lying in a confined space that felt like a coffin but was actually a storage bin down which a heavy cast-iron pipe was running; sewage, I wondered? My hands and feet were tied, and a rope from my upper arms was fastened to the pipe; they'd been very careful to be careful.

Von Brubeck said, mocking: "How's the head, Cain?"

I said: "It feels like someone hit it with a rifle butt, what did you expect?" I tried to sound as sullen as I could.

He smiled at me and walked to the door and opened it, and called up: "Kolchak!"

Four of them came in. Kolchak first, striding in like the Captain of a ship and standing there to stare stolidly at me; then Alvarado and the Indian, and between them, his face screwed up with pain and his left fist heavily bandaged, was Luther.

Von Brubeck spoke to Kolchak in German: "All the stuff is hidden in a tree out in the forest there somewhere. He thinks we'll let the girl go and then he'll lead us to it."

Kolchak said: "He'll lead us to it." His eyes moved to Leda, looked carefully over the length of her body. His expression did not change.

I heard Luther say viciously: "When I've finished with him he'll take us to hell and back. When I've finished with both of them." He struggled free of Alvarado's grasp and stood there swaying a little, swaying and coughing, doubling up and then straightening up again. He moved over to me and drove his fist repeatedly into my face. I heard Leda scream, and he leaned down and slapped her, hard. He said thickly: "I'll start on the girl, and Cain can watch what I do to her."

Kolchak said calmly: "No. I want the girl. Take her to one of the bedrooms."

Alvarado slung his rifle over his shoulder, bent down and picked up Leda and carried her to the door. I could see the revulsion in her eyes, though she was trying not to look at me. I could feel the ropes at my wrists almost cutting them in two as I struggled. The Indian put out his foot and slammed the door shut, and looked at Kolchak, waiting for instructions. Kolchak said to him: "Stay with Luther, he might need you."

He turned to von Brubeck: "He's got some friends somewhere, you'd better find out about that."

Von Brubeck smiled. "They're dead. Just these two left, and they're on their own."

Kolchak nodded, as though he'd half expected it. "Then stay here too. When I come back..."

Alvarado came down the stairs and looked at Kolchak and said: "She's in number five, the second door along the patio." Kolchak said nothing.

I felt one of the cords at my wrist stretching. There was blood greasing it, softening it. The cord round the pipe was nearly taking my arm off as I got a hitch on it and twisted; I could even feel the heavy pipe, embedded in concrete, shaking. There was sweat pouring down my forehead. As Kolchak moved to the door I yelled: "What do you want, for God's sake? I'll tell you anything you want to know! Leave her alone and I'll tell you everything!"

Kolchak didn't even smile. He said coldly: "What do I want? I'll tell you. I want her, Cain. And what I want, I take. Does that answer your question?" He turned back to the steps, and I yelled:

"You bastard, she's your daughter! You hear me? Your daughter, you bastard!"

It seemed as though everything froze. Kolchak did not move. I was conscious that von Brubeck was looking at him, a very gentle smile on his handsome face. Alvarado looked scared; the Indian, impassive. Only Luther seemed not to have heard. He had found a wine bottle and had smashed the bottom off it, and was standing there waiting for Kolchak to move out and leave the field to him.

Then Kolchak looked at me, his eyes very thoughtful. I think that in that moment, with the disclosure of something that was so irrelevant to the problems of jewel thieves and wartime loot, he suddenly knew that the whole thing was a lie from beginning to end, that I'd come there only to get him, that I was her husband, perhaps, or her lover, who had sworn to get the man who, so long ago, had so casually destroyed the ancient, noble family. There were thoughts of honor again, just as there had been in the forgotten, anachronistic world of the Zrinyi castle; it was as though the whole fragile fabric had been ripped open and brought to light a tissue of elaborate lies, with an elaborate plot, and nothing but vengeance behind it. It was as if everything, in that moment, had suddenly changed, and we were back where we started, with all the stories, the lies, never having really been told. Back where we started, only now all my cards were on the table and all his were up his sleeve, and he was omnipotent and I was powerless.

Was this the way it had always been? Fenrek had said: quietly, and stolidly, and constantly in control...And was this the way it was meant to be, always?

There's nothing more terrifying than abject helplessness.

I said again, very quietly, as he stared at me: "She's your daughter, Kolchak."

His eyes began to wrinkle up first, crinkling at the corners into thin, fine lines. The eyes themselves shone brightly, half-closed. And then the mouth twisted into a smile, and the great, barrel-chested body began to shake, and he threw back his head and laughed, and roared out his laughter, and then turned away and when the door had closed behind him I could still hear the sound of his heavy boots on the stairway; that, and the sound of the laughter.

There were four of them there. Von Brubeck, the Indian, Luther and Alvarado; in descending order of danger. As far as I was concerned, there could have been a hundred. I was blind, completely blind to anything except the need to get away from there.

The ropes had cut great hunks out of my wrists as I struggled against them, and my arms were numbed from straining against that iron pipe. I'd hardly used my legs because it was the shoulder-muscles that were required now. But all reason was gone, and I simply twisted and turned and threw myself every which way, meeting resistance, wherever it might be, with the maximum of force, not even bothering to hide my struggles. The ropes were strong, and I caught a glimpse of von Brubeck's face, quite unconcerned with my useless efforts, and Luther began to move in and I almost burst a blood vessel, and then...then I heard something crack; I didn't know if it was my own spine or the framework of the bins they'd tied me to. I heard someone yell in German—von Brubeck?—"Hold him!"

I was suddenly falling free, and the great oak structure was falling about me, with the iron pipe coming out of its junction at the wall and stinking water pouring out of it, thick with sludge and garbage and stench. Alvarado swung his gun at my head and I ducked sideways and heard von Brubeck again: "Hold him, hold his feet...!"

Somebody grabbed at them—Alvarado?—and I doubled up my knees and pushed out hard and heard a bone crack, and then Luther was on top of me, falling, a four-inch nail from a beam ripping across his face. I dug my elbows into his chest, hard, and heard the breath go out of his body. And then one of my hands was free; not free entirely, still fastened to the other but with a length of rope long enough to let me get a grip on it.

I wriggled sideways fast, keeping as much movement going as I could, and ripped it off my other hand, struggling in the water that was now flooding over the floor, and diving under the broken bin to keep my head out of the way of Alvarado's flailing gun. I heard the Schmeisser fire; von Brubeck had decided that perhaps he could keep me quiet with a burst of slugs in the feet. One of them tore into my shoe, and then I reached out and took the gun and wrenched it out of his hands and continued the movement to hit him with it, smashing it into him unscientifically, letting it land with monstrous force wherever it might be; it was the small of his back, and he fell and rolled over, and groaned, and then Alvarado was running for the door, the odds too high for him now. I shot out my bound legs and tripped him as he ran, then brought my fists, clenched together, down on top of his head. He doubled up like a concertina with the air gone out of it, and then...Then there was only the Indian, standing alone on the other side of the cellar, by the door, standing in a crouch with his long knife, the knife they call a *facao*, held quite loosely in his hand. I was on my feet, and my feet were still roped together, loosely; I kicked them free.

I kept my eyes on him while I flicked the cord from my wrist, watched his eyes, a brave man scorning to fight with the rest of them and confident in his own expertise whatever the odds; he had the knife, I had the size, he was thinking; and one was more than a match for the other.

The stinking water was up to my calves now, and the air was quite unbreathable. He stood there by the door, and I went to him and raised my fist, and slipped back as the knife whistled past my stomach, then reached in and took him by the shoulder and sent him sprawling with a blow behind the ear with my other fist. I was drenched to the bones and stinking like a cesspool, covered in blood and fury; and two seconds later I was racing up the stairs.

The air outside was fresh and clean and hopeful; it was a new lease on life. I raced through the deserted kitchen and across the patio and along the covered walk; no one was in sight or sound, anywhere. Slawata and Jao, where were they? I didn't need them now. Where was Mazlor and the pretty little serving girl who was looking after him? I didn't need him either.

And where were the honest folks of Urbana, if there were any? Asleep in their beds, or lying awake with the doors locked and their ears and eyes resolutely closed, not wanting to know what was going on outside, knowing only that it was part of the pattern that was their town and wanting no part of it unless it should profit them.

The smugglers are in town, so keep your eyes turned to the wall, what you don't see won't hurt you...

And so, the honest folk were lying abed and covering their heads with their blankets and hoping that it would all go away; the waiters, and the cooks, and the butlers and the floormen and all the others to whom Urbana and the jungle were a way of life; and outside, in the dark of the night, with the half-moon whitely bright, there was mayhem, and murder, and worse.

One, two, three, four...Five was at an angle of the courtyard, with a streak of light showing under the door, as I drew close, the faint sound of a whimper beyond it, like an animal crying. The door would be locked, if only as a matter of principle. That's all it would be, principle; for who would disturb the devil at his play?

I didn't even take time out to raise my foot and batter at the door. Moving fast, I simply slewed round and went through it shoulder first, bursting it open as if it had been made of paper. The window was smashed open, the drapes were fluttering, and Kolchak was gone. But Leda was there.

Hers was the whimpering I had heard out there; she was lying on the floor by the corner, curled up in the fetal position, quite naked, and softly crying to herself. There were great red welts over her shoulders, and, when I turned her over, across her lovely breast as well. I saw the thonged leather belt on the floor, the one with the fine decorations of gold wire woven into it.

I picked my Leda up gently and put her on the bed, its cover rumpled, and covered her over, and drew the curtains because a single shot from out there could still have been the end of everything, and went to the door and yelled:

"Marietta! Slawata! Jao! Anybody! Here, to me!"

Nobody answered my call, and I went to number two, Leda's room, and threw open the door and locked in, Marietta was there with Mazlor, and his eyes were open and looking at me, and he whispered: "What has been happening, Cain? I hear so much, I cannot move. The lady...Leda..." There was a broad bandage round his stomach now; his face was taut and white with pain, and Marietta was crying softly as she tried to restrain him. He was still trying to reach the door, and whispering: "You need me...I come...."

I said: "It's all over, almost. I want Marietta."

He nodded, and she came with me back to number five, and then Slawata and Jao were there too, running in from the castor field. I said to Jao: "There may be some cleaning up to do in the cellar. Just make sure nobody's around there with a gun. Then come back here, fast." Slawata looked a question, and I pointed and said: "Mazlor's in there. He's hurt but he's going to be all right. Better go to him."

He said: "Those men...the lady...?"

"The lady is all right now. Look after Mazlor."

He knew that something was wrong, but he nodded and moved away as silently as before. I watched him go into the room where Mazlor was, and I went back to see Leda.

Marietta was with her, sponging the wounds with cold water, and she looked at me with angry eyes and said: "*Quem o fez*, who did this thing?"

I said: "A man named Kolchak."

She looked at me, and the delicate movement of her fingers stopped.

"You kill him already?"

"Not yet. I will."

"*Bem*. Good." She handed me the wet towel, and stood looking down somberly while I sponged the soft, resilient, hurt body.

Leda opened her eyes and looked at me, and began to cry, and put a hand to her face and wiped away the tears and said, with almost a smile: "I'm glad to see that you're...you're free." She shuddered suddenly, and the tears came, and she said, trembling: "His hands...his great calloused hands."

Not knowing what to do, Marietta picked up the torn dress and the underclothes, and folded them up as though tidiness were all that mattered, and then went into the bathroom.

I took Leda in my arms and held her gently, and said: "It's all over, my darling."

"And you'll stay with me now?"

"I'll stay with you. There's one thing I have to do, and then I'll stay with you."

180

She looked at me, her eyes wide. "Kolchak...where is he?"

I said: "He's not anywhere near, he can't harm you anymore."

She looked away, and then lay back on the bed with her eyes closed. Marietta came up with a bath towel, soaked in warm water, and I laid it over her and said; "Get her some brandy, will you?" She nodded and was gone, and then Jao knocked on the door and when I let him in he said:

"*Que fedor*, what a stink down there!"

I said: "Trouble?"

He shook his head. "Two men dead, two men tied up like they won't go no place for long time."

"Who's dead?"

He shrugged. "I didn't ask their names. One man with bandaged hand, drowned in filthy water, what you call it?"

"Sewage, the best thing that could happen to him."

"One Colonel, Fuerte Quemado police uniform, his back broken, you do this, you my friend for always. One Indian unconscious I tie him up, I tie up too one Fuerte Quemado police Captain. Nobody give us no trouble no more."

Leda had heard. She looked at me with her eyes wide. "And Kolchak?"

I said: "On his way back home by now, scuttling like a scared rabbit. But how he's going to get there, that's another question."

She was worried about the expression on my face.

She said: "Forget him, Cabot, please."

"I can't."

She put her arms round my neck, holding me tight; and said: "Please, if I can, you can too!"

I said: "You'll never forget him, and neither will I."

"I've forgotten him already. With you beside me...don't leave me, please! Please?"

I took her arms very gently away. "It won't be for long. Jao is here, there's no danger any more. In an hour or two it will be daylight, everything will be all right then." I felt that if she'd insisted, I'd have stayed; I felt that she knew that too. But she said nothing, and nodded her head slowly, and kissed me with her arms round my neck and her eyes very grave, and then she lay back and pulled the cover up to her chin and stared at me.

Marietta came back with some cognac, and she took a little, and Marietta sat on the bed while Jao took up his position on a chair by the door, tilting it back and looking round the room. He saw the torn dress and the blood-stained towels, and the smashed window, and he went and picked up the thonged belt and touched it delicately and looked at the blood on his finger-tips, then tossed it down on the floor contemptuously and sat down again, and he looked at me and said clearly: "I see this man, Cain, I don't ask no questions. I just kill him for you, dead, like that. This—" he gestured toward the bloodied belt— "*Nao o quero aceitar*, I don't accept this."

I nodded. "You see him, you do that, Jao. Don't wait for me. You do that."

He looked at me sourly and said: "You tell me you want him arrested."

I said: "Not any more, I don't. He had a chance to stay alive, before. Now, he's lost it."

I kissed Leda, held her for a moment, and went out.

Far to the east, the sky was lit with a pale rose tinge, against which the trees and tangled vines of the forest were black, a solid black wall of impenetrable darkness. The early morning breeze was stirring, and the tops of the palm trees were bent over; the wind made a pleasant, whistling sound through them.

I said to myself: my name is Kolchak, I'm on the run from a man who wants to kill me, and all the help I can expect is at the top of the mountain, in a place called Fuerte Quemado which is my home and my refuge; my car's been sabotaged, there's no way to phone them, and if I stay here much longer, I'm a dead man; what do I do?

I said to myself: I can steal a car if I can find one, or I can get up-river in a boat and cut across country to the Doussa road and keep walking. I'm sixty years old or so, can I make a trip like that? I said: I can if I'm desperate enough; I'm a peasant, I'm tough in spite of my age...Yes, I can do it.

I went round to Mazlor's store first. The truck was still there, the only vehicle in the town. The river, then. I went over to the wharf, taking my time now because there was no longer any hurry, I didn't care how far he'd gone in the interim; it was all a question of patience, and though I don't have much of that I can call in an adequate reserve when it's necessary.

Mazlor's little canoe with the outboard was gone. The chain that tied it to the wharf had been wrenched out of the rotten boards and was gone, padlock and all. I hadn't heard the motor start, but he'd have paddled upstream for—how long?—ten, fifteen minutes?—to get out of sound range before starting up. I was dealing in likelihoods again; the hunted animal heads for his lair, and this was the only way he could go. I stepped on board the big launch, smashed open the locked door to the wheelhouse, started the big diesel, backed out carefully, pulled the wheel hard over, then pushed the throttle all the way home. The motor roared; a noisy great behemoth, and the white wave shot out round the bow as she surged forward.

Too much keel to go very far up-river, Mazlor had said; well, we'd see just how far very far was.

I held the wheel steady and waited. We touched bottom on mud once or twice, and once there was a sickening sound as we hit a submerged mass of granite; the boat heeled over, righted herself, forced herself on, a good fifteen or sixteen knots. She smashed into a submerged tree trunk, and I saw the roots coming up out of the water behind us, but she held her course like an angel, plowing forward under full power. The river ahead was dark, and it was just a question of pointing the prow in the right direction and hoping.

She rammed a sandbank and staggered over it, and the sky on my right was getting lighter; and when the sun showed its first, bright-red glow over the hills we were still moving. I cut the engine once and listened; nothing but the noises of the forest.

I started her up again and plowed on, pushing the throttle hopefully against the stop and trying to get another knot or two out of her.

And then it was daylight, and we hit the bottom with a thud that sent me sprawling. I got up and tried to back off, but we were stuck fast and groaning, so I jumped overboard and half-swam, half-waded to the shore; and then, I began to run.

I ran along the riverbank where there was any kind of a path, and where there was none I jumped over fallen trees and forced a way through the lianas, and twice got back into the river and swam, and at last I came to the porterage track up to the top of the first cliff where the waterfall was. I looked at my watch; eight o'clock, I'd made good time.

Could he have carried the canoe and its motor up there alone? I thought not; I was sure not. The boat was there somewhere then, unless I'd been wasting my time.

I thought it best to search before going any further, to make my likelihood a certainty. And in less than five minutes, I found it. It was carefully covered over with foliage, but the marks where he'd dragged it laboriously had been carelessly rubbed out with a branch, and the wet mud still showed the signs; not too long ago then.

And I'd been right. The elation was enormous; not merely because my reasoning had been correct, but most of all because he was here and Leda was back there, safe from him, a long, long way away, both in time and distance. And with the others out of commission, it was just the two of us now, Kolchak and me, and the end of all the wretched things I'd started.

I found his heavy footsteps, the prints of hurried, unfaltering feet. He'd climbed up to the top, and I followed; but where then? He couldn't be making for the cliff where Jesus was hidden, the cliff was unclimbable. Along the bank of the river, then, to...to where? Somewhere along the line he'd leave the river and strike out across country to the Doussa road. So why hadn't he taken it in the first place? Because I'd catch up with him more easily on the road...

I tried to remember the map Mazlor had drawn. The Doussa road curved round, and almost, but not quite, met the river again. Perhaps, then, he'd be better off taking the path along the secondary river to the deep gorge, and then striking across country? I could only hope that his tracks would tell me at the top.

I went up that path non-stop, running all the way, pumping my legs hard and forcing the pace to my very utmost, and at the top I searched for his tracks and found nothing; the ground was hard as rock. But I knew that he couldn't be far off now, perhaps only a few minutes ahead of me. Two more miles now along the bank, at a very fast run along the Indian track. I found the division of the rivers—and his footprints were there in the mud. So, too, were the marks where a canoe had been dragged down into the water of the eastern tributary, the long dark passage under the overhanging trees.

A canoe? Whose? And where from? I decided that it must have been left there by a stray Indian, and fortuitously found; or kept there under cover for just such an emergency as this. For supplies, perhaps, for the troops on the Doussa road barrier? It didn't matter very much; there'd been a canoe there, and Kolchak had taken it.

And how fast could he paddle upstream? I knew that by running where there was somewhere to run, and swimming where there wasn't, sooner or later could catch up with him, I stripped off my shoes and most of my clothes, dived in the water, and started a six-stroke crawl, taking it fast but conserving my strength. I swam for two hours, and then ran along the bank for forty minutes, and then...then, at last, I heard him.

I stopped to get some breath back, feeling the strain a little of pushing myself too hard, and as I leaned against a tree and took in deep and regular gulps of air, I heard the faint splashing of his paddle; only a little way ahead where the river swung lazily round a bend. I began to run again. I ran straight through the forest, tearing great hunks of flesh off my bare feet, to where the river's bend would bring me ahead of him, to where the white water was; and I lay down in the moss with a cluster of fern-fronds tight about me, and soon...soon, he was there.

Kolchak.

He was covered with sweat and grime, and he was panting hard. No wonder; he'd made extraordinary progress. I marveled at it, a man of sixty moving like an athlete in spite of the years of luxury with the drinks and the girls and all the little pleasures. I watched him pull the canoe into the shore by its rope, and drag it up onto the path to bypass the white water of the gorge where the deadly current ran so fast. The going was tough, and he had the rope over his shoulder, with his barrel-chest expanded and the sweat pouring down of his face, and his mouth set tight in a line of angry frustration. I looked at his eyes, and they were completely passionless. He was moving straight toward me, and we were not more than fifty feet apart.

And, suddenly, I knew that he'd seen me. He did not change his gait, or his expression, nor falter in the slightest. He pulled at his rope and grunted, and then he slipped and went down, and he swore and began to get to his feet and I knew exactly what he was up to; an able man doesn't slip quite so easily on dry ground, and I was racing toward him almost before his hand came out of his pocket with the gun in it. A small gun, a Walther .32 automatic that's only deadly in the hands of an expert who can hit a vital spot the first time.

He fired three times in that fifty feet. The first bullet went wide, the second hit me in the side of the chest, and the third went high in the air, because by then I was on him and had twisted his arm almost out of its socket. There were wild, untended thoughts racing through my mind; an old man, I was thinking, old enough to be my father. And then there was Leda lying on the floor with her dress ripped off her and the sound of her animal whimpering...And his gross laugh in the cellar when I had told him...

I hit him once, just hard enough, and yelled at him: "If I have to carry you down on my back, you bastard!"

I stumbled and fell then, and there was blood coming out of my mouth. I thought: my God, that bullet...There was no pain. I rolled over onto all fours, and then Kolchak's boot was coming at my head, kicking hard, and I thought: sixty years old and indestructible, and I grabbed his boot and twisted it, and he went spinning across the ground to land hard on his belly and, as I got to my feet, he jumped up with a log in his hands, a log so big I could hardly have hefted it myself. He hurled it at me, and I ducked and it went sailing into the water, and then he put his head down and charged, like a bull, a mad bull.

I stepped to one side and hit him scientifically on the side of the head as he went past me, and he still wasn't out, he was still full of fight, a tough old peasant up against it and battling for his life. He'd grabbed my fist as I hit him, and we went tumbling into the racing water, falling over each other and trying each of us to force the other under.

He never had much of a chance, really, from the very beginning, bullet or no bullet; once I stayed on my feet after that second shot, he must have known there wasn't any hope. But in the water...He soon saw there was nothing he could do; he doubled his back up, and put his feet under my chin, and kicked out and he was free of me and racing fast, swimming marvelously well, downstream on the fast current among the white spume of the water and the shining red granite of the boulders there, I coughed up blood and fell to the ground, and struggled to my knees and clutched at a tree, and then...

And then, in midstream, he screamed once; a short, staccato scream that was cut off almost as soon as it started. I saw him hanging there, on his back, in the river, with only one side of his head above the water, and the water tearing past him fast and not moving him at all.

I crawled to the river and swam, very slowly and carefully, over to the mangrove spears that were supposed to block the river's route from Fuerte Quemado. One of them had gone right through his belly and came out at the back, just to the left of his spine. I left him dangling there and swam slowly, painfully, back to the shore.

It took me a long, long time to get home. The bullet inside me was beginning to work its poison, and I took it slowly, easily, conserving all my energy for when I might need it. I took the canoe that Kolchak had used, and let the river carry me most of the way.

And when I came to the falls I crawled along the bank with the canoe on a rope behind me, and I lowered it slowly down the cliff, and when I put it into the water below, all I could do was lie in the bottom and let the river carry me all the way back to Urbana.

We bumped into the wharf at last. It was three o'clock in the afternoon, and Leda was there waiting for me, with Mazlor sitting painfully on the edge of her bed, and Marietta bustling around them both like the good little nurse she was.

I fell to the floor by the bed, and Marietta gasped and tore off my shirt and found the bullet hole, and the darkness came and went, and came again and went once more, and there were just the two of us lying side by side in the bed and the others had gone.

Her arms were around me and she was pouring *conhaque* between my lips, and looking at me with her solemn, pale-gray eyes, with lines of suffering around them now; and I lay back and stared at the ceiling.

And soon, the night came and took away all the pain.

CHAPTER 12

I woke up in the night; or was it the next day?

I was in a bed by myself, and there was a pain in my chest so severe that I nearly cried out, a knife twisting round in it, And that's what it was; when I struggled to fight the pain, I came to my senses and found that Jao was holding me down, or trying to, and that Slawata was digging the bullet out of my chest with the point of a dagger; there was time to see that he was laughing, and then the coma came again, and once more I was there with Leda and we were alone.

I remember Marietta flitting in and out of the room. I remember Mazlor peering down on me and hobbling painfully away. I remember that Leda was always there when I wanted her, and that when she was not I was suddenly in a panic, thinking that perhaps all that had passed was just a dream and that in reality the struggle was about to begin, and there I was tied down to a bed by a foolish wound from a gun that was, they had always said, not really big enough to harm anyone.

And then, all at once, the light of the day came and I was up and about, and we could walk together, quite slowly, Leda and I, along the river bank, and stop with Mazlor, still in pain but back on his wharf, for a bottle of his ice-cold beer. It seemed as if ten, fifteen days had gone by since I'd crawled down from the jungle, nearer death than alive; it was only two.

He said, Mazlor: "You go back now? I miss you, friend, we have good times together, no?"

188

I said: "What are we going to do about those bodies in the cellar?"

He grinned. "I tell my friend Jose Salvador, I tell him: 'Jose, lay off the bottle for one day, do what you supposed to do.'"

"There's a reward out, several rewards, for the man with the broken hand. His name's Luther Koch. And a lot more money riding on the other man, a man who used to call himself Anton Hans Ullmann. Only trouble is, they're both dead. What about the other two?"

He laughed. "One man, police Captain, Slawata kick his ass and send him home. Other man, Indian..." He shrugged: "Nobody don't hold Indian like that for long. He escape, go back to tribe in jungle, is best thing."

He never mentioned the fact that I'd been stringing him along all the time; as now, he must know. He just said reproachfully: "You not looking for this man Werther, after all, eh?"

"Werther was a pointer, an indicator, no more."

"Not Elena da Costa either, eh?"

I said: "My God, she's still up on the cliff with Jesus."

"And you not diamond thief, either. I know better now."

"No, I'm a relatively honest man. Does that make us enemies?"

He laughed and slapped me heartily on the back, and we winced, both of us, with the pain of it. He said: "No, good friends, you and me always." There was no mention at all of the loot I was going to cut him in on.

I climbed down under the wharf carefully, and retrieved the heavy canvas bag; I pulled out his rickety table and tipped out its load of brightly-shining baubles. He stared and almost yelled, and then he looked at me in awe and said: "My God, is not true."

Leda and I sorted out the Zrinyi jewels; they were all there. We put them carefully on one side. I pushed a careless handful of diamonds; rubies, emeralds, gold pins, and a dozen other odds and ends over to him, and said:

"All this stuff is loot. Some of it might have rightful owners, I don't know. After twenty-five years it's hard to know who owns what. Some of it has been stolen and recovered and stolen again over the past four hundred years, so whoever truly owns it is a matter of chance and nothing else. Split it up with the boys the way you think best."

That's when he started yelling. He yelled out: "Slawata! Jao!" and kept on yelling, dancing up and down and grimacing because it hurt him every time he moved. They came running, the two of them, and stared at the gems with their mouths open. I gathered up the rest of them and said to Leda:

"We'll give this lot to Fenrek. Most of it, anyway. If it all gets claimed, too bad; if not, it'll find its way back to us and were in clover for a little while longer."

She was picking up the Zrinyi collection, piece by piece, and looking at them sadly: "The pattern's never changed, has it? All the pain and the suffering for...for these baubles. I'm almost tempted to throw them in the river." She looked at me and smiled. "But not quite."

Mazlor dragged his eyes away from the shimmering collection, the ancient excellence lying there on the broken, grubby wooden table, and was staring at the river, a look of puzzlement on his face. He said: "Jesus."

Jesus it was. He was paddling in toward us silently, and sitting in the front of the dugout canoe was Elena.

Her beautiful clothes were ripped and filthy, her hair was all over her face, and there was a single bruise on her cheek, where, I guessed, Jesus had found it desirable, once, to teach her who was the master. There was a look of sullen, brooding anger on her white, still-lovely face.

The canoe slid up to the wharf, and Jesus shipped his paddle, and then Elena was climbing up the unstable ladder and staring, first at me, and then at the jewels, and then at Leda. Everyone was silent, watching, and Jesus came up, and grunted once, and sat down in the shade and said nothing. And then Elena leaped at me and ripped her fingernails down my face as I tried, not very hard, to fight her off.

Mazlor was staring at her and so was Slawata, and Jao was laughing and I was pushing her away; she was tearing at my face with her claws, and shouting out in a mixture of Portuguese and English, shouting things I hoped Leda would never understand, yelling obscenities in the kind of language that's often reserved for graffiti...And then Leda got up, quite calmly, and took hold of the long black hair and twisted her round, and then landed a haymaker on the point of the well-shaped chin. Elena staggered, and stumbled, and fell back, and there was a splash and she was in the water, yelling more obscenities at us. There were streaks of blood down my face, and I sighed and said to Mazlor: "Do something, for God's sake."

He laughed and said: "Woman like that, she take care of herself. She take care of herself good." Jao was helping her out of the water. She struggled, and he held her tight, and soon she was looking at him with a different kind of look on her face, her long fingers just resting lightly on his tight biceps.

I looked at Leda. "It's time to say our farewells."

The white-haired Carlos came for us, and I gave him a small, uncut diamond for his pains, and then there was the plane to Manaus and on to Belem, and a short wait and then the big Air France plane across the water to Paris, and when we arrived at Orly, Fenrek was there with my beautiful Jensen, just washed and greased and not a mark on it.

We sat in his rooftop apartment overlooking the Bois, and the couples were still walking arm in arm along the green verges, and the birds were still noisily hunting the insects that fed on the sap among the bursting buds. We talked about Cunha, plump and happy and still, no doubt, telling his wife about his trip up the mountain to Corcavado. I said: "Can you have him return Aarons property to him? And I suppose I'd better pay for that broken window. And come to that, I'd better stay away from Rio for a while."

He said cheerfully: "One of these days, Cain, you'll be running out of towns to visit." He poured coffee into the little Spode coffee cups. He'd acquired some new silver spoons, a set of Hester Bateman, very neat and uncluttered and beautiful. He said airily: "I'll send Cunha a cable, he'll take care of it."

A brace of pretty young women came to see him, and he shooed them away after a glass of wine, and we talked about the ethics involved in the chase that's gone on all over the world and down through the centuries for the beautiful, expensive things that have always intrigued man's imagination. He said:

"Zrinyi was planning on selling the necklace to pay for your services."

I shot a look at Leda. I said: "Don't worry, my pockets are well lined." More as a matter of principle than anything else, I gave him most of the stuff I'd taken from Kolchak. I said: "How much of this can be claimed, I don't know. Some of it, I hope, won't be, and that makes me the rightful owner. Possession is nine points of the law, all that nonsense."

I asked him about Vallence, and Fenrek exploded. He said wrathfully: "He's in prison."

"In prison?" I was only mildly surprised.

He said: "Yes, he tried..." His temper was making him gesticulate even more violently. He said: "A looted Rembrandt turned up in London, and somewhere down the line Vallence's name cropped up. So I called him into my office for questioning, and...By God, you know what he did? He came in grinning like an idiot, and he admitted he'd sold it, admitted he knew just what it was. And then he pulled a packet from his pocket and tossed it on the desk for me, and he said: 'Just a trifle, Colonel, to keep that fifteen thousand dollar automobile of yours running smoothly.' I opened up the envelope, not believing it, you understand? And there was a bundle of thousand franc notes a couple of inches thick. My God, whatever made him think he could bribe an Interpol man? And what did he mean about the car?"

I said happily: "Well, I was quite sure you'd never really catch him with his hands full of loot. I may, perhaps, have carelessly left an idea lying around...I don't know."

His mouth dropped open, and he said: "You son of a bitch."

We went back to Paperouse for a splendid dinner, the three of us, and spent the night at his apartment; and in the morning we set off for Budapest. We took it in turns to drive the Jensen, and we swept through the frontiers on Fenrek's Interpol card, and in two days we were in the Zrinyi castle.

The roses were all in bloom, and we wandered among them, the whole crowd of us, admiring the Tiffanies and the Jacques Verschurens and the brilliant scarlet Sarabandes. There was glorious Rosa Mundi, a Hybrid shrub that's been around since the fifth century. I said to Leda: "*Hic jacet in tumba Ros mundi*, here lies Rose the graced..." She squeezed my arm and Nicholas, the dark and angry man she said liked me so much, glared. The Count was smiling, moving along with us stiffly on his two artificial legs, his eyes bright and seeming to caress his wife with a kind of quiet contentment.

We talked of flowers, and of wine, and about the friendly, forested slopes of Transdanubia; we talked of the Colony the Romans founded and called Aquincum which later became Buda and then Budapest; we talked about the wars of the Jagiello Kings, and about the lovely gypsy girl Magda Zrinyi for whom the collection was made. And nobody said a word about Kolchak.

All that would come later...

We walked over the smooth lawns and watched the sun going down, and when we were apart from the others a little, just Leda and I and the lovely Countess; Leda said quietly to her mother: "Cabot asked me to marry him."

She was cutting a spray of Monique roses, long-stemmed, fragrant, silvery-pink. She turned to look at her daughter and said: "And will you?" The gray eyes were grave and sad. There were two worlds here, the old and the new.

Leda said: "No. I'd like to, but..." She sighed, and shook her head, and said: "I've told him I'll be his mistress if he wants. But I won't marry him."

Her world, and mine. For a while, she'd left hers; now, she was going back to it. Paris was behind her, the charming little apartment on the Left Bank with its sloping floor; and she was home again.

The sun went down over the distant plain, and the cool night breeze was coming in from the woods on the side of the hill, scented with pine and gorse and the rich, ripe smell of juniper.

And the red glow in the dark sky was the light of the distant, teeming city.

THE END

ABOUT THE AUTHOR

Alan Lyle-Smythe was born in Surrey, England. Prior to World War II, he served with the Palestine Police from 1936 to 1939 and learned the Arabic language. He was awarded an MBE in June 1938. He married Aliza Sverdova in 1939, then studied acting from 1939 to 1941.

In January 1940, Lyle-Smythe was commissioned in the Royal Army Service Corps. Due to his linguistic skills, he transferred to the Intelligence Corps and served in the Western Desert, in which he used the surname "Caillou" (the French word for 'pebble') as an alias.

He was captured in North Africa, imprisoned and threatened with execution in Italy, then escaped to join the British forces at Salerno. He was then posted to serve with the partisans in Yugoslavia. He wrote about his experiences in the book *The World is Six Feet Square* (1954). He was promoted to captain and awarded the Military Cross in 1944.

Following the war, he returned to the Palestine Police from 1946 to 1947, then served as a Police Commissioner in British-occupied Italian Somaliland from 1947 to 1952, where he was recommissioned a captain.

After work as a District Officer in Somalia and professional hunter, Lyle-Smythe travelled to Canada, where he worked as a hunter and then became an actor on Canadian television.

He wrote his first novel, *Rogue's Gambit*, in 1955, first using the name Caillou, one of his aliases from the war. Moving from Vancouver to Hollywood, he made an appearance as a contestant on the January 23 1958 edition of *You Bet Your Life*.

He appeared as an actor and/or worked as a screenwriter in

such shows as *Daktari, The Man From U.N.C.L.E.* (including the screenwriting for "*The Bow-Wow Affair*" from 1965), *Thriller, Daniel Boone, Quark, Centennial,* and *How the West Was Won.* In 1966-67, he had a recurring role (as Jason Flood) in NBC's "*Tarzan*" TV series starring Ron Ely. Caillou appeared in such television movies as *Sole Survivor* (1970), *The Hound of the Baskervilles* (1972, as Inspector Lestrade), and *Goliath Awaits* (198I). His cinema film credits included roles in *Five Weeks in a Balloon* (1962), *Clarence, the Cross-Eyed Lion* (1965), *The Rare Breed* (1966), *The Devil's Brigade* (1968), *Hellfighters* (1968), *Everything You Always Wanted to Know About Sex* (*But Were Afraid to Ask)* (1972), *Herbie Goes to Monte Carlo* (1977), *Beyond Evil* (1980), *The Sword and the Sorcerer* (1982) and *The Ice Pirates* (1984).

Caillou wrote 52 paperback thrillers under his own name and the nom de plume of Alex Webb, with such heroes as Cabot Cain, Colonel Matthew Tobin, Mike Benasque, Ian Quayle and Josh Dekker, as well as writing many magazine stories.

Several of Caillou's novels were made into films, such as *Rampage* with Robert Mitchum in 1963, based on his big game hunting knowledge; *Assault on Agathon*, for which Caillou did the screenplay as well; and *The Cheetahs*, filmed in 1989.

He was married to Aliza Sverdova from 1939 until his death. Their daughter Nadia Caillou was the screenwriter for the film *Skeleton Coast.*

Alan Caillou died in Sedona, Arizona in 2006.

DON'T MISS ANY OF MICHAEL KASNER'S
HARD HITTING MILITARY NOVEL SERIES

BLACK OPS

Formed by an elite cadre of government officials, the Black OPS team goes where the law can't - to seek retribution for acts of terror directed against Americans anywhere in the world.

3 BOOK SERIES

Armed with all the tactical advantages of modern technology, battle hard and ready when the free world is threatened - the Peacekeepers are the baddest grunts on the planet.

4 BOOK SERIES

CHOPPER COPS

America is being torn apart as criminal cartels terrorize our cities, dealing drugs and death wholesale. Local police are outgunned, so the President unleashes the U.S. TACTICAL POLICE FORCE. An elite army of super cops with ammo to burn, they swoop down on the hot spots in sleek high-tech attack choppers to win the dirty war and take back America!

4 BOOK SERIES

FROM CALIBER BOOKS
www.calibercomics.com

CALIBER
BOOKS

CALIBER COMICS GOES TO WAR!
HISTORICAL AND MILITARY THEMED GRAPHIC NOVELS

**WORLD WAR ONE:
MO MAN'S LAND**

ISBN: 9781635298123

A look at World War 1 from the French trenches as they faced the Imperial German Army.

CORTEZ AND THE FALL OF THE AZTECS

ISBN: 9781635299779

Cortez battles the Aztecs while in search of Inca gold.

**TROY:
AN EMPIRE UNDER SIEGE**

ISBN: 9781635298635

Homer's famous The Iliad and the Trojan War is given a unique human perspective rather than from the God's.

WITNESS TO WAR

ISBN: 9781635299700

WW2's Battle of the Bulge is seen up close by an embedded female war reporter.

THE LINCOLN BRIGADE

ISBN: 9781635298222

American volunteers head to Spain in the 1930s to fight in their civil war against the fascist regime.

**EL CID:
THE CONQUEROR**

ISBN: 9780982654996

Europe's greatest warrior attempts to unify Spain against invading foreign and domestic armies.

WINTER WAR

ISBN: 9780985749392

At the outbreak of WW2 Finland fights against an invading Soviet army.

**ZULUNATION:
END OF EMPIRE**

ISBN: 9780941613415

The global British Empire and far-reaching influence is threatened by a Zulu uprising in southern Africa.

AIR WARRIORS: WORLD WAR ONE #V1 - V4   *Take to the skies of WW1 as various fighter aces tell their harrowing stories.*
ISBN: 9781635297973 (V1), 9781635297980 (V2), 9781635297997 (V3), 9781635298000 (V4)

ALSO AVAILABLE FROM CALIBER COMICS

QUALITY GRAPHIC NOVELS TO ENTERTAIN

THE SEARCHERS: VOLUME 1
The Shape of Things to Come

Before League of Extraordinary Gentlemen there was The Searchers. At the dawn of the 20th Century the greatest literary adventurers from the minds of Wells, Doyle, Burroughs, and Haggard were created. All thought to be the work of pure fiction. However, a century later, the real-life descendents of those famous characters are recuited by the legendary Professor Challenger in order to save mankind's future. Series collected for the first time.

"Searchers is the comic book I have on the wall with a sign reading - 'Love books? Never read a comic? Try this one! ....money back guarantee...'" - Dark Star Books.

WAR OF THE WORLDS: INFESTATION

Based on the H.G. Wells classic! The "Martian Invasion" has begun again and now mankind must fight for its very humanity. It happened slowly at first but by the third year, it seemed that the war was almost over... the war was almost lost.

"Writer Randy Zimmerman has a fine grasp of drama, and spins the various strands of the story into a coherent whole... imaginative and very gritty."
- war-of-the-worlds.co.uk

HELSING: LEGACY BORN

From writer Gary Reed (Deadworld) and artists John Lowe (Captain America), Bruce McCorkindale (Godzilla). She was born into a legacy she wanted no part of and pushed into a battle recessed deep in the shadows of the night. Samantha Helsing is torn between two worlds...two allegiances...two families. The legacy of the Van Helsing family and their crusade against the "night creatures" comes to modern day with the most unlikely of all warriors.

"Congratulations on this masterpiece..."
Paul Dale Roberts, Compuserve Reviews

DEADWORLD

Before there was The Walking Dead there was Deadworld. Here is an introduction of the long running classic horror series, Deadworld, to a new audience! Considered by many to be the godfather of the original zombie comic with over 100 issues and graphic novels in print and over 1,000,000 copies sold, Deadworld ripped into the undead with intelligent zombies on a mission and a group of poor teens riding in a school bus desperately try to stay one step ahead of the sadistic, Harley-riding King Zombie. Death, mayhem, and a touch of supernatural evil made Deadworld a classic and now here's your chance to get into the story!

DAYS OF WRATH

Award winning comic writer & artist Wayne Vansant brings his gripping World War II saga of war in the Pacific to Guadalcanal and the Battle of Bloody Ridge. This is the powerful story of the long, vicious battle for Guadalcanal that occurred in 1942-43. When the U.S. Navy orders its outnumbered and out-gunned ships to run from the Japanese fleet, they abandon American troops on a bloody, battered island in the South Pacific.

"Heavy on authenticity, compellingly written and beautifully drawn."
- Comics Buyers Guide

SHERLOCK HOLMES:
THE CASE OF THE MISSING MARTIAN

Sherlock is called out of retirement to London in 1908 to solve a most baffling mystery: The British Museum is missing a specimen of a Martian from the failed invasion of 1899. Did it walk away on its own or did someone steal it?

Holmes ponders the facts and remembers his part in the war effort alongside Professor Challenger during the War of the Worlds invasion that was chronicled in H.G. Wells' classic novel.

Meanwhile, Doctor Watson has problems of his own when his wife steals a scalpel from his surgical tool kit and returns to her old stomping grounds of Whitechapel, the London

CALIBER PRESENTS

The original Caliber Presents anthology title was one of Caliber's inaugural releases and featured predominantly new creators, many of which went onto successful careers in the comics' industry. In this new version, Caliber Presents has expanded to graphic novel size and while still featuring new creators it also includes many established professional creators with new visions. Creators featured in this first issue include nominees and winners of some of the industry's major awards including the Eisner, Harvey, Xeric, Ghastly, Shel Dorf, Comic Monsters, and more.

LEGENDLORE

From Caliber Comics now comes the entire Realm and Legendlore saga as a set of volumes that collects the long running critically acclaimed series. In the vein of The Lord of The Rings and The Hobbit with elements of Game of Thrones and Dungeon and Dragons.

Four normal modern day teenagers are plunged into a world they thought only existed in novels and film. They are whisked away to a magical land where dragons roam the skies, orcs and hobgoblins terrorize travelers, where unicorns prance through the forest, and kingdoms wage war for dominance. It is a world where man is just one race, joining other races such as elves, trolls, dwarves, changelings, and the dreaded night creatures who steal the night.

TIME GRUNTS

What if Hitler's last great Super Weapon was - Time itself! A WWII/time travel adventure that can best be described as Band of Brothers meets Time Bandits.

October, 1944. Nazi fortunes appear bleaker by the day. But in the bowels of the Wenceslas Mines, a terrible threat has emerged . . . The Nazis have discovered the ability to conquer time itself with the help of a new ominous device!

Now a rag tag group of American GIs must stop this threat to the past, present, and future . . . While dealing with their own past, prejudices, and fears in the process.

www.calibercomics.com